VAMPIRE ROYALTY:

Raven's Blood

by
Valerie Hoffman

ISBN 9780979247637

Published in the United States of America
Publisher:
VG Press
595 W. Granada Blvd., Suite H
Ormond Beach, FL 32174
386-677-3995
drval@bellsouth.net

VAMPIRE ROYALTY:

Raven's Blood

Contents

Other Books By
Valerie Hoffman

VAMPIRE ROYALTY:
The Rebellion

VAMPIRE ROYALTY:
Resurrection

Dedication

This book is dedicated to my brother Andrew —"To be or not to be that is the question."

This book is also dedicated to my husband, Norm, without his continued dedication and support this series would not exist.

I would also like to make a special dedication to all the fans who protested on Andrew Gabriel's behalf.

Acknowledgements

I really do have to acknowledge some special folks who helped bail me out in my time of need. First, foremost and always there's my husband, Norm. In addition I would like to say thanks to the folks at Z-graph for the outstanding cover. Also to the folks at Florida Graphic Printing Co. for all their hard work.

Special appreciation goes to my new editor Robin Smith. Her editing skills have taken the "Vampire Royalty" series to a whole new level. Great Job!

Prologue

VENGEANCE QUEST
Cornwall, England

Lightning split the moonless night sky, briefly illuminating the blackness. An ear-splitting boom of thunder accompanied a second streak. The turbulent clouds rolled and tumbled across the heavens, broadcasting the storm to come. The black-clad figure clung precariously to the side of the cliff, salt water spraying her face and peppering her skin as it perpetually dampened the surface of the cliff. A hundred feet below the roaring surf crashed against the jagged rocks.

Laural Gabriel, Marchioness of Penbrook, glanced forlornly up at the foreboding structure looming another yard above her. The castle appeared no more then a dark silhouette against the darker sky. She gritted her teeth as she continued to climb.

It would be very risky to get caught out here in the rain.

Another bright flash lit the sky, throwing the glistening surface of the wet rocks into sharp relief. As darkness descended again, Laural continued to pull herself up the cliff. Her perfect night vision enabled her to work through the gloom as she grappled for her next handhold. Using each crevice and crack, she painstakingly inched her way up several more feet.

The stone beneath her right boot crumbled. Before she could compensate, her left foot slipped off the slick overgrown algae covering the protruding rocks. Dirt and gravel rained down on her as she slid toward the edge of the cliff. The skin on her fingers was scraped raw. Her blood trailed across the stone as she dug her fingers into the craggy cracks. Her erratic heartbeat drowned out the roaring surf while she hung suspended over the raging sea, ragged gasps escaping from her as she clutched the rocks.

While resting her forehead against the unyielding stone she took stock of the damage. Scratches stung her face and imbedded dirt burned her eyes, but, otherwise, she was uninjured. She blinked rapidly several times in an attempt to clear her vision. Her efforts only succeeded in making her eyes water.

"Damn!" she exclaimed. She couldn't keep climbing with impaired vision, and she couldn't release her hold to wipe her eyes--either way she would face certain death.

An idea struck, and she turned her head to peer down into the waves. Despite her blurry vision she experienced a moment of vertigo as the ground seemed to be rushing up to meet her. Laural briefly closed her eyes and clenched her jaw.

This is no time to give in to my fear of heights.

The thunder boomed and the ocean roared. Frothy mist spewed over her as a huge roller broke against the cliff. Laural took a deep breath, knowing her idea would work if she could just—

Another wave washed over her. Taking a deep breath she turned her face full into the spray of salty water. The water washed her eyes clean but tried valiantly to take her with it as it withdrew.

Resolutely, she refocused on her goal while keeping her gaze locked on the open window. Another giant wave hit the cliff, washing over her, trying to drag her away in its wake. Grunting, she threw herself against the Cornish cliffs and splayed flat. Her cuts and scratches burned as salt water sprayed into the wounds. She gritted her teeth and ignored the injuries. There was no time to worry about the pain. Besides, within minutes, the abrasions would heal.

She looked longingly up at the window. A soft glow emanated from the opening, offering evidence of its occupant. The sword dug into her side but she didn't dare let go of her handhold. Slowly, she slithered upward. The gun in her waistband dug into her skin. A drop splashed against the top of her head.

Mist from below or rain from above? No rain, please.

If she got soaked her route would become even more treacherous, preventing her from reaching the castle and also providing her quarry an opportunity to escape. Another drop. Lightning blazed, giving credence to the rain. Setting her sights on the small square opening, she redoubled her efforts.

THE DEFECTOR

Inside the castle Lord John Edwards stood in the center of the master bedroom, nervously surveying his surroundings. Dark shadows hovered in the corners of the large gloomy quarters, giving him even more reason to be on edge. He started as another streak of lightning tore across the sky. He winced at the crash of thunder that followed. His eyes jerked apprehensively from the window, around the room, then back to the phone.

To hell with waiting.

He strode to the liquor cabinet; he needed something to steady his nerves. He poured brandy from one of the decanters. His lips twisted as he watched the liquid fill the glass.

I probably shouldn't risk clouding my mind and dulling my thoughts before the call comes in. But will my caller even know?

He laughed mirthlessly, realizing the absurdity of that thought even before he finished it. His caller would surely know, he always knew.

His hand shook as he lifted the glass. Another boom of thunder shook the room as he downed the drink. There was too much at risk for him to remain calm. This project was full of potential problems, and, by embracing it, he was betraying his people's mores; customs they had lived by for thousands of years. This path he had chosen presented a huge risk to the survival of his species. Still, if his leader was on the right track, the potential benefits could not be ignored.

He poured a second drink, this time sipping more cautiously. It wouldn't bode well for his leader to detect any reservations. The possible threat to his own survival was his heaviest concern. Taking another sip from his glass, he reflected on the reason for his present predicament. When he had originally been recruited by the Loyalists he had been convinced of the validity of the cause. He was tired of his people's traditional approach, which had placed them in a subjugate role in society. He had, however, begun to reconsider the wisdom of his choice since the Loyalists were slowly but steadily being assassinated.

He grimaced as the strong liquor burned a fiery path down his throat and settled in his stomach. He twirled the drink in his hand and watched the amber fluid slide around the glass. Unbidden his mind flashed onto the image of the last Loyalist discovered in her Italian villa--decapitated. He shifted his gaze to the fireplace, hoping the hypnotic dancing of the flames would distract him from the pain. He had been the one to discover his lover, and by the time he had found her, all that had been left of her body had been a smoldering pile of ashes. A note had been found with the remains stating that any porphyrian wanting to defect from the rebels would be welcomed back into the mainstream--but those who stayed in the Loyalist camp would meet a similar fate.

His lip curled in derision. Obviously, whoever had made that offer didn't know who they were dealing with.

As if those who defected from the Loyalist cause would be dealt with any less severely.

Scowling, he topped off his drink. At this point he was beyond caring how he came across during the upcoming phone call.

He had to admit the cause really meant nothing to him.

But the power! Now there's motivation.

Power was a natural aphrodisiac, providing more excitement then even money or sex. And if power was measured in ruthless determination, then his leader certainly had the edge.

As he mulled over his decision he wondered if, in the end, he had made the right choice. The phone rang, cutting off any further speculation. He spoke the prearranged code words into the receiver while his eyes probed the shadows. His caution seemed overzealous considering he was alone. Even if he hadn't been by himself in the castle, the volume of the storm would have made eavesdropping impossible. Still, a lifetime of wariness could not easily be put aside.

His eyes roamed restlessly around the room. This castle had been in Loyalist hands for years. Its location remained secluded and virtually inaccessible. He had been flown in by private plane. His lodgings in the keep were luxurious and well-appointed. Expensive furnishings intermingled with priceless artwork. Ancient tapestries and historical portraits hung on the walls. The large stone fireplace cast a cozy glow over his surroundings. The setting was designed for serenity, so why was he so anxious?

His gaze strayed to the window. The wind howled, the lightning flashed and the thunder crashed. The storm offered even more security then his isolation. No one would be able to approach in that weather.

The draperies blew frantically as if trying to break free. He considered closing the leaden panes, but just then his connection went through.

"Hello?"

He refocused. "Edwards here."

Silence.

He cleared his throat. "I believe I've discovered the location."

"Where?"

He pulled nervously at the cuff of his pale grey smoking jacket. Any interaction with his leader always made him uncomfortable. "Penbrook Castle."

A deep chuckle echoed across the line just before the phone went dead.

THE PROMISE

Edwards slowly hung up the receiver. A chill coursed down his spine when a loud crash sounded behind him. He paled.

Just the shutter banging against the wall.

The tension drained from his body. Remembering the open window, he turned, took one step and froze. A black-clad figure stood just inside the opening. Shocked, he stared as she raised her pistol. A burst of lightning pierced the room. He gasped, "You!"

She nodded grimly. "So, Edwards, you recognize death when it stares you in the face."

Icy fingers gripped his heart while his brain tried to negate the apparition standing in front of him. "I never expected you would do the killing."

She glared at him, disgusted. "Unfortunately, you didn't foresee a lot of things. Unlike your leader, I wouldn't expect someone else to take risks while I play it safe. Nor would I ask others to do what I wasn't willing to do myself. Besides," she continued, taking aim at his head, "I made a promise."

His shock subsided as he registered his imminent peril. Like a dark avenging angel she faced him. The wind whipped her cape out behind her, the excess material trying to take flight like the wings of a bird of prey. The woman appeared to be no more than twenty, with smooth skin, a well-defined body and blond hair cascading in a long braid to her waist. Despite the youthful appearance, her set features projected unyielding determination.

Another clap of thunder boomed. The pregnant clouds burst open, giving birth to torrents of rain. Drops drummed against the castle, all but drowning out the report of her pistol. Just as she fired he dove for her. They grappled. She was fast and strong, but so was he. The gun flew from her hands. She quickly drew her sword. Realizing he couldn't reach the fallen weapon quickly enough, he snatched a sword from the coat of arms above the mantle.

THE WRONG SIDE

Laural jumped to her feet just in time to see her adversary snatch a sword from above the mantle. Flourishing the weapon he advanced. She brandished her own weapon as she stepped back a pace to gain maneuvering room. Sword-fighting wasn't her first choice. She preferred the less complicated, straightforward bullet to the head. For a moment her eyes fastened on her gun lying on the floor several feet away, but gave up the thought of retrieving the weapon when her opponent made his first slash at her.

She ducked, fainted, parried, then spun as he lunged. Sweat poured down her face and into her eyes. Adrenalin coursed through her veins as her sword sliced crisscross patterns through the air. Going on the offensive, she lashed out. A crimson line slashed across the man's chest.

Edwards looked down in disbelief, his fear evaporating into fury.

I'll be damned if I'm going to let this slip of a girl get the better of me--no matter who she is.

Swinging the sword viciously he bellowed obscenities at her as he charged.

Taken aback by her adversary's ferocity, Laural hesitated. In that instant, Edwards sensed his advantage. A malicious smile curved his lips as he struck. She threw her arm up to cover her throat. Edwards, however, aimed low rather than at her neck.

She gasped in pain and shock as blood spilled from the gash in her abdomen. Edwards pushed his advantage and struck again. Laural clamped down hard on her agony. If she were going to win this battle she couldn't afford any distractions. Edwards lunged but this time she parried the blow. She could feel the rivulets of blood running down her body, but despite the profuse bleeding, she knew the wound would quickly heal. Edwards swung toward her head. She countered with several quick short cuts to his face and neck. He raised his arm to shield his vulnerability. She arched high and sliced down, cutting off his arm just below the elbow.

Transfixed, the man stood, staring in stupefied fascination as the blood poured from his body. The severed limb fell, hitting the floor with a sickening thump. The sword clattered as it dropped onto the stones. The sound jarred Edwards from his trance. He dove for the gun. Curling his fingers around the stock he yanked it off the floor and fired.

The bullet passed harmlessly over Laural's shoulder. She pounced. He aimed. She held the sword high, driving down with all her strength. The sword sliced through the man's neck just as the gun went off a second time.

Staggering she fell back onto the hard stone floor. Edwards's severed head rolled then rested inches away from her face. She blinked. The angry eyes seemed to be accusing her.

It's your own fault. You picked the wrong side, she thought as she slipped into unconsciousness.

Chapter 1:
One Less Threat

Washington, D.C. and London England

The shrill ringing pierced the stillness of the quiet room. Jordan Rush, Earl of Rockford, snatched the receiver from the phone on his desk. His anxiety was high and his nerves were shot.

My reaction is the same every time my cousin puts herself in danger, he thought as he strangled the receiver. *So far she's been lucky. Will this be the call letting me know her luck's run out?*

He raked his hand through his chestnut brown hair, then pulled at the collar of his dress shirt. Fear overwhelmed him and he couldn't speak.He sat motionless as the seconds ticked by. His heart raced while his mind conjured up the different types of disasters that could have befallen his cousin.

I should have gone with her. Hell, I should have gone instead of her. I should have--

"Jordan?"

As he released an explosive breath his jade-green eyes rested on the photo of the vibrant beautiful blond woman poised on the far side of the desk. Closing his eyes he allowed his tense muscles to relax. He knew the cause was important and the need great, but every time Laural went on another mission he was a basket-case until he had reassurance of her survival. He ran an unsteady hand across his face. He would be relieved when the threat was over.

"Are you okay?"

"Of course." She hesitated. "I got shot in the shoulder, but it's healing."

The green eyes flashed as he banged his fist on the desk. The pen holder toppled and several papers slid to the floor, but he didn't notice. "You need to be more careful," he admonished. "One of these guys could get off a lucky shot to the head, then where would you be?"

"Dead."

He was silent. Picking up his glass he took several long gulps of the reddish-brown liquid. Setting the glass back on the desk he said more calmly, "Edwards?"

"We now have one less threat to worry about."

"Did he tell you anything?"

Laural paused as she registered the tension in his voice. She knew this was a sensitive area. They had been searching for Jordan's child ever since his former fiancée, Dana Maxwell, had become pregnant, then intentionally disappeared thirty years ago. At this point, however, finding the child was only part of the issue. There was a serious concern that Jordan's child, who was a direct descendant of Craven Maxwell, would be used by the Loyalists to continue the demented legacy of his grandfather.

Over the past three decades, a group of porphyrians, loyal to the ideals practiced by Laural's long-dead uncle, Craven Maxwell, had managed to infiltrate into diurnal society. They were using the very foundation Laural's father, Andrew Gabriel, Sixth Marquis of Penbrook, had helped to create half a century earlier. The Craven Loyalists had penetrated the Willow Grove Foundation by passing themselves off as porphyrians eager to integrate into diurnal society. Since that was one of the primary purposes of the Foundation, their duplicity had initially gone undetected.

Her father had discovered the true nature of the infiltrators only after it was too late to prevent their assimilation. Before he died Andrew's last request had been for Laural to make it right. She had made that promise to him with every intention of keeping it.

Jordan's interests were divided. He also wanted the Loyalists eliminated and the threat neutralized, but he wanted to find his child too. Many hours had been spent contemplating the fate of his progeny. Eventually they had agreed that Either Jordan's offspring was being used as an unwilling figurehead by the loyalists or the child was intentionally heading the group. The first possibility was less likely since the lineage of Craven Maxwell was too powerful to be controlled. Even so, Jordan clung to the hope that this particular descendant hadn't inherited the Maxwell penchant for evil.

"Mortal combat tends to dampen conversation."

He grimaced at the reminder of her peril. "Where are you now?"

She smiled into the phone. "Where else would I be? On my way to work."

He grunted. When she wasn't off eliminating Loyalists, Laural was completely immersed in her duties as director of the Willow Grove Foundation's London office. After achieving longstanding success with integration in their Washington headquarters, they had agreed several years ago to open another branch in England. It was the next logical step toward their goal of interspecies integration.

The Foundation had several mission statements. Providing financial assistance to needy students pursuing secondary education was one of the agency's main functions. The Foundation also offered assistance in relocating displaced immigrants. Covertly, the relocation and integration involved porphyrians as well as diurnals.

Opening an overseas extension of their program allowed them to expand in order to accommodate those of their kind, who, after living centuries in Europe, might not want to migrate to America. Starting a London office also provided Laural with an opportunity to relocate to a place where no one knew how old she really was. This was a key issue since porphyrians did not age at the same rate as diurnals.

Descended from the ancient legendary lineage thought at one time to be vampires, porphyrians were, in fact, a sub-species who had several abilities and liabilities their diurnal counterparts did not. Their lifespans were prolonged, their physical strength enhanced, and they enjoyed the ability to communicate telepathically. They also had extremely improved immune systems with an innate ability to heal their own wounds. They could, to varying degrees, mentally manipulate diurnals, and a rare few of their kind could also mentally dominate each other. Each porphyrian's powers varied, and were only able to be used unilaterally.

The countercheck to these enhancements was their dependence on PS4, a supplement which provided the necessary electrolytes and chemicals to counteract the lack of enzymes in their hemoglobin. All porphyrians drank PS4, for without it they would become victims of the blood sickness. Laural had fallen prey to this disease thirty years ago when her porphyrian powers had first manifested. The illness had driven her to derive the necessary electrolytes by drinking human blood. Jordan knew, maybe better then she did, that part of her quest was to prove her redemption and reassure herself that she would never be a victim again.

"Jordan," she offered, pulling into her private parking space and waving to the on-duty guard, "there's only a few more Loyalists left."

He frowned. "I know."

Laural strode toward the contemporary office building and stepped into her private glass elevator. As she rode to the top floor she felt the mild apprehension her fear of heights always provoked. Refusing to acknowledge her weakness, she deliberately studied the view, just as she did every morning. She hoped saturation would cure her affliction, but so far it hadn't worked. Subduing her nerves she relished the sight. The building was a monument to her parents' dream of integration with its maze of offices dedicated to the advancement of both species. She was sure her parents would have been proud.

"With only a few names left we've got to be at the inner core of the conspirators. So far I haven't come across any who've known anything about your child or an underlying plot to use a descendant of Craven's for a major conspiracy. I've encountered many, however, who've had ambitions of their own."

Jordan's eyes lifted to the grandfather clock against the opposite wall. "I have a meeting with Tim in a few minutes. He claims he has some updated news about the search."

"Great!" Laural exclaimed as she entered her office. Let me know." Distracted, she dropped the cell phone back into her purse and sat down behind her desk. Her eyes swept slowly around the ornate office. Fondly she reflected on the fun she and Jordan had had locating and decorating the room with antiques and exotic furnishings brought in from their favorite places around the world.

She stood then walked past her rosewood antique desk and matching bookcase until she was in front of the globe. Absently, she spun the gift her cousin had given her as an office-warming present. While studying the continents, land masses and oceans she wondered where they would finally catch up with the grandchild of Craven Maxwell. More importantly, once they found Jordan's child, she feared they might have to kill him or her in order to prevent the poisonous legacy of Craven Maxwell from continuing. She spun the globe one final time.

Chapter 1: One Less Threat

Will Jordan be able to do what's necessary--even if it means slaying his own child?

Chapter 2:
Devoted and Deadly

"Come in," Jordan replied to the knock at his office door.

The door opened, admitting a tall broad-shouldered man with red hair and a smattering of freckles dotting his handsome face. A slight bulge, barely discernable under the jacket of his grey herringbone suit, bore evidence of his shoulder holster. Smiling affably at his boss, he entered the room. His friendly open features belied the deadliest and most devoted member of the Willow Grove Foundation's security team.

Tim Cooper had been head of security, as well as assistant director, for the past three decades. He had inherited the first position when his previous superior, John Carpenter, had been killed by Jordan's former fiancée, Dana Maxwell. When Andrew Gabriel, Jordan's long-time friend and head of the foundation, had been murdered by Dana's father, Jordan had become the director. Losing the marquis had left a void, not only in Jordan's heart but also within the foundation.

After taking over the running of the facility, Jordan had promptly promoted Tim. His original intention had been to delegate the position of security chief to someone else, but Tim had insisted he could do both jobs without short-changing either. Due to the highly sensitive nature of some of their programs, Jordan had agreed to the arrangement.

The muscular, red-haired man advanced further into the room. Jordan indicated a chair then reached into the cabinet next to his desk to extract a bottle of reddish-brown liquid. He filled a glass with the PS4 supplement for Tim and replenished his own drink.

"You said you had news?" he asked eagerly while studying the investigator's composed features.

Tim nodded as he accepted the drink. He took a sip then set the glass down on the edge of Jordan's desk. Lifting his notebook, he said, "I just finished interviewing Mrs. Emma Berkley. Mrs. Berkley is an elderly woman that lives in the Bronx. She reported that she used to be a midwife. About thirty years ago she delivered a baby for a woman fitting Dana's description on board a cruise ship. To the best of her recollection, the baby was a boy and the ship was headed for England."

The earl steepled his fingers. He gazed steadily at his head of security while attempting to rein in his excitement. "How reliable is this information?"

"Knowing how important this is, I followed up on it myself. I didn't detect any duplicity."

Jordan nodded, but remained skeptical. Better to play the devil's advocate then to gain false hope. "Why did it take thirty years to find this woman?"

"She's only recently returned to this country to retire. Before that she was a traveling midwife, providing services to those in need who couldn't afford modern medical care. Her calling seems to have taken her to the more remote parts of the world. And, I have to admit, I didn't think to investigate the rain forest of Costa Rica or the tundra of Antarctica."

"Did she have any other information?" he asked, trying not to let his hopes soar too high. He had been in this position many times in the past three decades. So far none of their leads had ever panned out.

"Yes, but she wasn't sure," he hesitated, but he could tell from his boss's look that if he didn't divulge the rest he would be probed. "She thought the mother made reference to the baby being anemic."

Jordan straightened in his chair and pierced him with a penetrating glare. "How is it that she remembered such a detail after all this time?"

Tim shifted uncomfortably but maintained eye contact. "I wondered the same thing. She said it struck her as odd since the woman had just given birth and the doctor on board hadn't had time to verify the condition. But the mother insisted that it was an inherited trait. The new mom had even planned ahead by bringing a special infant formula she claimed she got from her own doctor prior to the trip."

"Special formula," Jordan mused.

"We're checking the records to confirm her story and following up in the UK. I thought you'd want to know what we have so far. I really have a strong hunch that this time the lead will prove to be accurate. Jordan, it looks like you have a son."

Jordan leaned back, briefly closed his eyes, then exhaled. "A son," he whispered. Despite his best intentions he still felt a spark of hope begin to flicker. After all these years to seriously consider he had a son. He opened his eyes. "Set up an appointment for me with the midwife, I want to talk to her myself. And Tim," he called after the retreating porphyrian, "the sooner the better."

Tim quietly closed Jordan's office door before pausing in the hallway. He stared for a long moment at the Executive Director plaque. He was aware that as directors of the Willow Grove Foundation, both Jordan and Laural had had to make some tough decisions over the years. He knew firsthand about the heartbreak and losses suffered by both. He understood the crusade they were on to purge the agency of the cancerous growth that was spreading by way of the Loyalists. He agreed they must be stopped in order to prevent the infiltration and poisoning of the society they were pledged to protect. But as he walked down the corridor, Tim couldn't help wondering if it ever came down to it would Jordan actually be able to kill his own son?

The elderly woman grinned as she opened the door of her apartment. Her smile broadened and her eyes sparkled as she took in the affluent appearance of her visitor. She stepped aside in order to allow her guest access to her home. The man entered and walked into the dingy, sparsely decorated living room.

Mrs. Emma Berkley followed him into the room while flashing another smile. She was proud of her even white teeth. They were all her own and the only thing she had left that was still in prime condition. Even though she ached with arthritis, and her vision and hearing were deserting her, she could always count on her smile.

"You mentioned you would make this visit worth my while, your lordship," she said, coming directly to their reason for the meeting. No point in offering refreshments she didn't have. She squinted at the man's well-tailored suit and arrogantly set features.

He doesn't look like the type to be interested in staying for tea. No, the likes of him would never soil his clothing by sitting on my old, tattered furniture.

Self-consciously she tugged at the folds of her faded housedress while she continued to watch him. Her uneasiness grew as he disdainfully surveyed her small shabby apartment. A hot flush suffused her cheeks as the visitor turned to scrutinize her with a gaze that was as filled with the same contempt he had bestowed on his surroundings. Fervently she wished that they could quickly conclude their business.

"Did I say I'd make it worth your while? Sorry, Mrs. Berkley, I must have misspoken. I meant you would make it worth mine."

Emma Berkley's eyes rounded as the tall elegantly-clad man produced a dagger from beneath his suit jacket. She began backing toward the door, but before she could escape he interposed himself between her and the exit.

She blinked rapidly several times.

He moved so fast—how did he move that fast? Where else can I go?

She began frantically backing away in the opposite direction. Maybe if she could get the bedroom or bathroom door between her and that wicked-looking knife. He smiled almost affably at her and she had the absurd notion he was reading her thoughts. Her eyes flicked from his face to his hand. Her gaze was caught and held captive by the gleaming blade.

The predator stalked his prey. Matching his pace with hers he followed her across the living room. He always enjoyed the look of terror and helplessness on his victims' faces when they realized their fate. This time was no different. The old hag wasn't smiling at him anymore, he noted with sadistic satisfaction. Normally, he would take more time, tormenting his victim before killing her, but today he couldn't afford to indulge himself.

"My lord," wailed the old woman, "maybe we can renegotiate? I'll give you the information for half the price we agreed."

He continued to advance. The steel blade glistened as it reflected the light.

"For free!" she screeched, cowering in a corner.

As the dagger sliced the air she realized she wouldn't have a chance to make it to the bedroom or bathroom. In desperation, she threw up her arms to ward him off.

Raising the weapon high, he plunged repeatedly down into her arms, chest, and stomach. He watched with perverted pleasure as her skin ripped open and her flesh turned crimson. The crimson rivers flooded the dingy carpet with pools of blood. "The problem is, old woman," he said as she crumpled to the floor, "you've got nothing to negotiate with. I don't want your information, and, unfortunately for you, I don't want anyone else to have it either."

He drove the dagger deep into her chest. The hilt stood at attention, poised like a lone sentinel several inches above her heart. Cataracts and pain clouded her vision as her gaze swept back and forth between the dragon-decorated hilt and the glittering jade-green eyes of her killer. Emma Berkley's last thought as the man's head descended toward her gaping chest wound was that she had seen those eyes somewhere before.

Chapter 3:
The Explosion

Laural seated herself behind her antique rosewood desk. As she pulled her appointment calendar closer she considered her schedule: two business meetings, a charity luncheon, and a trip to the Raven's Nest. She studied the last entry for several seconds. The temporary shelter for porphyrians who were in the process of transitioning into diurnal society was going to have a couple of new arrivals this week. The program had provoked a lot of interest among her people and was most likely the primary reason for the upsurge in inter-species integration in Europe.

Allowing herself a momentary reprieve, she pulled open her bottom desk drawer and extracted her PS4 supplement. She poured a drink and carried it over to the full-length window behind her desk. Mild dizziness and nausea surged up, but she quelled the feeling as she gazed down at busy Bond Street.

London, the city that never sleeps.

She smiled as she watched the early morning traffic, taxi cabs, double-decker buses and pedestrians streaming along.

As the first sip passed her lips she idly wondered where the steady stream of travelers were headed. Many, of course, would be going to work in the numerous office buildings scattered throughout the city. The casual clothes, cameras and shopping bags proclaimed that there were also quite a few sight-seers determinedly seeking the glories of London's tourist attractions.

Sighing, she wished for a moment that she could join them. There was nothing like the impressive experience of walking through Parliament, Big Ben or Westminster Abbey, where Queen Elizabeth I was buried. Viewing the exhibits at the Victoria and Albert Museum, as well as the Crowned Jewels at the Tower of London, was like sharing a piece of the past. She took another sip from her drink while she remembered how impressed she had been to discover that the Tower Of London had actually been erected by William I after he had conquered England in 1066.

She sighed again as she continued to observe the bustling throng from her office window. Ten years ago she had permanently relocated to England, for both professional and personal reasons. Prudence had demanded she either start to show signs of aging or absent herself from their Washington office. She could have employed the same camouflaging techniques Jordan used to make herself appear older, but coming to London had provided the simultaneous resolution of several issues.

Now porphyrians on this side of the Atlantic could have the option of enjoying the benefits of assimilation without having to go halfway around the world. Expanding overseas had also allowed the agency to provide promising European university students in need of financial assistance a chance to benefit from their services.

Laural continued to drain her glass while staring into the last vestiges of the early morning fog. If she was completely honest she'd have to admit that at least part of the reason for leaving Washington had been to escape from her disastrous social life.

Not that I had much of one to escape from. Or at least not since--

Snatching her thoughts away from past regrets, she refocused firmly on the present. So far their plan for assimilation had worked out well. They had integrated twelve of their kind into society in the past decade, a virtual record. Word was getting out and it would only be a matter of time before her parents' dream of porphyrian assimilation into diurnal society would be completely realized.

She lifted her glass in a memorial salute to her parents. Victory and Andrew Gabriel had both been killed thirty years ago. Her mom had been a victim of her depraved uncle, Craven Maxwell. Craven had been a powerful porphyrian who had relished delusions of grandeur. After his half-brother, Andrew Gabriel, had deprived him of his opportunity to dominate the country, Craven had retaliated by murdering Andrew's wife and trying to destroy his child. Victory had paid the ultimate price but Craven's plans for Laural had eventually been thwarted. Unfortunately, Andrew had died in the process. Sometimes her heart still ached with the loss, and she wondered if she would ever heal.

She turned back to the desk, ready to begin the day by returning phone calls. The intercom buzzed. Frowning, she slipped her empty glass back into the cabinet, glanced at her watch then depressed the switch.

"Excuse me, Lady Gabriel, but there's a Tami Baily here to see you."

Laural checked her appointments; Miss Baily was scheduled for the next day. "There's been a mix-up, Colleen. Let Miss Baily know her appointment is tomorrow."

"I did, but she's become extremely upset and is insisting she can't come tomorrow." When her secretary paused Laural could hear the loud crying in the background. "She's quite distressed," murmured Colleen into the receiver.

"I can hear that," she said, glancing at the pile of unanswered messages. She had come in early with the intention of catching up. She blew out a long breath. "Alright, send her in."

A few seconds later the door opened to admit a young pretty brunette. Laural admired her navy skirt and crisp white blouse.

She obviously wants to make a positive impression.

The young woman approached the desk with her hand outstretched, her eyes still brimming with tears. "Thank you so much," she enthused, as she wiped the tears with the back of her free hand. "I don't know how I got the days mixed up, but tomorrow I have to meet with the staff of the daycare center my son will be attending. The slots are so hard to get--I've been on the waiting list for six months. If I cancel tomorrow's appointment they're liable to put me at the bottom of the list again."

Her heart went out to the young mother as she took the proffered paperwork. According to her file Tami was a single parent, struggling to raise her baby while putting herself through school. "That's alright," Laural smiled as she shook the young woman's hand. "I have some time before my first appointment of the day, but you'll understand if the interview has to be condensed."

"I understand," she agreed while seating herself in front of the desk. She arranged her skirt, then folded her hands on her lap while she waited for Laural to speak.

Laural sifted through the application, autobiographical sketch, references, and transcripts. She was impressed that Tami had managed to stay on the Dean's List for the entire four years of her undergraduate studies. Laying the transcript aside she picked up the autobiography. Skimming the text she smiled at the last line. Looking up she asked, "What's your son's name?"

"Bryan," Tami responded with a return smile. Trying to bring the director into better focus she squinted, then blinked rapidly several times.

Watching the other woman, Laural became aware that sunlight from the open drapes was shining directly into her face. Tami's eyes began to water again but this time Laural was certain it was from physical discomfort rather then emotional distress.

She'll probably suffer through the entire interview with the sun beaming into her eyes rather then ask for another concession.

"A little too bright for you?" she asked as she stood and headed toward the window.

Tami blinked rapidly several more times. "Well, now that you mention it…"

Laural drew the outer curtain closed. The lacey fabric would still allow light to penetrate while warding off the direct rays of the sun. "How's that?" she asked, turning back to her client.

The young woman smiled. "I'm truly sorry about the confusion," she reiterated, "but ever since my baby's father disappeared, I've been doing double-duty trying to fill the role of both parents for my little boy. I'm afraid sometimes it gets overwhelming trying to keep everything straight."

Laural's heart constricted as she finished straightening the curtains. Crossing the room she gazed at the determined yet vulnerable face. Something about Tami reminded her of a younger version of herself.

Disappeared is probably a polite way of saying he bailed on them.

She smiled reassuringly as she approached her desk.

A bright flash followed by a deafening roar exploded through the room. Temporarily blind and deaf, Laural futilely reached out a hand in Tami's direction. Above the roar in her ears she thought she heard another noise. It sounded like a scream.

Desperate to find Tami she tried to focus her vision. Through a haze of dust and falling debris, she sought a glimpse of her client. As she tried to move forward the floor shook and shifted beneath her feet.

A second explosion tore through the building.

Glass shattered and shrapnel flew by as she was propelled through the office window. The ground seemed to be rushing up to meet her.

I'm not going to make it.

She was frantically reliving her drop from the top of Penbrook Castle--the cliff, the fall, the rocks. Her father's broken body. These images had played over and over again in nightmares. Only this time she wasn't dreaming. For an instant she knew only pure terror as her fear of heights overwhelmed her then blackness.

Chapter 4:
Chaos and Destruction

The red button on the black phone blinked repeatedly. The shrill ring pierced the stillness of the dark room. The receiver was lifted and a deep voice reverberated across the line. "The mission has been accomplished."

"The instructions were followed precisely?"

"To the letter."

"Complete chaos and destruction of the Willow Grove Foundation's London branch. Edwards and the others have been avenged by devastation beyond repair."

"Good. A lot depends on this—there must be no mistakes."

He cleared his throat. Apprehension seized him as his trembling almost caused the phone to slip from his grip. "An unforeseen development has occurred."

"What kind of unforeseen development?"

The caller hesitated.

"I'm waiting."

"A couple of staff members and a client were in the building when it exploded."

"Are they dead?"

"Yes," he admitted reluctantly, wondering how long he would have left to live.

"Any of ours?"

"No, only diurnals."

A soft chuckle echoed across the line. "That is an unexpected bonus. The House of Penbrook has a reputation for taking good care of those in their service. The blood stains on their honor will be even more devastating then the destruction of the Foundation."

The caller swallowed hard. He hoped his leader would still be in a good mood after he learned all the facts. "One of the diurnals was the mother."

A low rumble flew across the line.

The caller sighed with relief when he realized that instead of the anticipated fury his leader had actually found humor in the situation.

"Another unexpected bonus. It saves us the trouble of eliminating her later." He sobered. "And the marchioness?"

A long pause ensued while the caller listened to the rapid beating of his own heart. He had managed to make it through the first two admissions, but he had a feeling his luck was about to run out. For the second time he wondered what form his execution would take. "Unfortunately, she arrived earlier then expected. She was in the building when it exploded."

"My instructions were specific. The marchioness was to remain unharmed."

"There was a miscalculation," he rushed on. "She wasn't delayed as originally planned."

"Then you've failed at your assignment," he growled.

The caller wiped the sweat from his brow with the back of his sleeve as he quickly explained. "She's only moderately damaged, I'm sure she will heal." He tried to sound confident but when his voice cracked he subsided into silence.

"She better. The Marchioness of Penbrook is imperative for the next phase. If my plans are ruined due to your incompetence the consequences for you will be dire," he warned before abruptly breaking the connection.

Chapter 5:
The Dragon Crest

"She can't be dead," Jordan erupted into his portable phone, needing to refute what he had just heard. Agitatedly he paced back and forth across the Turkish rug covering the living-room floor of his Georgetown brownstone. Flickering flames cast elongated shadows across the wall every time he passed the brick fireplace. He approached the ornately-carved full-length mirror next to the hearth, pausing to glare at his image before turning to retrace his steps.

"I'm really sorry," Tim said in a hushed tone. "She was murdered some time last night. The police and media are swarming. I was able to get in and out just ahead of them. I went through the apartment but couldn't find any additional information about Dana and the child. All we have is what Mrs. Berkley told me originally. I've been following other leads, but it seems, after they disembarked in London, they just vanished."

He paused briefly as another car with flashing lights and NYPD emblazoned on the side whizzed past. He consulted his notes while striding briskly down the street. "They registered on board under assumed names, but they weren't hard to trace since Dana was the only one who gave birth on board. The records confirm the midwife's story. But, after they reached port in England, it's a dead end."

Jordan sat down hard on the tan leather sofa in his living room and raked his hand through his chestnut hair. He let out a long frustrated breath. "Any ideas on who killed the old woman?" he asked, shaking his head. It was likely their interest had inadvertently brought about her death.

"No, not specifically," Tim sighed, placing his notebook in his pocket as he approached his car. Holding the phone between his ear and shoulder he took out his key and opened the door. Sitting behind the wheel he placed the key in the ignition but didn't engage the engine.

Pulling out the object he had found at the crime scene, he stared down at the dagger for a long moment. "But I've got a couple of things you need to know about."

Jordan narrowed his eyes and sat up straight. "What are they?"

"The first is the murder weapon. I'll be bringing it in as soon as I'm done here, but in the meantime…" He flashed Jordan a mental image of the dragon-handled dagger.

Jordan's eyes widened. "The Maxwell family crest," he whispered as his face blanched.

So, the Loyalists are finally putting their cards on the table. Up until now they've remained much more covert. What's brought them to the point where they're ready to admit their game plan?

"Yes," Tim agreed, being careful to keep the weapon below window level as he turned it over in his hand in order to inspect it from all angles. "I thought it would be prudent to remove it before the police took it in for evidence."

"Good thinking. I need to see it as soon as possible. What else did you find?"

Tim chose his words carefully. "The body was completely devoid of blood."

For a moment he was perplexed. "From the knife wounds?"

Tim pressed on. "There was quite a lot of blood loss due to the multiple stabbings but not enough to account for the corpse to be totally drained."

Jordan inhaled sharply. "A blood drinker," he said hoarsely.

"Should we contact Laural?" asked Tim. He shoved the dagger back into his inside pocket and turned the ignition key.

Jordan's eyes flicked to the photo of his cousin on the end table. "I'll handle it." He paused to collect his thoughts. "Did you get a chance to search the midwife's apartment well enough to insure there was nothing that would connect the murder to any porphyrians?"

"I did as thorough a job as I could before the authorities and press arrived," he confirmed. "My search didn't turn up any revelations about the motive for the murder or information about your son. Whatever data this woman had must have been kept in her head."

"Damn," he exploded, slamming his fist down on the coffee table. He had been so close to obtaining the first real clue he had ever had about his son, and now he was no closer then before. "Tim, this investigation's been going on for thirty years, and now you're telling me all we've got to show for it is a renegade blood drinker and a Maxwell memento?"

After pulling out of the mainstream traffic and onto a side street of the dilapidated Bronx neighborhood, Tim dragged the dagger out again. He studied the blade with its dragon hilt. The malevolent ruby eyes glared back at him. "I think this may be more of a clue then you think. The design appears authentic, and it's my understanding that only members of the Maxwell family had the originals."

Jordan went very still. He stared blankly into space while trying to assimilate what he had just heard. Craven's family were the only porphyrians who ever used the dragon emblem on their personal correspondence and family heirlooms. The last time Jordan had seen an authentic Maxwell dragon crest had been on Craven's journals. Those journals had contained personal notes on research he was conducting--research which would have enslaved porphyrians and destroyed humanity if he and Andrew hadn't put a permanent end to Craven's diabolical plans.

Up until that moment he had assumed Tim's find had been a replica used by the Loyalists to symbolically represent their lost leader. That would have been bad enough, for it would insinuate that the rebels had every intention of pursuing Craven's schemes to dominate the diurnals. He closed his eyes against the implications. "Bring it to me now." Silence hung suspended on the line for several seconds.

"You know both of these matters have to remain completely confidential."

"I understand," confirmed Tim, while slipping the dagger back into his inner pocket.

Jordan reached up to yank off his tie. He hadn't even had time to change before the call had come through. Expecting good news he had been disappointed to be confronted by another failure. "Now that the Loyalists have raised the stakes by killing a diurnal, I want all available manpower diverted to this investigation. There's obviously more at stake here then just finding my--"

He stopped short as the doorbell rang. He waited expectantly, and then remembered Mable, his part-time cook and cleaning lady, had already left for the evening. Stomping over to the door he jerked it open. Annoyance gave way to surprise when he saw his cousin standing on the threshold.

"Tim, get on it and let me know."

He disconnected the phone as he followed Laural to the living room. Collapsing onto the sofa, she buried her face in her hands and burst into tears.

Chapter 6:
Loyalist Vendetta

Jordan sat on the couch next to Laural and gently pulled her into his arms. Rubbing her back, he probed and then waited for her to speak first.

Finally she lifted her head. Tears continued to pour from her sapphire eyes as she searched his face. "It was awful."

"Want to tell me about it?" he asked offering her a handkerchief.

"You probed," she said dabbing at her eyes.

"Only far enough to check how deep your distress went."

She leaned back and stared silently into the distance for so long that Jordan felt compelled to probe a second time. His mental enquiry brought her back into focus. Her eyes started to fill with tears again but she rapidly blinked them away. "Have there been any problems at the Foundation?"

Confused, he frowned. "You come halfway around the world without notice, dropping yourself on my doorstep ready to collapse, just to get a status update?"

Her eyes sought his. "Someone's trying to kill me."

He went rigid as every muscle in his body tensed. His green eyes flashed while he studied her intently. "I think you better start at the beginning," he commanded in a steely voice.

Noting the carefully controlled fury, she hesitated. "You haven't seen the news today?"

He stared back curiously. "No, I've been tied up in meetings all day. I just got home and have been on the phone with Tim ever since. Laural, what's going on?"

She closed her eyes, wishing for a way to prepare him for the shock. Knowing she couldn't put it off, she opened her eyes and confronted him directly. "After I spoke to you this morning, the building was bombed. There's nothing left but rubble. I was blown through my office window and thrown clear. Since there was no corresponding attack here, I think it was personal. I know I face death all the time when I go after the Loyalists, but this was different. It was so covert and subversive it undermined my feeling of security. I was too afraid to go home so I came here."

"Oh, my God!" His jade green eyes scanned her face then ran up and down the length of her body. "Were you seriously injured?"

She smiled weakly and shook her head. "Nothing that won't heal. But it was difficult getting out of the hospital without letting the doctors give me a thorough examination. "

Jordan looked alarmed.

She placed a reassuring hand on his arm. "Don't worry. I left quickly enough to prevent them from checking too closely. Because of the condition I was in, the medical staff protested, but when I insisted on leaving against medical advice there was nothing they could do."

Jordan's jaw hardened as his fists balled in impotent rage. "Just how bad were you hurt?" he repeated more sternly, certain she was holding back.

She squeezed his hand. "I know you feel responsible for me but, really, I'm okay." He still looked unconvinced so she continued, "Mom and Dad couldn't have done a better job of protecting me, Jordan, but even they would recognize they couldn't guard me all the time."

"Maybe opening the branch so far away wasn't such a good idea."

She pulled back to look up at him. "You know better, and besides you and I are the strongest among our kind. In that lies my safety."

"Being the most gifted doesn't protect you from bombs."

She nodded solemnly. "There are some things that we just can't guard against." Her eyes roamed over his tense features. She felt a warm glow at the concern he projected. For the first time in several hours she began to feel safe. "Even though I believe this is a Loyalist vendetta against me, we can't rule out the possibility you may be at risk too. The best course of action is to eliminate the remaining Loyalists before they cause more damage."

He pulled her into his arms again, hugging her fiercely. He couldn't imagine life without her. "You're right. If the worst is that our building is a pile of rubble, I'll consider we got off lightly."

She stiffened in his arms. Pulling back, she shook her head. "That's not the worst part," she sobbed, her eyes haunted by the memories.

He waited as his green eyes probed hers. Whoever had darkened those sapphire eyes with such abject misery would pay dearly.

"Three diurnals were killed. I was in early so most of the staff hadn't yet arrived, but my receptionist and the security guard were on duty. And," she continued, her voice breaking, "there was a young mom, Tami. She was only twenty-two and had a baby boy. She was a single parent struggling to provide everything so her child could enjoy the benefits of life. She was full of hope and plans for making a better future for herself and her son. Now all that remains of Tami won't even be enough for a decent funeral."

Jordan's heart ached as he considered her words. Obviously, the Loyalists were becoming so bold they didn't care about the risk of exposure. His phone rang.

"Hello." He paused. "Yes, she's here. She told me. No, she's alright." He listened for several seconds. "Yes, she's unharmed. I know, she just filled me in. I want you on it right away. We'll have to postpone that for now. I want to know who's behind this. Work with Ben Fletcher and the local London authorities whenever you can, but do whatever is necessary to insure I get a full report as soon as possible. "

She tapped her finger against his arm.

"Hold on a minute, Tim." He looked at her expectantly.

"Let's not assume that because the same thing hasn't happened here yet means it isn't going to. Have Tim check for explosives."

He turned back to the phone, but again she touched his arm. He looked up and gasped.

Laural nodded as she held the dragon pendant in front of him. The malevolent ruby eyes flashed as they caught the light. "I was wearing this when I woke up in the hospital."

Chapter 7:
The Heirlooms

"So what do we have, Tim?" asked Jordan from behind his office desk as he stared hard at his assistant director.

Tim stretched his shoulders as he tried to work out the kinks brought on by the long drive back from New York, followed up with hours spent hunched over his computer screen. He looked down at his notepad, then up to confront his boss's steely gaze.

"After consulting with Ben Fletcher and drawing from the information he's gathered so far, we've come to the following conclusions: The explosives appear to be made from components which could be obtained providing you had the right connections. They had the capability of being detonated from almost any location within a certain radius. There were six bombs in total, and they were placed in strategic points designed to cause the most structural damage.

"Since the explosion occurred prior to business hours, Ben and I are in agreement that the most logical conclusion at this point is that the target was the building itself rather then either clients or employees. We believe it was *not* part of the plan," he turned to face Laural, "that you or anyone else would be in the building at the time of the explosions. Of course, all these suppositions are only preliminary and subject to change as we gather more information. Ben's very concerned and asked how you're holding up. I told him you were still shaken about the incident, but that physically you were fine. He recommended you remain here for a few days until he gets a more complete picture of what's going on."

Laural stood and walked over to the wall-length window. Parting the drapes she stared down at the city street below. Anxiety threatened but she quickly pushed it away. *How long will this acrophobia continue to plague me?* She smiled sardonically to herself. *Probably at least until I stop dropping off cliffs or falling from skyscrapers.*

She could certainly understand Ben Fletcher's concern. He had been the assistant director and head of security of their London branch, as well as her personal friend, long enough to accurately guess how deeply the tragedy would affect her. Tears blurred her vision as she thought of her staff and the young woman who had been in her office when the bomb went off. She couldn't imagine how they would explain to Bryan that depriving him of his mother had not been part of some demented psychopath's plan, but just a horrible accident of Tami being in the wrong place at the wrong time.

What comfort would that give to a child growing up without his mother? None at all!

Pulling Jordan's handkerchief from her pocket she firmly brushed away her tears. She had tried to return the handkerchief to him last night but now she was grateful he had insisted she keep it. Staring at the crumpled cloth she wondered how many more times she would need it. Shoving the cloth back in her pocket she pivoted to face her companions. Blue sparks shot from her eyes and her chin rose resolutely as she walked back toward them. "Unintentional or not, people were killed. The Loyalists will pay with their heads. I owe Tami's son and the families of my staff retribution."

"If it was the Loyalists," Jordan inserted. He was watching her closely, and recognized that defiant stance. She had been in the same state of mind right after her parents had been killed. A vengeance quest could warp her judgment and cause her to get sloppy; just as it had all those years ago.

Reading the projected thought, she glared at him. "This time is different. I'm no longer a naive fledgling unfamiliar with her own abilities."

He searched her face and reached for her hand to tug her back toward the couch. For a moment she resisted then allowed herself to be reseated.

"It most likely was the Loyalists," he said out loud, glancing toward Tim for confirmation. The big man nodded and Jordan went on, "but we've got to be sure and then make a strategic plan. We are not going to do something rash just to get revenge."

"Tell that to Tami's baby," she shot back hotly. Then she leaned back, closed her eyes and took a steadying breath. She knew all too well what it was like to lose parents to a psychopath, but Jordan was right: She couldn't allow her personal feelings to cloud her judgment. Opening her eyes again she caught Jordan watching her intently. She said more calmly but with complete conviction, "The culprits will be brought to justice."

They all sat silently for a few moments. "How long before we get confirmation on who's behind it?" Laural asked.

"We're still in the elimination process. The Loyalists are the most likely, but there are a few publicity-hungry terrorist groups already taking credit," Tim reported as he shuffled his paperwork. "Ben and I don't want to jump to conclusions and miss something vital in a rush to blame Craven's supporters."

"Do you think any of the other terrorist groups would have left this?" she demanded, lifting the large dragon pendant from where it lay next to the dagger on the desk. The heavy gold links felt oily and slick in her hand. Mesmerized, she gazed into the blood-red eyes. A sense of malignancy emanated from the heirloom, penetrating, then boring into her. Like venom from a viper she could feel the poison spreading through her veins, wrapping its coils around her mind and crushing her spirit. She dropped the chain abruptly. It landed with a loud clink back on the desk.

"No," Tim admitted. "And I don't think any other terrorist group drained Mrs. Berkley's body of all its blood, then left a dagger with the Maxwell crest at the midwife's murder scene either. But I need to be sure. Any mistakes we make in this investigation could prove catastrophically fatal."

Laural wiped her hands on her skirt while continuing to stare into the dragon's eyes. Jordan placed a hand on her arm. Shaking free of the pendant's hypnotic hold she turned her attention back to Tim. Giving him a long level look, she said, "Be thorough but be quick. We need to exterminate the blood drinker as soon as we get confirmation its one of our own and not a deviant diurnal. I'm also not going to wait long to make up to Tami's baby or the families of my staff for the loss of their loved ones."

"You have to stop persecuting yourself. It wasn't you're fault," Jordan projected silently.

Her eyes locked with Jordan's. She nodded before giving her attention back to Tim.

"I don't expect it will take long to get to the bottom of this," asserted Tim while gathering his notes.

Relief flooded through her. She ached to get her hands on the culprits. Despite Jordan's protestations she felt powerless to assuage her guilt until she did.

Frowning, Jordan glanced from his cousin back to the head of security. "What makes you so sure?"

"Because nothing else makes sense. Other then that one group, the two of you and the foundation have no other enemies. If it were an act of random violence there are a lot more illustrious targets then a philanthropic agency geared toward providing student scholarships and training programs for immigrants. Besides," he continued, staring at the pendant and dagger lying on the desk, "as Laural just pointed out, these," he jabbed his finger at the objects, "were not left by random perpetrators or a terrorist organization. They were left as specific calling cards. Although we need to be thorough, checking into other options is basically going to be just a formality."

Laural and Jordan exchanged a long look. "I guess," started Laural slowly while watching Jordan's face, "this puts a whole new slant on finding your child."

He stared back. They both knew the implications of the Maxwell calling cards. "Or his mother," he conceded. "After all, it wouldn't be the first time Dana's switched sides."

Tim nodded his agreement. "The last we knew she had realigned herself with her father."

"And even though Craven's been dead for three decades," Jordan said bitterly, "there's never been a sign from her to indicate a change of heart."

Laural winced. During her childhood she had been good friends with Dana Maxwell. "She acted that way only because of her father's influence." Jordan and Tim both stared at her, but she continued staunchly, "And even after he was no longer a threat she had her newborn to consider. She had no way of knowing how you'd react to a baby born addicted to blood. I know if I were a mother I'd do everything I could to protect my child--even if I had to hide the baby from its own father."

Weariness darkened his eyes as he responded, "I want to believe in her as much as you do, but we can't ignore the evidence." He waved a hand at the objects scattered on the desk. "As difficult as it is, we've got to be realistic—only Dana would have access."

"Or your child," she said softly.

He looked at her then turned back to Tim. "What about the search for my son?"

Tim heaved a heavy sigh. "We've run into a brick wall. The very few leads we've obtained from the midwife have led to dead-ends. I have a hunch we won't find your son until he wants to be found."

Jordan studied the Maxwell heirlooms for a long moment, then stood and walked to the window Laural had stared out a few minutes earlier. The seconds ticked by but no one spoke. He considered how the situation might have turned out if he had been able to raise his own child. His son's life could have turned out so differently if he had grown up in a loving, caring environment instead of under the shadow of the Maxwell legacy.

However, he could no longer afford to indulge in speculation. People were dying and he had responsibilities. Massaging the back of his neck he turned to find them both watching him. He smiled slightly as he noted the concern and compassion on their faces. "I'm aware that we have to consider that he could be leading the Loyalists and may very well turn out to be the blood drinker."

Relief flooded their faces. Tim rose and headed for the door. "I'm back on it. I've got all available manpower on it too. Until we get a clearer idea of what's going on, I'm assigning bodyguards to both of you."

At their startled expressions he held up his hand. "I know you both like to think your invulnerable, but if one or more of the Maxwells is involved, both of you are at risk. You both know as well as I do that their mental and physical strength is comparable to your own."

"So much for this being an attack against the agency instead of us personally," Laural grumbled.

Tim nodded. "I'm still convinced whoever is behind this didn't want you dead, at least not yet. Otherwise," he stated emphatically as he pointed at the pendant, "whoever was with you while you were unconscious would have cut off your head or set you on fire instead of just leaving you a memento."

Heat flooded her face as his words hit home.

He pressed his point. "Whoever this is seems to be playing a game of cat-and-mouse with the two of you. They're starting out by toying with you but we all know what happens to the mouse once the cat tires of the game."

Chapter 8:

Instinct

After the head of security left the room Laural faced her cousin. "Are we really going to allow him to place bodyguards with us?"

He stared at her for a long moment while the thought of how she had nearly been killed played through his mind. "We should at least consider the idea."

She raised her brows.

"You're right, I suppose not, at least not yet. It's just too cumbersome and there are certain activities that we need to attend to alone."

She nodded, glad they were in agreement. Then she frowned. "You didn't tell me you found out your child was a male."

Jordan exhaled as he sat back down behind his desk. "I didn't get a chance. When you showed up last night it kind of slipped my mind. Don't take this the wrong way," he said eyeing her speculatively, "but why come here instead of staying in England?"

She gave him a long searching look, leaning forward in her chair. "As I told you last night, I didn't feel safe."

He raised his brows. "But there were plenty of places for you to seek refuge which were much closer, including your own estate. And I'm sure Ben Fletcher would have provided a security detail."

Hesitantly, she explained. "Despite Tim's instincts, I think the attack was meant to kill me."

His first impulse was to deny it. After all, Tim's evidence was pretty conclusive. But he also knew Laural was very intuitive. Her instincts had kept her alive despite all the years of combating Loyalists. "Why?"

She stared hard at the pendant and dagger, as if expecting them to lend credence to her supposition. "Because I've been killing off too many of their group to remain unnoticed. I'm sure terminating me is one of their top priorities. And if it was only the agency they were intent on destroying, why not attack here too?" She didn't add that she felt less exposed and more secure with Jordan's protectiveness shielding her. She knew it was irrational but her cousin always made her feel safe.

"Alright, let's go with your theory for a moment. If whoever did this wanted you dead, then why not just kill you at the scene?"

She shrugged. "Maybe they were interrupted. Or it's possible they spontaneously changed their mind in favor of a different plan. I don't have all the answers—I just know what I feel, and my instincts are telling me this was personal."

He frowned. "We don't know for sure this facility hasn't been targeted. Just because we came up clean for explosives doesn't mean there wasn't a plan—or still is one, for that matter. Maybe whoever it is was just waiting for us to be in the same place so he can kill two birds with one stone. Besides, you can't discount the murder of the midwife." He nodded toward the dagger. "I'd say that part was personally aimed at me."

The intercom buzzed. Jordan depressed the button. "Yes, Betty?"

"There's a professor from Georgetown University insisting on seeing Lady Gabriel."

His brows lowered. "We're in an important meeting and are not to be disturbed."

"Yes, sir, I told him, but he's quite insistent that he schedule an appointment with her before she returns to England."

Jordan raised his brows, glancing toward Laural. "How would he have known you were here?"

Laural shrugged.

He turned his attention back to Betty. "Did he explain what he needed that's so urgent?"

"Professor Ravensblood said he's the head of the archeology department at Georgetown University and wishes to discuss an on-site project for the upcoming semester."

Green eyes clashed with blue as they both sat back—stunned.

Chapter 9:
The Professor

Laural's pulse raced as she sat behind the large mahogany desk in Jordan's office. Her heart pounded erratically as she stared steadily at the man across from her. He had coal black hair, bright green eyes and appeared to be in his early thirties. His face was lean with a strong square chin and aquiline nose. The determined set of his jaw was offset by his friendly smile as he gazed directly back at her.

A warm glow suffused her as she tried to pinpoint the reason behind her response.

He's certainly attractive--but is my reaction purely physical?

When her eyes lifted back to meet his she paused. A moment of disorientation gripped her as she was mesmerized by the intensity of his gaze.

Subtly, her visitor cleared his throat. Her composure slipped a notch as her mind snapped back into focus. His expression left no doubt that he had been aware of her perusal. Mortified she swiftly turned away to hide the bright flush staining her cheeks.

Out of the corner of her eye she continued to covertly study the professor. He certainly didn't remind her of any instructors she had had when she was in college. He was too damned good-looking and sexy. Dressed in penny loafers, khaki fatigues and an oxford shirt he exuded both casual charm and raw masculinity. The shirt was rolled back at the cuffs and open at the neckline to reveal muscular arms and a strong throat. His frame was lean and the exposed skin on his forearms, throat and face was deeply bronzed, offering testimony to many hours spent in the sun.

Despite her best effort to appear neutral, her eyes were drawn back to his of their own volition. The air between them crackled with suppressed tension. A force like a low-grade current vibrated through Laural as his intense jade gaze sent an unspoken promise from their fathomless depths. She swallowed hard past the lump in her throat while she continued to drown in the enigmatic sea-green pools.

"Let me get this straight, Professor Ravensblood," she ventured in a voice she hardly recognized as her own. Clearing her throat she continued more steadily, "You'd like my permission to take a group of post-graduate archeology students on a field excursion to Penbrook Castle?"

Professor Nicholas Ravensblood leaned forward to prop his elbows on the desk. His eyes gleamed with so much excitement that Laural felt herself being drawn into his zeal. "This is much more then a student excursion, Lady Gabriel."

She wrinkled her nose. "When in the States I prefer to drop my English title."

"Alright, Ms. Gabriel."

"How about Laural?"

He raised his brows.

She stared back, unable to determine why she had extended such familiarity.

His green eyes darkened as he studied her. His expression was inscrutable as he continued, "I don't want to offend you, especially since I'm asking for such a favor, but I'd prefer to keep this on a more professional level."

Color rose to her cheeks. "As you wish," she agreed stiffly.

His eyes searched her face. "As I was saying, it's much more then a field trip. My students are highly trained and experienced, only one step away from their doctorates. Some of them have been involved in important excavations and a few have even co-authored papers on their field work. I can assure you we take our excavations very seriously. This would be much more then just a bunch of amateurs poking around your estate."

She frowned. "My family's ancestral home is in a secluded area for a reason. The Gabriels have always valued their privacy. I'm not sure that I would be interested in allowing strangers to excavate parts of my property, no matter how professional they are. Surely there are other sites in England that would suit your needs."

He leaned back, crossing one ankle over the other knee while continuing to gaze intently at her. He nodded toward the papers on the desk. "As you can see by my proposal, I have several sites planned for excavation field work. Yours is one of the most appealing because it's never been explored. The idea of a fresh site is every field archeologist's dream. In addition, my research indicates there's a good chance we could make some historically significant finds in that area."

His eyes glowed with an inner fervor as he spoke. Beguiled by his enthusiasm, Laural felt her resolve weakening.

"Besides," he said, grinning, "I think I can make it worth your while."

She arched her brows but before she could speak her cousin interjected, "How could you make it worth Lady Gabriel's while?"

Slowly, the other two turned toward Jordan who was sitting on the leather couch. As her eyes met and held his, Laural realized he had been aware of the effect the professor was having on her. Awkwardness overwhelmed her and she dropped her eyes. Heat flooded her face as she continued to feel the weight of her cousin's gaze boring into her.

She had been so involved with Ravensblood that until Jordan had spoken up she had all but forgotten his presence. Regaining her composure she lifted her eyes. Jordan was still studying her. The look on his face made it clear he was aware of her preoccupation. She turned away when she began to blush again.

What's wrong with me? I'm allowing these two men to make me blush like some sort of schoolgirl with a crush on the teacher. Or like someone with a guilty conscience.

But she had nothing to feel guilty about, and regretted the impulse that had prompted her to request Jordan remain for the interview. Not that she could have kept him from it, she realized, while glancing back and forth between the two men.

"I offer," replied Ravensblood, dividing his attention between the earl and the marchioness, "the same thing I offer all my benefactors: the opportunity to recover lost artifacts from their ancestors, and sometimes even some of the ancestors' remains. You'd be surprised at the amount of buried artifacts recovered from these sites--living utensils, plate ware, ancient coins, documents, even bones. You never know," he smiled and shrugged, "we could uncover your great-great grandfather."

She had to admit she was intrigued. But she didn't know if her interest was in the project he proposed or the man behind the project?

"I don't think it's a wise idea," Jordan communicated silently.

Her eyes flew to the couch. Jordan was scrutinizing their guest with a look on his face Laural couldn't quite identify. She threw him a telepathic question, "Why not?"

"Because if he and his students were to go digging up Penbrook property, who knows what they might uncover. What if there are some long buried porphyrians out there?"

"What if there are? Our bone structure is the same so they'd never realize what they'd found. Besides what about the documents the Loyalists are searching for? Couldn't they be buried on the estate?"

During her quest to wipe out the Loyalists she had recently been receiving telepathic images indicating the group was looking for documents they considered important to their cause. No details had been forthcoming, however, and she had been left frustrated and confused.

"If there's a possibility they are then that's all the more reason not to allow his request."

Ravensblood coughed discreetly. Terminating the telepathic discourse with Jordan, she smiled at the professor. "What happens to any artifacts found on the site?"

Recognizing a crucial point, he grinned. "They become the sole property of the owner. Of course," he added lightly, "if we find the missing link or Noah's ark, I'd expect to write a paper on our findings. Even though I'm optimistic, I have to admit the vast majority of the time the artifacts found are of interest only to the family."

She nodded then stood. "Your proposal requires further consideration. I need to review the paperwork you've provided and think about it a little longer before I decide."

He stood and held out his hand. As their hands clasped their eyes locked. For several heartbeats neither spoke. Laural felt as if the entire world had constricted to a focal point in this one moment. Finally, Ravensblood smiled. The smile caused tiny creases at the corners of his eyes.

He's too young to have crow's feet.

She continued to stare.

"Thank you for your time and consideration. I'll be waiting eagerly for your decision."

He gave her hand a final squeeze. He shook hands with the earl and left the room. After he had gone Laural stood for a long moment, staring thoughtfully after him.

Chapter 10:
Connections

"Are you out of your mind?" demanded the Earl of Rockford several hours later as he paced agitatedly across the office floor. "I can't believe you'd allow a group of college students to go tramping through Penbrook's grounds. What if they actually made a significant discovery?"

Laural shrugged her shoulders. "What if they did?" She leaned back in the swivel chair and pushed back from the mahogany desk. Eyeing her cousin warily, she continued cautiously, "You heard Professor Ravensblood. Anything they find will be handed over to me. If there are any artifacts from my ancestors buried on the estate, I'd like to have them. And you never know," she finished as she continued to watch him pace, "they might find something we can use in our battle against the Loyalists."

"That's exactly my point," Jordan objected, halting in front of her and leaning his hands on the desk. "If they find anything of relevance, the existence of our species would be exposed. We'd become the next media frenzy. How would you like to try and explain their discoveries and our existence to six billion curious diurnals watching CNN?"

She leaned back further in her chair and arched her eyebrows. "Really, Jordan, don't you think you're being a little melodramatic? I've had time to thoroughly read over the proposal, and unless you have a better reason to deny the request, I don't see any harm in it." He still looked unconvinced, so she went on in a more placating tone, "Maybe letting them explore the area will be to our benefit. If the documents the Loyalists are searching for are buried on the estate, I can't think of a better way to find out then by letting a group that won't arouse suspicion do the checking for us. If we hired a team of professionals to do it we'd attract unwanted attention and publicity. This way it looks like nothing more then a philanthropic gesture."

He stared hard at her expressive face and excited sapphire eyes. She was so young and naive despite her forty-eight years. "I've got a bad feeling about Ravensblood. Are you sure your interest isn't more in the professor than the project?"

As the telltale flush stained her cheeks she dropped her eyes to the papers covering the desk.

Did he read my thoughts? No, of course not. Jordan would never violate my privacy.

She frowned while skimming over the dossier Tim Cooper had provided on the background of Nicholas Ravensblood. "I don't know what you mean," she hedged. Avoiding his penetrating glare she flipped through the papers. A pair of bright green eyes seemed to stare back at her from the pages.

Jordan threw himself into the wingback chair in front of the desk. When she finally looked up, he said gently, "Laural, you're allowed to be attracted to him. Just because things didn't work out between you and Jim doesn't mean you can't have another relationship."

Her eyes glittered. "Having a relationship with someone who's going to grow old and die before I physiologically age past my twenties is not my idea of a viable option."

"But you were attracted to him?" he pressed.

She raised her chin defiantly. "I can control my emotions. I won't allow a physical attraction to cloud my judgment."

"Good, because there's something about him that doesn't feel quite right."

"That's the second time you've mentioned concerns. Do you have anything specific?"

"I took a cursory reading, nothing beyond the surface level," he reassured her, noting her startled glance. "The name was so obvious I had to check him out."

"And?" she prompted.

"And nothing. He reads clean, at least on the surface." He shrugged.

Laural nodded. Porphyrian ethics would never allow for the intrusion into a diurnal's thoughts without extreme provocation.

Jordan changed the subject. "What about the documents you mentioned? If the Loyalists are searching for them, they're sure to be detrimental to humanity as well as problematic for us. What makes you think they might be buried on the estate?"

She frowned and shook her head. "I have no idea whether anything of significance is buried on the estate. I'm not even sure what we're looking for. All I have to go by are some vague thoughts I've picked up about the PS4 supplement and research into our people's past. If Ravensblood and his students find anything like that, the idea is that they'll hand them over to me as ancestral junk mail. Maybe we should have had the grounds checked before this, but having them do it for us now is too good an opportunity to pass up…" Laural trailed off when she noticed Jordan staring vacantly into space. She was sure he hadn't heard most of what she had said.

"Not again," he mumbled to himself.

As Laural watched him, his eyes snapped back into focus, boring into her with an intensity that made her uneasy.

"Tell me everything you can remember about the thoughts you picked up from the Loyalists," he demanded.

She frowned, concentrating. "Well, for one thing, I think imminent death muddled their thoughts because, in their minds, they kept referring to the supplement as PS3. I also got several mental images of a picture of a dragon. It looked exactly like the design on the dagger and the pendant."

Jordan reached into the desk drawer, withdrew the dagger and pendant and placed them on the desk. "Are you sure this is the same emblem?" he asked, tapping the dagger.

She lifted the pendant with its heavy gold links and stared as the dragon twirled on the end of its chain. The malevolent blood-red ruby eyes stared back. Hesitantly she reached for the dagger in her other hand. She held both artifacts tightly for several long moments before dropping them onto the desk, where they landed with dual thuds in the center of the papers on the history of Nicholas Ravensblood. "One and the same," she asserted, unable to tear her gaze away from the glittering ruby orbs.

"This one," he said, tapping the pendant, "shows up around your neck after the explosion, and this one," he indicated the dagger, "just happens to wind up buried deep in the chest of the midwife who delivered my son. Not likely a coincidence."

Dragging her eyes away from the dagger she stared at her cousin. "How do you think all these pieces fit together?"

"I'm not sure, but I'm starting to make a few connections and I don't like where they're leading." He held up a hand to forestall more questions. "I'll let you know as soon as my theory takes shape. Are you sure, where Ravensblood is concerned, you can remain objective?" he asked softly.

She flushed but gazed steadily back. "I'm sure I can control my raging hormones," she stated firmly.

"Good, because I would hate to have your decision based on a physiological reaction."

She dropped her gaze from his probing eyes. Her glance fell back on the blade. She studied the handle as an uneasy feeling settled in the pit of her stomach. He wouldn't probe if she didn't want him to, one of the porphyrian moral codes she was especially grateful for.

She handed the dagger back to her cousin. Her voice shook with outrage as she reflected on the unfortunate soul who had died just so the Loyalists could keep their secrets. "Have Tim or Ben come up with any leads on Mrs. Berkley's murder?"

He shook his head. "Except for the obvious conclusion that the two events are related."

"Yes," she nodded. "It's also obvious the Loyalists don't want you to find out about your son. With a blood drinker appearing at the same time as the Maxwell heirlooms, they might as well have taken out a front-page ad." Laural fought for control. Her rage was always piqued whenever innocent lives were sacrificed. Trying to cool her temper she scanned the documents before her. "You know, if I didn't know better, I'd have put money on this Professor Ravensblood being your son."

He sighed as he slipped the dagger and pendant back into the drawer. Loosening his tie he said, "So would I."

"You were right about the surname. It's just begging to be recognized."

"Along with the eye and hair color."

"But the skin tone, I never saw a porphyrian with a tan."

He chuckled. "Ultra-violet rays are not our best ally. However," he continued, sobering, "I suppose if someone wanted to take the time to build up solar tolerance it could be done."

"But you didn't get any reading from him indicating he's anything other then what he professes?"

He shook his head. "Besides," he said, nodding toward the report, "Tim's very thorough dossier shows this guy's complete history."

"I know. Born and raised in Syracuse, New York. Parents, siblings, schools he attended, friends and activities. Attended Syracuse University for undergrad with dual majors in anthropology and archeology, then Georgetown for his masters and doctorate. This report even states he was on the school ski team and broke his leg in a skiing accident ten years ago." She looked up. "The broken leg certainly casts doubt."

"Read on--there's more."

She sifted through the pages. "More medical records going all the way back to childhood. Immunization records, medical reports on chicken pox and other childhood illnesses. Sprained wrist in seventh grade from gymnastics." She let the papers slip through her fingers. "He certainly seems to be physically active and academically proficient."

"But unless his whole life is an illusion we're back to square one."

"I'm sorry," she said softly, her eyes glowing. She knew how important it was for Jordan to find his son.

The intercom buzzed. "Professor Ravensblood on line one."

She lifted the receiver. "Hello, Professor."

"Please call me Nicholas."

She raised her brows. "I thought we were staying on professional terms."

"I've reconsidered. If we're going to be spending a lot of time together, I think Lady Gabriel and Professor Ravensblood would be rather cumbersome."

"You're assuming we're going to be spending a lot of time together. Isn't that rather presumptuous?"

"Yes, but hopeful."

"Alright, Nicholas."

"Actually that still sounds too formal. My friends call me Nick."

"I've come to my decision, Nick."

"I actually called to invite you to dinner."

"Dinner?" Her eyes flew to Jordan. He scowled. "I'd like to have dinner with you. We can discuss the details then."

"Am I to assume you've agreed?"

She studied her cousin for a long moment before answering. She knew his objections, and even considered his points valid, but something inside compelled her. "Yes," she answered softly.

Chapter 11:
Laural's Lesson

"As your mentor and guardian I insist," Jordan stated firmly while tugging Laural by the hand through the steel double doors.

Rolling her eyes she humored him and allowed herself to be pulled into the training room. "You haven't been my guardian or mentor for a long time."

"True," he agreed while keeping a firm grip on her hand, "but now I'm wondering if I relinquished that role prematurely."

Laural was taken aback. Halting abruptly she dropped his hand. "I was under the impression that I had far exceeded the proficiency level a long time ago." Certainly after battling Loyalists for well over twenty years she was beyond the need for any additional training.

What's Jordan up to?

Her eyes swept around the spacious security training area. Pummel horses, trampolines, flying rings, balance beams and a fifty-foot climbing wall took up one side of the spacious gymnasium. Another portion was dedicated to fencing. A weapons cabinet containing several swords, rapiers and daggers of various types stood in the far corner. A shooting range surrounded by sound-proof walls completed the training room.

She had a similar training area in the London branch and worked out diligently six days a week. Or at least she had, she amended frowning, before the explosion.

Dark thoughts continued to plague her as her attention was drawn to the gun range. Tim was instructing a new security employee. Pleased by his performance, she continued to watch as the pair pumped rounds into the target. She was gratified to see that their program was proving so successful. This was the third new security guard added to their staff in the past sixty days. With the increase in Loyalist attacks they couldn't have enough protection.

Tim looked up, saw her and waved. She smiled and nodded. Returning her attention to Jordan, she asked, "Why did you bring me down here?"

His eyes flickered toward the shooting range, then back to her. "Because the surge of anger you were feeling earlier in the office projected itself like a tidal wave when you spoke about losing your staff and the young mother in the explosion. And when I told you about the midwife your fury was so intense it was almost tangible."

She stiffened. Her eyes turned an electric blue. "The young mother's name was Tami, and she, as well as Colleen, Joe and Mrs. Berkley, were innocent bystanders slaughtered by psychopathic cowards who are going to pay for their deaths and for making an orphan of Tami's son," she finished, her voice shaking with rage.

"This is the first time I've seen you so vehement since your parents were killed. I think you're over-identifying with the situation—and that's why you're here. If I could sense your emotions, so will your adversaries. When I took on the responsibility of training you thirty years ago, it was to prepare you emotionally as well as physically for your conflicts. Before I allow you to continue your missions, I have to be convinced you can put your emotions aside in favor of keeping your mind clear and focused."

"There's no need for the lecture; I remember your lessons."

"Really? Do you also remember the reason why I insisted on formal training in the first place?"

She stiffened. It was difficult even now to remember the period right after her parents had been killed. Pain and rage had been her constant companions. For a while she had become emotionally erratic. Her method of coping with her grief had been to invest her emotional agony in revenge. Anyone associated with Craven Maxwell had been annihilated--until she'd come up against Robert.

Robert had been the head of the Loyalist movement in Europe and almost as diabolical as his predecessor. His porphyrian powers had been formidable, but it was his long years of honing his skills to razor-sharp precision which had almost caused her demise. She hadn't bothered to develop her own abilities before embarking on her vengeance quest. Instead she had relied on the force of her fury to defeat her opponents.

A miscalculation which almost cost me my life.

Robert had been different then her previous foes. He had possessed the mental clarity to remain focused which had given him the edge during combat. His ability to control his feelings allowed him to maneuver and strike with the precision of a true predator while she raged like a wild bull. If Jordan hadn't arrived on the scene just in time to slay Robert as he was about to decapitate her, she would have ended up like the bull on the wrong side of the matador's sword.

After rescuing her, Jordan had rounded on her with fury. Sometimes her ears still rang with the blistering lecture. Ashamed at her failure she had humbly elected to become his pupil.

He looked quite stern as the shared memory passed between them. "I didn't save you from Robert all those years ago just to lose you now. In case you've forgotten, your lessons weren't designed just to teach you how to shoot and fence. If all you received from my guidance was the technical skills, then I failed and your training was incomplete."

He strode over to the weapons cabinet. Opening the door he selected a lightweight razor-sharp rapier. Balancing it from hand to hand, he finally nodded. His eyes sought and captured hers. "Until I'm convinced you won't let your feelings cloud your judgment, I can't let you go after any more Loyalists. You're strong, fast, and have innate healing abilities--but so do they. One careless moment when your emotions supercede your judgment could get you killed."

Guardedly she glanced from her cousin to the weapons. She shook her head. "I don't think this is a good idea."

"Why not?" he challenged.

A spark of understanding passed between them and she softened. After all, Jordan wasn't the enemy; he was just trying to look out for her. "Because in my present mood I might unintentionally hurt you." She exhaled loudly. "Look, give me about a half hour to calm down and I'll gladly spar with you."

He shook his head. "That's my point. You need to be able to control your reactions no matter how you're feeling at the time." She glared at him. She hated it when he took on that patronizing tone. He made it sound as if she was some green novice starting her first training session. She'd been at this for over two decades, and although Jordan had originally been her instructor, role model and guide, she had a natural aptitude that had quickly placed the student's level of expertise above her mentor's. She would really like to knock some of the condescension out of him and work off some of her anger, but her conscience was insistent that if she allowed him to goad her into it she probably would hurt him. "And if I refuse?"

"Then I won't let you go."

They glared at each other. "You don't have the power to stop me."

"No," he agreed, knowing they were too evenly matched, "but you don't have the power to keep me from trying." She raised her brows and he amended, "Not for long. We'd be at a stalemate and you wouldn't get very far with me on your trail every step of the way."

Her blue eyes glittered like shards of glass as she stalked over to the cabinet. She selected a matching weapon and growled, "Be aware that in my present mood you could get hurt if you push me to do this now."

He nodded gravely. I've been forewarned," he acknowledged, saluting with his sword.

They took up opposite positions, facing each other across a wide gym mat. Laurel warily eyed her opponent. She wasn't sure what Jordan was trying to prove, but the sooner they got this demonstration over, the quicker she could get back to tracking and dealing with whoever had murdered all those innocent people.

Just then an image of the building being blown up flashed into her mind. Her eyes widened in shock and she stared at Jordan in disbelief. Unable to believe what he was doing to her, she stood rooted to the spot. Jordan was completely focused on her as he advanced.

Another image accosted her and she saw herself digging through the rubble, searching for survivors as unchecked tears flowed down her face. She gasped as the memories surged. She had been forthcoming with her cousin regarding her pain.

How dare he use those disclosures to exploit my emotions!

Rage blazed like wildfire through her veins as she rushed forward. She lunged, missed, and spun around to face Jordan on the opposite side of the mat. Anger at her miscalculation infuriated her even more and she stalked her opponent while considering her next move. If she needed to defeat Jordan in order to convince him, that's what she would do.

Metal clashed against metal as Jordan backed away from the fury of her onslaught. "Look," he said, "I know you care about the people in your charge, but they were only diurnals. The staff is replaceable, and as for Tami," he waved disparagingly with his free hand, "she'd only have lived another forty or fifty years. The midwife was at the end of her life span. She was poor and diseased, so whoever killed her probably did her a favor."

Heat suffused her face as her blood boiled. Part of her mind recognized he was goading her but she was past caring. At that point defeating Jordan became the symbol for vengeance. Her breathing quickened. She lashed and slashed. Jordan parried easily, not even out of breath from defending her attack. The need to show him she couldn't be trifled with drove her as she raised her sword to slash at his shoulder. Nothing too serious, just a reminder that, despite her feelings, she could still defend herself and defeat her opponents.

She gasped in surprise. Glancing down she grimaced at the crimson line of blood streaking across her jumpsuit from her left shoulder to right hip. Aghast, she looked up just in time to see Jordan's next move. Too late, she realized her mistake, and before she could react she was on the ground. Lying flat on her back, she glowered up as her cousin gave her his hand.

"Get the point?" Jordan asked as he grazed her neck with the tip of the rapier.

Chapter 12:
Dana's Message

Jordan held out his hand. Laural accepted the offer. As he pulled her off the floor their eyes locked. "Truce?" he asked.

Smiling, she nodded. Despite her embarrassment she had to admit he had been right. Her sense of fair play pushed her to acknowledge the truth. Until she learned to master her emotions--instead of allowing them to dominate her--she was not fit for combat.

"Why did you invade my mind with those images from the explosion?" she asked, confused and still a little hurt by the intrusion.

He slipped an arm around her waist. "The enemy isn't going to fight fair. They won't hesitate to exploit any weakness."

"Still, that was a bit harsh."

On the verge of responding, Jordan paused. Tim Cooper was heading in their direction, a serious expression fixed on his face while he spoke rapidly into the cell phone glued to his ear. After terminating the call he flipped the phone shut.

His already grim expression darkened when he spied the tear and dried blood on Laural's jumpsuit. She winced when he threw an accusing glare at Jordan. "You should have kept the safety tip on."

Jordan shrugged. "This way brought the point much closer to home."

The head of security glowered. Laurel quickly placed her hand on his arm. Although completely loyal to both of them, Tim had been extra protective of Laural ever since she was eighteen and he had been her personal bodyguard. He had failed at that first assignment. He had made a mistake which had allowed her to be kidnapped and almost gotten her killed. Ever since then he had been overcompensating in an attempt to make up for his near fatal error.

"Jordan's right," she admitted, stopping further protests. "Did you have something you wanted to tell us?"

He nodded and relaxed a little. "I just got off the phone with our computer analyst. We've received an e-mail from Dana Maxwell."

Jordan stiffened and Laural's mouth dropped. After quickly scanning the room, she said, "Let's go into the office where we can talk in private."

They had barely entered the room before Jordan exploded. Slamming the office door he demanded, "What do you mean an e-mail from Dana?"

Laural sank onto the couch, sweeping her focus back and forth between the two men. Shock prevented her from assimilating the full import of Tim's news. Dana had been out of touch for so long they had always assumed she had a vested interest in remaining secluded.

Why would she initiate contact after all this time?

An image of the dragon pendant and dagger flashed into her mind. Laural's feelings were in such a confused state that she decided to let Jordan take the lead.

The Earl of Rockford stalked over to the bar and poured three glasses of PS4, using the diversion as an opportunity to regain his composure. He returned to the others, his emotions firmly in check. After handing a glass to Laural and Tim he returned to the bar for his own drink. He paused to take a long swallow of the reddish-brown liquid before seating himself behind the mahogany desk.

Tim perched on the wingback chair in front of the earl. Jordan stared expectantly at him as he took a healthy sip then sat his drink on the desk. "At about ten o'clock this morning we received an encrypted e-mail. We've had our experts working on decoding and tracing it. I didn't want to bring it to your attention until it was authenticated."

Laural leaned forward on the sofa. Her hands were shaking violently. When she put her glass down on the end table some of the contents sloshed over the rim of the glass. She watched Jordan as he, too, slowly set his drink aside. She could sense the tightly suppressed emotions he was keeping carefully contained.

Jordan was right. I do have a lot to learn about control.

"What did she have to say?" he asked in a deceptively calm voice.

The assistant director shifted uncomfortably, not deceived by Jordan's mild tone. "According to Dana's message, she and your son were being held prisoner in a small Liberian village in Africa."

"What do you mean were?"

"In her message Dana claims that at first both she and her son were being held prisoner by Loyalists, but eventually they were separated. She has no idea where her son is now."

Laural sat up straight as memories of her own captivity at the hands of Dana's father surfaced. "Why hold them prisoner all this time rather then just kill them?" she demanded.

Both men glanced at her then Tim replied, "Dana alleges that a group of porphyrians loyal to her father were holding them as figureheads to rally the cause. They're putting together a plan which, according to her, makes Craven's schemes seem paltry in comparison."

"I don't believe it!" she cried, shaking her head. "Craven Maxwell wanted to destroy the diurnals and rule the world. It doesn't get more grandiose then that."

Tim shrugged. "She wasn't forthcoming with the details. She was much more focused on being rescued. She claims that the Loyalists tried to get her to head their cause, but, when she refused, they pinned their hopes on the young man. He also refused at first, but ever since the Loyalists separated them she's feared the worst."

Jordan's calm demeanor was breaking down. "How long have they supposedly been prisoners?"

"She wasn't specific, but I got the impression they'd been there for a while."

"And where have they been the rest of the time?"

"Trying to stay hidden from you. According to Dana she felt there was a strong possibility you'd feel obligated to kill the child."

Laural and Jordan exchanged glances. Memories passed between them of how he had tried to kill her when she had been in the throes of the blood sickness. He stood and walked to the bar again. This time he poured a shot of brandy. Carrying the glass to the window, he stood for several seconds, sipping his drink and staring into the dusk. "She's right." He pivoted to face them. "What's the plan?"

"She specifically requested that you head the group that comes to rescue them. She claims she can only trust you and can't be convinced that whoever else comes aren't traitors unless you're with them."

"That's a switch," Jordan sneered as he walked back to his chair. "What happened to her concern that I'll kill our child?"

Tim shrugged again. "At this point it seems she's more concerned about being rescued. Maybe she decided she'd take her chances with you rather than her captors. Maybe she's figured since the child is a young man and has, by now, come into his porphyrian abilities, he has less to fear from you. Or it's possible she's just tired of running. She must realize that they can't remain hidden forever." He exhaled sharply. "It's all conjecture and theory on my part because the message ended abruptly, as though someone had interrupted her--but that's also more of my own interpretation."

"Do you buy her story?" Jordan asked quietly.

Tim looked back and forth between his employers for a long moment. "No, the timing is too fortuitous. The request for you specifically makes some sense, but with the recent bombing, the murder and Maxwell family heirlooms turning up at the crime scenes, it's just too coincidental." Tim paused. "There's also been another murder fitting the same description as Mrs. Berkley's."

"Damn!" Jordan exploded, slamming his fist on the desk.

So much for control.

Laural struggled to rein in her own emotions. "We've got to eliminate that threat."

"We're working on it," Tim asserted.

"Work harder."

Tim nodded. "Getting back to Dana's message, I think it's more likely that if the Loyalists did have Dana and her son, they would have had to kill them by now rather than run the risk of being overpowered by them. There's a much stronger possibility that this is a Loyalist hoax, designed to isolate the two of you from each other. It's a foregone conclusion that they want nothing more then to destroy both of you. Not just because you're responsible for Craven's death, but also because you represent the biggest threat to their long-term plans. And let's not forget that Laural's been doing a rather good job of exterminating Loyalists lately." Tim stated, gazing at her with a mixture of admiration and apprehension. "I think you've gotten their attention."

"Have you consulted with Ben Fletcher about this development?"

Tim nodded. "Ben believes that this is part of a Loyalist ploy designed to lure you to the other end of the world while they destroy this building just like they did the London branch. They seem to be intent on terminating the assimilation program, but not the leaders—

at least not yet. We agree that it's only a matter of time before that changes, but, for the moment, their desire to spare the two of you is blatantly obvious, but I'll be damned if either Ben or I can figure out why."

Jordan studied Laural for a long time before responding. "I'm not going."

"But what if this provides the link you need to find your son? And what if Dana and your son really are in danger?" she protested.

The green eyes were grave as he gazed back at her. "You heard what Tim said. I agree with most of his analysis. It's clear that the assimilation programs are the primary target at the moment. However, I think it is much more likely the whole thing is a red herring designed to draw me to some remote area of the world while, at the same time, isolating you. Then the Loyalists can attempt to eliminate us separately, which would be much less risky then facing us together."

"But there still might be a chance the request is genuine."

"There's also another possibility." They both refocused on the head of security. "If Dana's message is valid, there's a good chance the Loyalists have corrupted her son. That would explain the timely appearance of the Maxwell heirlooms as well as the increase and heightened boldness of recent Loyalist activity. I'm sorry," he looked at Jordan, "but each new link strengthens the case for your son being the Loyalist leader. And we can't rule out the possibility that he might be the blood drinker."

Jordan mulled over everything he had heard. He could no longer afford to indulge in unlikely fantasies. "I want you to lead a team and go out there to check it out."

Tim rose. "I thought you might feel that way. I've already been assembling my team."

"Tim," Jordan warned as the big man opened the office door, "be careful."

Chapter 13:
Uncovering the Past

Laural cast one more sidelong glance at her companion before emerging from the racy red McLaren Mercedes. The valet held open her door.

Salaries must be pretty good at Georgetown University.

Spying the long line of dinner guests, she sighed. She was rather hungry but it looked like they were in for a long wait.

Nicholas Ravensblood escorted her into the foyer of the restaurant. A striking woman dressed in a beautiful kimono top and silk pants was standing a few feet away, speaking quietly to another customer. Recognizing Nick, the hostess excused herself, and, approached them with outstretched hands.

"Professor, we're delighted you could join us this evening. You've been away too long," she chided gently, encompassing both of them with an ingratiating smile.

"Forgive me, Margarite," he returned the smile while squeezing her hands, "but my responsibilities call me away quite frequently."

She beamed at him. "Maybe sometime you can fill me in on your latest adventures." Turning to Laural, she continued, "And you've brought a lovely dining companion to join us this evening."

Nick lifted Laural's hand to his lips. She blushed when he brushed a light kiss against her fingertips. Nick chuckled softly. Laural glanced up in time to catch the humorous gleam in his eyes before he turned back to the hostess.

"Margarite, this is Lady Laural Gabriel. Lady Gabriel and I are going to be working on a project together."

"How fascinating," she offered, looking at Laural with renewed interest. "I'll add that to the long list of stories I'm still waiting to be told. I expect you to come in one day for lunch and fill me in. Right this way, please."

"I didn't realize the Carriage House was open for lunch," she said in an undertone to Nick as the elegantly-clad hostess moved ahead of them.

"It's not," he returned as they followed Margarite through the dining room.

Startled into silence, Laural followed as the hostess led the way to a cozy table for two. Candlelight shimmered and a vase with one perfect rose bloomed in the center of the linen-cloth-covered table. After seating herself she looked around. The inside of the Carriage House was just as impressive as the exterior. The restaurant was intimate and decorated with understated elegance. She was glad she had decided to wear her black sheath and diamond studs, a decision which had been prompted by her companion's secretiveness regarding their destination.

The corners of her lips lifted as she examined her escort by candlelight. The golden glow set off sparks in his ebony hair and was reflected in his jade green eyes. The subdued lighting also cast a burnished gleam to his tanned skin, setting it off dramatically against the starched white of his dress shirt. His black suit fit him to perfection. Laural admired the way his broad shoulders filled out the lines of the suit jacket and how his lean torso narrowed to accommodate the form-fitting pants.

Her gaze moved slowly back up his frame until their eyes clashed. With a start she realized he was watching her watch him. She blushed. "Sorry for staring, but you seem full of surprises."

"Do I?"

She nodded. "First this," she said, indicating the corsage decorating her shoulder, "then the fancy car, and now I find out you're a preferred guest at the Carriage House." She let her eyes travel appreciatively around the elegant dining area. "I've been wanting to come here for months, but it's always been so crowded I could never get past the front door." Her gaze swept past several other couples engaged in quiet conversation. Very romantic, she mused before refocusing on her companion. "If the perks are this good," she said lightly, "maybe I should become a university professor."

He smiled easily as he lifted his scotch. "I was left a rather large inheritance when my parents died. It allows me to live in the lap of luxury while still being able to pursue my dreams."

"Which are?" She was having difficulty concentrating on the conversation with his bright green eyes delving into hers, causing her heart to beat faster.

"Not the family mining business, much to my parents' regret. My first and only true love lies in uncovering the past."

She felt vaguely uncomfortable with something he had said but couldn't quite determine what it was. She was having a hard time focusing on anything save the erratic beating of her heart. She hadn't felt like this for a long time.

He observed her for several long moments. His eyes traveled over her face, lingering on her lips. When his gaze met hers again, her doubts dissolved. His eyes darkened as he studied her intently. Laural felt her face growing warm under his prolonged scrutiny.

"Thank you for coming out to dinner with me," he said huskily as he laid his hand over hers.

"You're welcome," she murmured softly. A light tingling like a low-grade current began emanating from the spot where his hand came in contact with her skin, suffusing her entire body with a warm inner glow. She glanced sharply at him, probed, then relaxed. "Speaking of the past, I've decided to grant your request on two conditions," she stated, disengaging her hand so the waiter could place their meals in front of them.

"I hope you don't mind," he said, noting her surprised expression, "but I took the liberty of calling ahead and asking the chef to make a couple of his special lobster tails stuffed with lump crab meat for us this evening. He gets pretty busy around this time so I thought I'd make the arrangements in advance."

She grinned appreciatively as she inhaled the mouth-watering aroma of her meal. "It looks and smells delicious." She spread her napkin across her lap.

He followed suit then raised his eyes to meet hers. "Your conditions?"

"The first is that you do turn all artifacts over to me."

He took a long pull on his drink. "I personally have no problem with that, but if the excavation lives up to my expectations, the decision about what to do with the artifacts maybe taken out of my hands."

"What do you mean?"

As he explained her eyes grew wide.

While she was still pondering this new prospect, he asked, "And the second condition?"

"That you only work on the site while I'm in residence."

He frowned. "I was hoping to start right at the beginning of the semester, which is only a few weeks away. If that doesn't meet with your time frame, I need to know so I can look elsewhere."

She set down her fork and took a sip of champagne before answering. "I should be ready to head back to England shortly. I have some business to attend to in London first, and then I should be free to return to my estate in Cornwall."

He lifted his glass and clinked the rim against hers. "To our professional and personal association. May they both prove to be mutually satisfying."

Three hours later Laural decided she couldn't have had a more enjoyable evening. Dinner had been superb, the conversation stimulating and her companion both entertaining and solicitous. Now, as she relaxed against the leather seat, she couldn't help but admire the way Nick maneuvered the McLaren roadster into the parking spot outside Jordan's townhouse.

Leaning into the red leather seat she gave an inward sigh of regret that the evening was over. After Nick turned off the ignition they sat in silence for several seconds. Nick's eyes roamed a sensual path down then back up her body until his gaze finally came to rest on her face. His desire was so obvious that Laural's breath caught in her throat, and for a moment she couldn't move.

His hand cupped the back of her neck. Strong arms imprisoned her and drew her firmly into his embrace. His kiss was gentle but insistent. She felt lightheaded as the kiss deepened, becoming more demanding. Just as she was beginning to lose herself he pulled back.

Feeling bereft she stared at him in confusion. Bemusement soon gave way to nervous tension. She wasn't sure she liked the overwhelming effect this man was having on her senses.

So much for keeping my emotions under control.

Only now did she remember her promise to Jordan.

"You'll find, Laural, that I'm very direct," he said, linking his hands with hers. "I've been feeling a strong physical attraction to you ever since we met. Unless I'm totally missing the mark, I'd say you've felt it too," he murmured, stroking her arms all the way up to her shoulders.

Laural inhaled sharply, mesmerized by the depth of passion reflected in his jade green eyes.

"I'd like to come in for a while," he murmured, his voice husky with desire.

She moaned and leaned back. She looked from the apartment back to her companion, already regretting her next words. "I don't think that would be a good idea right now."

He straightened and studied her for a long moment. Something flitted across his enigmatic green eyes, but before she had time to consider it, he was out of the driver's seat and opening her car door. She stepped out into the balmy night air.

"Thank you for a lovely evening," he said, kissing her cheek.

Before she could recover from the rapid switch of mood he was gone. As she watched the glow of the Mercedes tail lights recede she wondered if she had made the right choice. Sighing, she turned toward the townhouse.

Chapter 14:
The Conspirator

"Did you see her? Wasn't she magnificent" demanded Nick Ravensblood as he ripped off his tie and entered the living room of his luxurious penthouse.

"Of course I saw her," responded Cynthia lazily. Yawning, she stretched her long lean body across the grey leather sofa. "I followed you all evening."

He eyed the red-haired beauty suspiciously. "Back off, Cynthia." She arched one delicate eyebrow and he continued, "I have special plans for the Marchioness of Penbrook and I don't want them jeopardized by her sensing your presence."

She watched him from under half-closed lids. "I'm aware of your plans, remember I helped develop them--but I still think it's a mistake to prolong your exposure. Either she or Rockford are bound to get suspicious eventually."

He shrugged. "I'm sure they are already, but thanks to a fabricated history and a healthy tan their suspicions have been allayed."

"Yes, your forged documents and years of building solar tolerance are shielding you for the moment, but they're both too astute to be fooled for long."

"By the time they figure it out, it'll be too late. The Marchioness of Penbrook," he said adamantly, "is an integral part of my plan. As for the earl," his shoulders lifted then fell, "he serves no purpose other then to be eliminated."

Cynthia narrowed her glittering green eyes. "I have my own plans for the Earl of Rockford. He murdered your grandfather in cold blood and almost killed me too. He also helped Andrew slay Thomas, and I've told you what Thomas meant to me. Unfortunately, it looks as though I'm going to have to come up with another idea in order to get my revenge."

"What are you talking about?" he demanded.

Her eyes widened. "You didn't know? While you were distracted courting the Marchioness of Penbrook, I was informed by our sources that Jordan didn't take the bait."

"He didn't go to Africa?"

Copper tresses swept her shoulders as she shook her head. "He sent Tim Cooper along with a special reconnaissance team to check out the story."

"Damn!" He pounded his fist into his hand. "I wanted them separated and out of touch with each other. Seducing Laural is going to be difficult enough without the interference of her overprotective mentor."

She shrugged one shoulder and propped herself on her elbow. "As soon as you lure the marchioness back to England, they'll be separated. As for the earl," she licked her full red lips, almost purring, "leave him to me. Playing deceptive games with two of the most powerful porphyrians on the planet is taking an inordinate risk. I'm in complete agreement that the sooner they're out of touch with each other the better."

"Don't worry about Laural. Once my plans come to fruition, she'll no longer pose much of a threat."

She raised her delicately arched brows as her perfectly manicured nails drummed against the back of the sofa. "I hope you're right. That bitch is making everyone nervous. There's been talk of disbanding and abandoning the cause before she has a chance to kill off the rest of us." White hot rage scorched her at the mere thought of the cause being lost. "I've managed to subdue any concerns, but it's not like she's the only available source for testing your theory. There are others who'd be both willing and honored."

His fury faded as he recognized her ploy. "Are you offering?" he scoffed.

She pouted. "Why not? I'm certainly willing."

His eyes raked over her voluptuous curves. "Take care how you make your proposals—for a moment I thought you were implying dissension." She squirmed uncomfortably under the penetrating green glare. "As for your offer--you're always willing, maybe that's the problem." He studied her chastened expression. "In order to achieve the ultimate success I have to test my theory on the most powerful porphyrian I can find, and that is Laural Gabriel. Besides you're not the only one with a vengeance quest."

She grinned back, relieved to move away from the dangerous discussion of dissension. "And the earl, are there any plans you have for him I should know about before I implement my own?"

He tore off his jacket and shirt, kicked off his shoes and pants, then leapt on top of her. "There's only one plan you need to be concerned with right now. As for the earl—do what you want with him. Just be quick about it. The sooner Jordan Rush is out of my way the better."

Her eyes sparkled with delight as she chuckled, giving herself over to his brutal lovemaking.

You have your plans, my prince, and I have mine.

Chapter 15:
The Proposal

"You did what?" demanded Jordan as he paced restlessly around his living room.

"Please try to relax," requested Laural from her position on the sofa. "After all, I'm not handing over the keys to the estate; I'm going to be there. And I have to admit," she looked back at the documents in her lap, "Nick's theory has aroused my curiosity. There are a lot of old myths that have surrounded the area for generations and I'd like to see if any of them are true."

Halting abruptly, he stood in the center of the room. Running his hands through his hair, he eyed her skeptically. "I think you've been reading too much fiction." He raised a hand to halt her rejoinder. "There's the distinct possibility that what you've read and heard are all just outlandish theories and suppositions used by Professor Ravensblood to make his proposition more appealing."

She raised her chin, annoyed by his insinuation. "Nick did not make up those theories just to impress me. And you know as well as I do that the myths and legends which have circulated through Camelford have nothing to do with Nicholas Ravensblood. For centuries they've provided the basis for many bona fide articles which have appeared in respectable journals. I read his proposal thoroughly and so did you. His hypothesis is very well-researched and documented."

"Alright," Jordan conceded reluctantly, "but it's still just a theory and only one of many. Aside from the debate over whether or not Ravensblood is trying to impress you, did you forget what Tim said before he left?"

Her eyes glittered like jewels as her excitement escalated. "He said to be wary of anything that lured us into positions of isolation. But, Jordan, I'd just be going home."

He frowned. "Even your own head of security advised you to stay here until they can gather enough data to determine conclusively that it was the building and not the director that was the primary target. It may only be a precaution but I still don't like the idea of us being separated so soon after the bombing and murder. It's all happening too fast and seems too coincidental."

She smiled gently at him. "I understand you're worried, but we both knew I'd have to go back eventually. I can't stay here forever. Even without the Professor's project, I'd still need to go back to England in order to supervise the rebuilding of our London office."

"You said you didn't feel safe in England," he reminded her.

"Initially I was pretty badly shaken up. I'd be lying if I said I didn't have concerns for my safety as well as yours—but I can't hide from life because the Loyalists have gone on the offensive. The stakes are too high. Now that we've backed them into a corner it's to be expected that they would retaliate."

"And what about the blood drinker?"

"I agree that problem has to be taken care of as soon as possible, definitely before he strikes again and before the diurnals figure out what's going on. But you don't need me for that. We have long-established protocols for handling that sort of problem. Methods which our special-operations unit is quite capable of carrying out."

Jordan turned his back on her and walked over to the fireplace. Gazing into the flames he brooded over what they had discussed and what was still left unsaid. Although her statement about their security detail being able to cope with the blood drinker was true, he knew that, at any other time, Laural would have insisted on heading the investigation. Uneasily, he contemplated the effect the archeology professor was having on his cousin.

Laural was also silent while she gave more thought to an idea Nick had proposed at dinner the previous evening. After listening to him and reading his proposal, his suppositions had given credence to an idea which had been taking root in her subconscious for years. His research and documentation had taken her disjointed thoughts and formulated them into something much more cohesive. She had to decide if she should bring it up with Jordan.

With an effort she refocused her attention on her companion. It was important to her that she and Jordan maintain a united front. She was deeply concerned that if there was dissension between them their enemies would have the advantage. She looked at him; his rigid posture and taut muscles gave evidence of his emotional turmoil.

She walked over to join him and laid a hand on his arm. He kept his gaze firmly fixed on the burning logs. Laural waited patiently until he looked up. "I don't want this to cause a rift between us, but I have to go."

Jordan clasped her hands as he searched her face. "Why?"

"For several reasons," she hedged. "I'm tired of being on the defensive and I want the Loyalists to understand that they haven't destroyed our dream of assimilation. The best way to do that is to rebuild as soon as possible." She paused to choose her next words carefully. "I'm also intrigued by a theory the professor presented to me at dinner. Everything I've read seems to support Nick's hypothesis, and I think it would be an injustice not to at least explore the possibility."

Jordan looked at Laural closely, his concern and affection for her evident. "Laural, I don't know what theory you're referring to. There have been so many, each more outlandish than the next."

Laurel's face turned pink.

I was so excited, I forgot to tell him. Or maybe I was just afraid to tell him for fear he'd laugh at me.

"Well, a lot of evidence and historical data point to the possibility that my grandfather may actually have been the legendary King Arthur."

·

Chapter 16:
Cloak and Dagger

Jordan dropped Laural's hands and moved away from the fireplace, stunned by the idea. He began pacing again as he considered all the angles.

Laural watched him for a moment before returning to the couch. She intended to press her point. "The similarity of Camelford to Arthur's kingdom of Camelot, the story of how the ancient king died in the battle of Slaughter Bridge, and the legend that whenever wounded in battle Arthur miraculously healed all lend credence to the theory. Folklore attributes the lack of blood loss in war to the scabbard of Excalibur, but it sounds suspiciously like King Arthur may have possessed the healing ability of a porphyrian."

Jordan waved his hand dismissively. "You and I both know that King Arthur was not a myth but a real flesh-and-blood man. He fought for the rights of the English people and against the Roman subjugation of Great Britain."

"Everything I've heard about my grandfather's character and convictions, along with the historical rendition, only serves to strengthen the case."

"There are other points to consider."

She raised her brows. "What other points?"

"Two. First, are you sure Ravensblood is legitimate?"

Her eyes softened. "I'm sorry, I know you were still considering the possibility that he was your son, but I get no reading from him. He's either the best-kept secret there ever was or he's really who he claims to be."

"Didn't you get any more information?"

"Only that his parents are dead and his family is in mining."

Jordan's eyes narrowed.

She studied his expression. "What's the matter?"

"Nothing, go on."

She shrugged. "That's it. I don't want to push too hard too soon. That's one of the reasons I'm going to be on-site."

"And what's the other reason?"

Their eyes locked. "I think your demonstration the other day was enough to keep me from allowing my emotions to impair my judgment."

"I hope so."

"Until we find out for sure that he isn't your son, my relationship with him will remain platonic."

"And then?"

She shrugged. "What was your other point?"

He stared back at her for a long moment. At last he decided to allow himself to be distracted. "I'm still concerned about what could be found while digging up Penbrook property."

She watched him closely. "Is there something you're not telling me?"

He sighed, dropped into the wingback chair facing the fireplace and took several moments to mull over everything he had learned. At last he spoke. "There's another myth about your grandfather that's more directly relevant to our situation then whether or not he was King Arthur."

She watched him with interest, but her growing excitement was quickly quelled as she read his troubled expression.

"After careful consideration it's become clear to me that this myth has a direct bearing on what the Loyalists are seeking. Your grandfather, as you know, perfected the porphyrian supplement we've been drinking for several generations."

Her eyes took on a haunted look as she nodded. "Craven gave me that piece of family history when he abducted me."

"Prior to PS4, there were other supplements."

She smiled slightly. "Let me guess, PS1, 2, and 3."

He didn't return her smile. While watching the play of the flames he admitted, "Originally Arthur Gabriel thought he had the supplement perfected on the third attempt."

"What happened?"

"You're aware that our kind has an extremely difficult time procreating."

"Yes," she responded, puzzled at the change in subject.

"You've been told that problem is due to a flaw in our physiology."

She frowned. "I was lead to believe it was nature's way of offsetting our extremely long life span."

His green eyes studied her thoughtfully. "Until now I was the only one left who knew the truth. It's a Penbrook family responsibility to perfect the supplement and to guard the most important porphyrian secrets. I'm sure your dad would have told you if he had known his time with you would be cut short. He told me when we were young, just in case he died with no offspring."

"Enough with the cloak and dagger," she snapped impatiently. He was making her nervous and she was sure she wasn't going to like what he had to say.

He nodded. "The Penbrooks have always been responsible for making and distributing the supplement. The formula is traditionally handed down from generation to generation."

"I know all this already. Even though my dad wasn't able to provide me with the details before he died, I was aware of my family's responsibilities, and then you made sure I was informed so they could be implemented. The procuring and distribution of the supplement hasn't ever been interrupted--despite the unexpected death of my father."

He briefly shielded his eyes with his hand then dropped it to his lap.

How can I tell her the rest?

"That's only half of the responsibility. The other half is the knowledge of where Arthur Gabriel is buried. The story handed down is that the Fifth Marquis of Penbrook is buried somewhere on the estate, along with the journal detailing his first three attempts at making a supplement and all the problems that arose with each version. Most porphyrians believe the tale to be a myth."

She looked at him blankly, unable to comprehend. "I've heard those rumors," she mused, "but if they're true and an important part of my family history, how come neither you nor my dad ever mentioned it?"

"I'm sure your dad didn't mention it for the same reason he didn't tell you the rest: he thought he'd have more time. As for myself, I didn't tell you because Andrew never confirmed it."

Now she was confused. "If my grandfather is buried on the estate with records on his person, I would think my dad would have told you."

Jordan shook his head. "If I'd known all those years ago, there's a good chance that Craven would have pried the information out of me and used it to further his schemes."

She nodded as his eyes delved deeply into hers. They shared an understanding and acknowledged each other's past experiences with the depraved porphyrian who had left both of them scarred for an eternity.

Holding eye contact, Jordan walked across the room and seated himself next to her on the sofa. Taking her hands in his, he continued, "PS3 almost became the final supplement. It seemed to meet the criteria of properly balancing our minerals and electrolytes. After extended use, however, it was determined to have an extremely undesirable side-effect: Any porphyrian who drank it for more then six months went mad. They deteriorated to a state very similar to what you went through when you had the blood sickness."

Chapter 17:

Trade-Off

Laural fell back hard against the sofa cushions. Stunned, her mind dropped back thirty years, to the time when her insane uncle, Craven Maxwell, had kidnapped her and injected her with diurnal blood until she deteriorated into a depraved blood-drinking monster. She had rampaged through Washington, killing and maiming several people before her father had finally captured and cured her.

She shivered. "No one is going to voluntarily drink PS3 if they have any idea about the side-effects, which must surely be included in my grandfather's notes on the formula."

"Then how do you explain the blood drinker?" asked Jordan.

Her brows drew together. "Come on," she scoffed. "We both know there could be many explanations, having nothing to do with PS3. If it turns out the blood drinker is your son then he was given blood prenatally during Craven's experiment. Or it could be one of our own who either was accidentally exposed or intentionally started drinking blood. Once begun, the desire becomes addicting. But there's a vast difference between a renegade deviant and an organized plot to reinstate a supplement that drove those who drank it insane."

"We're not talking about people in their right minds; we're talking about Craven Loyalists who are possibly being led by his own grandson."

She swallowed her disgust.

"Besides," he continued, dropping his gaze to stare into the fireplace, "there's one very desirable benefit from using PS3 and I believe it's the purpose behind why the Loyalists want to get their hands on the recipe for the formula. The real reason porphyrians rarely reproduce is not due to any physiological deficiency. It's a side-effect of PS4. Kind of a trade off: only a ten-percent reproduction rate instead of going mad and craving human blood."

"You mean--" She hesitated, confused again.

"Yes," he affirmed, meeting her eyes, "when using PS3 porphyrians were quite prolific. I dare say, considering our extended life span, that if we'd been drinking it all this time, we'd have overrun the planet by now."

Laural considered the implication for a long moment. Inevitably that would have led to a direct confrontation with the diurnals and the possible genocide of her species. "But if PS3 was so problematic, why keep the documents at all? Surely my grandfather and father must have realized the potential threat those records would pose if they fell into the wrong hands. Why not just destroy them once they perfected the supplement?"

Jordan sighed. "Your father never confided where his father was buried. I questioned him once about it and he told me that he was keeping the site secret so as not to encourage desecration by his enemies. I thought he was being overly cautious, but if Arthur was buried with those documents, it makes more sense. As to why the journals weren't destroyed, the only reason I can figure out is that they act as a back-up system. If something were to happen to the last Penbrook holding the secret of how to make the supplement, the records could still be obtained by digging up Arthur's grave."

"Not if no one knew where to look or even that the journals existed," she interjected doubtfully.

He shrugged. "I didn't say I had all the answers. Most of this is pure conjecture on my part. As I said, your father didn't share that information with me. I've only been reconsidering it as a serious possibility since you started collecting thoughts about a conspiracy involving PS3 from the minds of our enemies."

"I still don't understand why the formulas for all the supplements would be kept. If some were known to pose a threat why not just keep the one that worked?"

"My presumption is so that there would be a complete history of the drink in case some descendant wanted to improve on it. That way whoever tried to improve the supplement in the future wouldn't fall victim to past failures, unless--"

"Unless the failures are their intent. Jordan, you don't think—"

"That's exactly what I do think!" He slammed his fist on the back of the sofa. "If those journals fell into the wrong hands some unscrupulous maniac--like the grandson of Craven and great-grandson of Raven Maxwell—could use them to turn a whole slew of psychopathic prolific porphyrians loose on the world."

Chapter 18:
The Cryptic Text

Two weeks later, the Marchioness of Penbrook sat in her study at her Cornwall estate. She turned on the computer then switched over to her e-mail. Smiling slightly, she clicked onto the message from Ben Fletcher. As expected, in addition to the business update, her assistant director and head of security had advised her that the castle had been cleared for explosives. He had left a message earlier on her cell, but since she hadn't had time to respond he was following up. True to form Ben had also included a stern reprimand to her about returning to England prematurely. Her grin broadened. She could almost picture Ben shaking his head as he wrote. Her long-suffering friend would have realized, even while writing the message, that trying to impose any restrictions on her would be a lost cause.

Her grin faded when she clicked onto the next message. Agitated, her fingers tapped against the antique writing desk. She read the message from Jordan a second time. It didn't make sense. Again she scanned the brief contact but could gain no additional clues from the cryptic text.

Briefly she raised her eyes from the screen. They came to rest on an armored knight standing sentinel in the corner of the room. The metal-clad figure reminded her of the discussion with her cousin about her grandfather.

Could he really turn out to be King Arthur?

A tiny furrow etched itself between her brows when she recalled Jordan's objections. Her gaze slid over the knight until it rested on the coat of arms, a symbol of loyalty, chivalry, and integrity, all time-honored traditions standing at the heart of the Penbrook moral code.

The same ideals held by the Knights of the Round Table.

Tucking her hair behind her ears, she returned her attention to the enigmatic note. According to the message, Tim had contacted

Jordan from Africa. He had written to inform the earl that his team had surprised a small band of porphyrians holding two prisoners, Dana Maxwell and a young man, claiming to be her son. Tim had gone on to report that during the ensuing conflict, Dana had been killed.

Laural leaned back and closed her eyes. Sorrow overwhelmed her as she tried to come to terms with the loss of her cousin. Mental snapshots of Dana flashed through her mind. Her heart ached as she recalled the good times they had shared when they had all lived in Washington. Now Dana Maxwell was dead.

Remorse tore through her as she considered whether anything could have been done to prevent the tragedy. She wished her cousin had chosen to get in touch at some point during the past thirty years. If only Dana had trusted them rather than fleeing, maybe she would still be alive. The Willow Grove Foundation would have made the problem of Dana's child's addiction to hemoglobin their top priority. With their entire staff of scientists and advanced medical equipment devoted to the project, Laural was certain they could have found a solution.

Once the issue of the baby's addiction to human blood was resolved, Jordan, Dana and their son could have lived as a family. Instead--

Her thoughts stopped short. Of course there had been too many variables and no easy answers. No matter how hard she tried she couldn't imagine Jordan and Dana as a contented couple. Despite her fond memories she had to admit Dana had always been temperamental. At the first sign of trouble her pattern of abandonment would probably have resurfaced.

She opened her eyes. The ancient knight was still on guard at his post, offering neither advice nor solace as he kept his lonely vigil. Sighing, she read the message again, hoping that if she studied the message more thoroughly it would make more sense.

Apparently after determining the young man was who he said he was, Tim had requested that Jordan join him in Africa. Jordan, of course, was so eager to find his son he was catching the next flight.

Why would Tim ask Jordan to travel to Africa when he was so firm about us not taking chances? He could just as easily have brought Jordan's son to Washington instead.

She shook her head. Of course, there were more details that Jordan hadn't had time to explain. He'd promised to call in a couple of days to give her an update. Since Tim had given the all-clear for the trip. She just had to hope her misgivings were misplaced. It seemed, for now, that waiting was her only recourse.

A knock sounded at the study door. Lines of confusion were still nestled between her brows when she turned to confront the visitor. Her face cleared when she saw Nick casually standing in the entrance. Even if Tim and Jordan had needed her she wasn't free to leave while a group of outsiders were deeply involved in exploring her property.

"Is your group settling in?" she asked a little breathlessly. Firmly taking control she quickly stifled the physiological response this man had on her while sternly reminding herself of Jordan's last lesson. Recalling her cousin brought him again to the forefront of her thoughts and her lips tightened as she glanced briefly back at the computer.

Slowly her confusion was replaced by a dawning realization. If Jordan's son was in Africa, then Nick was completely cleared. The main roadblock for keeping her distance had just been eliminated.

Hold on. Just because he's not Jordan's son doesn't mean my attraction to him won't cloud my judgment.

He nodded. "Everything is above and beyond my expectations. I wanted to thank you personally for the consideration you must have taken insuring we were accommodated. Your staff has been wonderful helping us get set up." His eyes roamed over her face. "Did I interrupt something? You looked very intense."

She eyed the e-mail one more time, exhaled a long sigh of frustration, and hit delete. "Just a message from my cousin."

"Is there anything wrong?"

She drank in the sight of him for several moments before answering. He was almost irresistible in his linen shirt and khaki trousers. The shirt was open at the neck, revealing the upper portion of his broad chest. The pants emphasized his taut leg muscles. His ebony hair was windblown and his eyes were sparkling with enthusiasm.

Swallowing hard she tried to focus on what he had said. "No, he's just letting me know he's going to be out of town on a business trip for the next several days."

"You two seem very close," he offered as he walked up beside her.

Laural almost forgot to breathe as he approached. Captured by his gaze, she watched her reflection in his jade green eyes. "We are."

He raised his brows. "How close?"

She thought she heard a possessive note in his tone, and her voice hitched slightly as she explained, "Aside from being close personally, we run this international corporation together. We need to keep in close contact in order to assure the smooth operation of our business. Unfortunately," she glanced back at the computer as though it were somehow responsible, "sometimes unexpected situations arise. However, I'm sure Jordan is quite capable of dealing with his own business problems."

As she spoke her mind raced again.

I can't imagine what's come up that changed Tim's protocol so drastically he would countermand his own advice by insisting Jordan come to such a remote area. Perhaps the Loyalists have caused Tim such a problem he had to call in for reinforcements—but usually that's my domain, not Jordan's.

Her thoughts skidded to a halt. She stood and pinned a cheery smile on her face. Jordan must have felt obligated to go. After all, he knew she wasn't free to leave and it was his son they had rescued. And even though Jordan would be out of touch due to the contact limitations in the third-world environment, she was confident of his capabilities. He had, after all, taught her everything she knew.

Her mind traveled back over the years of hard training and rigorous routine. The job of teaching her how to hone her abilities should have fallen to her dad, but since he had died prematurely, Jordan had taken on the responsibility of being her mentor. Throughout the years of training she had always felt spiritual guidance from her dad aiding her in her quest. Forcing her mind back to the present she refocused on her guest.

Sensing he finally had her full attention, Nick grinned. "I'm glad your cousin can manage because I'd prefer not to share you. Come with me," he insisted, reaching for her hand. "I want to show you our site."

She laughed. Shaking off her misgivings she allowed herself to be dragged along in the wake of his enthusiasm.

Chapter 19

The Abyss

Jordan's brows drew together as he puzzled over the e-mail Laural had sent him earlier that morning. By deciphering the encrypted code he was able to determine that she had information about the dig site on her property which she didn't want to disclose over the phone or electronically.

Leaning back in his swivel chair, he pondered the possibilities. At last he reviewed the lines again. Apparently Laural needed him to come to Cornwall immediately in order to obtain his input on the discovery. Since he was the expert regarding this part of porphyrian history she was waiting for his opinion before determining the next course of action.

Pushing away from his desk, he dropped his head against the top of the chair. Steepling his fingers he stared absently at the screen. He was aware that there was much more left unsaid. They had intentionally designed this style of communication to be very difficult to interpret.

The corners of his lips lifted while he recalled the fun they had had creating the coded messages. It had felt like a scene out of an espionage movie, but now he was glad of the precaution. If Laural had found something truly significant he could see why she wouldn't want it to be sent over normal channels. He was also the only one she could consult and confide in.

And what about the professor's theory that the fifth Marquis of Penbrook was King Arthur?

His lips compressed. There were certainly skeletons in the Penbrook family closet but to the best of his knowledge that wasn't one of them.

He depressed the intercom button. When his secretary responded, he requested she send Tim Cooper to his office. After cutting the connection he leaned back again and closed his eyes. Having just returned from Africa, Tim was due in for a briefing on his findings. He would get an opinion on the cryptic e-mail from his second-in-command.

Jordan massaged the back of his neck while he continued to wait. Tension racked his body and frayed his nerves as he hung suspended over the abyss of his wildly churning thoughts. Ever since receiving word Tim had returned, his mind had been conjuring all sorts of scenarios. He hadn't even allowed the poor man time to go home and get some rest before demanding he present himself at the office. He grimaced. Impatience had superseded consideration and Jordan could only hope the big man would excuse the lapse in light of the circumstances.

His mind turned back to the mysterious message.

Could the team of archeologists have uncovered something significant so soon? They've only been on location for a few days. Of course, they could have gotten lucky and just hit the right spot. I hope the secret of PS3 is still secure. The discovery of Arthur's long-lost journals would explain Laural's resistance to openly communicate, especially if she suspects her phone lines and e-mail might be compromised.

A knock at the door interrupted his speculations. Jordan's eyes flew open and he called out. He observed Tim Cooper closely as the big man seated himself on the other side of the desk. As usual, he had come prepared with a thick case file as well as a pen and pad.

Jordan smiled slightly as his head of security raised questioning brows. Even though his clothes were rumpled and his face was drawn taut with fatigue, he was always ready to do his part for the cause. A warmth suffused him as he realized what a loyal and sincere friend he had in this man. Not since Andrew had died had Jordan really felt a spark of true friendship. The thought of Andrew brought pain and loneliness just as it always did.

"What did you find out?" he asked, pushing aside his melancholy thoughts.

Tim laid the pen and pad aside and opened one of the two files he had laid on the desk. His red hair fell forward as he bent his head to study his notes. "We found Dana, or at least what was left of her," he said bleakly, looking up. His eyes glistened and he cleared his throat before continuing. "Her body was burned to ash but she'd been decapitated, and whoever committed the atrocity made sure to leave her head intact so we would be able to identify the remains."

Chapter 20:
The Golden God

Jordan inhaled sharply then shut his eyes tightly to ward off the visual image. It didn't stop the pain. The picture of his former fiancée imprinted itself on the inside of his eyelids. Once he had truly loved Dana Maxwell and it still hurt to think that she hadn't trusted him enough to confide in him and seek his help rather then flee.

If she had come to me, would she be alive or would the outcome have been the same? If our son couldn't have broken his addiction to drinking diurnal blood, I would have been obligated to kill him. In that case she would have needed to escape anyway, in order to protect her child from his own father. Damn Craven Maxwell!

It had been Craven who had injected Dana's baby prenatally with diurnal blood, insuring the child would be born addicted. It had been part of his grand scheme to develop a superior breed of porphyrians. All it had bred so far was misery, heartache and death.

He opened his eyes. The sorrow he felt was reflected in the face across from him. "What about my son?"

Tim's shoulders slumped as he shook his head. "We questioned every native in all the nearby villages. No one provided any specific information about your son."

Jordan stared in amazement. "No one saw anything the entire time Dana and my son were there?"

"I didn't say that," Tim refuted. "I said they didn't admit to it. Personally, I think they were too scared to admit anything. Whoever was there ahead of us put the fear of the devil into them. We did everything we could think of to get them to talk and got nothing. We followed other leads, but after several days it became clear they were intentional misleads. Obviously, this was well-planned. Whoever's behind it wanted us to find Dana, but that's all. They've vanished again with your son, and I have a feeling they won't be found until they're ready to make their next move."

"Any idea about why they'd want to kill Dana after thirty years?"

"I don't think she was there that long. As to why they killed her," he shrugged, "either she outlived her usefulness or she was causing them a problem."

"Any speculation on why they would leave identifiable remains?"

"Several possibilities. It could be a warning to other traitors in their own group. It could be a ploy to lead us on a wild goose chase. It could be an implied threat that if you don't back off your son will be next. There could be many more possibilities," he rubbed his hand over his face, "but, honestly, I'm too tired to think of them right now."

Jordan winced. "Sorry to do this to you, but I couldn't wait."

"I understand," he conceded graciously.

The earl eyed him thoughtfully. "Is that the entire report?"

Tim sighed wearily. "I should have realized you are too perceptive for me to hold anything back."

"Tim," he admonished sternly, "I don't want you taking it upon yourself to edit the information you have. If I'm going to operate effectively as the head of this agency and conduct my private life appropriately I need to know everything."

The other man looked offended. "I'd never hold back anything that would compromise you either personally or professionally. But I'm not in the habit of providing information until I have a better understanding of it myself."

Jordan waited.

Tim studied his notes for a long moment before confronting his boss. "Although I couldn't find anyone who could provide any news regarding your son or the Loyalists I did find several villagers who were quite willing to discuss," he hesitated briefly and consulted his notes again, "a Golden God."

Jordan looked at him, curious. "What does that mean?"

He shook his head. "I'm not sure exactly, that's why I was hesitant to bring it up. I don't know if it has any bearing on our interests or if it's something entirely different. I'm not even sure if this Golden God is real or some part of a local legend. The only reason it even factors into my notes is because the reference kept coming up every time

I enquired about the Loyalists. It was as though the villagers were connecting the two."

"Do you think they could be referring to my son?"

"Anything is possible but I got the feeling it was related to something else. What that something else is I'm not sure."

Jordan mulled it over. "Any details we can link?"

"That's the other reason I didn't want to bring it up. I haven't had time to thoroughly work over my notes yet."

Jordan nodded, dismissing the issue for the present. "Keep on it. Any update from our covert-ops team on the status of the blood drinker?"

Tim flipped to his second file. "It's difficult to eliminate a problem you can't find. As in the case of your son, after last week's second murder, the blood drinker seems to have vanished." He looked up to confront his boss. "Based on the timing and background data we've collected so far, it's highly likely that your son will turn out to be the blood drinker."

Do you think there's any chance this Professor Ravensblood could turn out to be my son?"

Tim looked pensive. "Aside from the fact that he's sporting a healthy tan, you read the report."

"Could it be fabricated?"

He raised his brows. "The tan or the background?"

"I know it's a long shot. But even if he's what he claims…"

Tim studied him for a long moment. "Is she that serious?"

Jordan blew out a breath. "I don't know."

"I'll do some digging."

He nodded curtly then changed the subject. "Now that you're back, I'm leaving you in charge for a few days while I go to England." He waited but Tim said nothing. "Laural sent me an e-mail requesting I come to Cornwall."

"Due to the upsurge in Loyalist activity I think I should go instead," Tim asserted while making notes.

He shook his head. "I'm not sure exactly what's going on, but I'm relatively certain after reading her message that it isn't a Loyalist issue--at least not directly. Laural specifically requested my presence and I don't think it's due to any physical threat."

Tim glanced up, his pen poised in mid-air. Deliberately he laid the pen and pad on the desk then asked, "May I see the message?"

Jordan hesitated. Even though he had considered showing the message to Tim only a few minutes ago, he was ambivalent about divulging Penbrook family secrets. But Cooper might determine a threat he had overlooked, and his concern for Laural outweighed his caution. He nodded. "Yes, but hold on a minute. Laural and I encrypt our more sensitive messages, so I'll have to decode this before you'll be able to make sense of it." Jordan pressed several keys then moved aside.

Tim studied the screen intently. After a few moments he looked Jordan directly in the eye. "Do the two of you code all your messages?"

"No, only the interesting ones," he smiled briefly, then sobered. "I'm sorry to leave you out of the loop, but it's necessary."

Tim shrugged. "Whatever private codes you and Laural have is your own business--unless it compromises security."

Jordan remained silent.

Tim stared at him levelly. "I know you don't want to hear it, but I'll remind you that someone recently tried to kill Laural and we just discovered the dead body of Dana Maxwell. I think I should send some of our best to England with you, just in case."

His gaze sharpened. "Then you do believe the explosion was an actual attempt on Laural's life?"

"I didn't think so at first. The logical conclusion was to assume that if the perpetrators had wanted her dead, they could have killed her while she was unconscious. But after finding Dana's remains I can't be sure of anything. I've alerted Ben Fletcher but I'd still feel better if some of our special-ops people joined Laural's security detail."

Jordan waved the objections aside. "Laural's security detail in England is as good if not better then our own. I understand your concern but, in case you've forgotten, you and I hand-picked her team. Besides I need our best here to ferret out the blood drinker and keep our facility, along with our employees, safe and operational."

"I still want to place personal bodyguards with both of you."

Jordan shook his head as he shrugged into his jacket. "We can't spare anyone right now and we haven't got time to wait. I appreciate what you're trying to do but Laural and I are quite capable and I'm sure we'll be fine."

"Laurel may be fine—she has protection. You're planning to travel halfway around the world alone."

Jordan said nothing. There was no sense in increasing Cooper's uneasiness by letting him know that once he joined Laural they would both be unprotected--at least until they insured the secrets of PS3.

Tim blew out a frustrated breath as Jordan pulled out his briefcase.

And Jordan thinks Laural's stubborn?

A sharp glance from his boss indicated he had caught the stray thought.

"Well," stated Tim emphatically, "it's very difficult to protect people who won't let themselves be protected. I also get the feeling that there's an underlying issue related to this trip that you don't want exposed. Guarding the two of you as well as our interests is going to be very difficult if I'm not provided with all the crucial information."

Jordan stared. He was impressed with the astuteness of his head of security's observations. Still, he couldn't afford to confide in Tim or take extra porphyrians along on his trip in case the discovery Laural had made was about PS3. He was determined to keep that bit of information as confidential as possible.

Recognizing the stubborn set of Jordan's jaw, Tim headed for the door. "Let me know if you need me."

"Tim," Jordan called as the porphyrian entered the hallway, "go home and get some rest."

Chapter 21:
Abduction

The chauffeur held open the door for Jordan as he quickly crossed the sidewalk and approached the limousine.

"Where's Jack today?" he asked politely as he hefted his briefcase then climbed into the back seat.

"On vacation, sir," responded the driver before closing the door.

Jordan nodded absently as he checked his watch. He should have plenty of time to reach the airport. His thoughts strayed to Cornwall. He had been continually plagued by a sense of foreboding ever since Nick Ravensblood had intruded into their lives.

He pulled open a bottle of spring water from the bar. Sipping slowly he gazed out the side window. As they passed the Capitol building he again wondered what could have caused Laural to send such an enigmatic note.

Well, I suppose I'll find out soon enough.

Upending the contents of his glass, he poured a second glassful.

I must be thirsty.

Distractedly he watched the pedestrians and landmarks of the capital whiz past while he speculated on the potential problems awaiting him in England. As he continued to survey the scenery he frowned. He found then pressed a button and the partition slowly lowered.

"Yes, sir?" enquired the driver respectfully.

"You're heading in the wrong direction," he asserted, his voice slurring slightly. Hastily he glanced from his glass to the bottle. The label read Evian.

"I beg your pardon, sir?"

"You're not heading toward the airport."

"Yes, sir."

Jordan tried to shake free from the shrouds of mist clouding his mind. He couldn't concentrate. He tried to look out the window to get his bearings from the landmarks. No, he thought shaking his head sluggishly, this couldn't be right. His voice echoed hollowly when he spoke. "I'm going to Reagan International and you're headed the wrong way."

"The plans have been changed, sir."

Jordan felt like the driver's voice had taken on a menacing tone. He glanced into the rearview mirror to try and gauge the chauffeur's expression. To his dismay the placid features became distorted. The nondescript straw-brown hair and watery grey eyes hardened into a vibrant red mane and glittering green eyes.

That face--where have I seen it before?

His heart raced and his blood pounded as the face swam in and out of focus. His brain felt as if it were being dragged through cement.

Is this another Loyalist attack?

Belatedly he regretted not heeding Tim Cooper's warning. Sweat drenched his skin. He could feel himself slipping. He groped for the door handle.

I need to get out of here. I need to get to a hospital before…

He fumbled for the handle, missed, tried again. His hand wouldn't obey his command. Another glance out the window confirmed the car was heading away from the city to God only knew where. On the verge of protesting again, he slumped forward. His head hit the opposite seat as he slipped into unconsciousness.

Chapter 22

In Good Conscience

Tim Cooper took another sip of coffee while he waited for the overseas connection. Finally the line cleared and the call went through. The deep baritone voice of Ben Fletcher came on the phone.

"Hey, Tim. The receptionist said it was important. Have you got some news?"

the mug thudded as he laid it on the desk. "Yes, but not the type you're expecting." Briefly he wondered if his boss would approve of divulging this information but Jordan's safety--not his approval--was his top priority. He also couldn't deny the possibility that Laural, too, might be at risk. In that case, he couldn't, in good conscience, leave Ben in the dark. "Jordan just left here a few minutes ago, supposedly to meet with Laural."

Ben was silent for a few moments. Finally he said, "If they're meeting it must be out at the castle, but are you sure? Laural hasn't mentioned it."

Tim lifted his pen, tapping a staccato beat against his note pad. "I'm not surprised. Jordan was acting quite mysterious about his plans."

Suddenly alert Ben asked, "What do you mean by mysterious?"

"He wasn't open about why he felt the need to drop everything and rush off to Cornwall. I got the distinct impression there's more going on with this situation then we've been told."

"Damn it!" Ben exploded. "How do they expect us to protect them and the agency if we don't have all the information?"

Tim traded the pen for the mug. He took a long sip before answering. "I don't believe either Jordan or Laural are looking at it that way. And I'm sure they've never been completely comfortable with the idea of having to be protected. However, in this case, I think there's more to it then just that issue."

"Besides the foundation being blown up, attempted assassinations, and a renegade blood drinker on the loose?" Ben asked incredulously. "Maybe I should confront Laural about Jordan's visit and whatever it is they're keeping from us."

"I'm not sure that would be a good idea at this point. I'm just as concerned as you are, but we have to draw the line between being body guards and prison guards. I also think she'd be just as evasive as Jordan was. I'm basically calling to make sure you're on the alert."

"Thanks," Ben grumbled. "Now instead of Laural staying on your side of the Atlantic until I get a better handle on the situation, I'm going to have both of them here." He hesitated. "Can I pick your brains for a minute on a different subject?"

Draining the last dregs, he laid the mug aside. He leaned back in his chair and unbuttoned his suit jacket. "Go ahead."

Ben took the plunge. "It's about dating."

Tim chuckled. "I'm hardly an expert on the topic but I do my fair share."

"You date diurnals, right?"

Tim's brows drew together. "Yes," he said, wondering where the conversation was headed.

Ben cleared his throat. "Well, I've been dating a woman named Lindsay for about two years."

"Two years isn't dating, it's a relationship."

"Exactly my point. We're pretty serious and it's time to make a complete commitment. We're both thinking marriage but there's a problem."

Tim smiled. "Sounds to me like there could be several. Personally, even though I date diurnals, I keep it light. If I ever settle down it's going to have to be with someone who I can be myself with, and that would only be another porphyrian. For me it would be too heavy a burden to have to go through life worrying about exposure. And that doesn't even take into account the issue of the life-span discrepancy."

"Neither one of those issues is the problem--or at least not the main one. I'm fine with keeping part of who I am a secret. I'm used to that since covert ops is part of my daily routine. I've thought about how to best use camouflaging techniques, and I've even considered ways to stage my own death when the time comes."

"Sounds like you've put a lot of thought into this. Your Lindsay must be a really special woman."

"She is."

"So what's the problem?"

"Lindsay wants children."

"That's not possible."

"I know, but I'm afraid if I tell her that we can't have kids, I'll lose her."

"Why not adopt?"

Ben drew in a sharp breath. "Would you believe I've been doing all this work on the case for the adoption of the kid whose mother got killed in the explosion and I never thought of that solution for myself?"

"Sometimes," said Tim, "it's hard to see the forest for the trees."

Chapter 23:
Buried on the Estate

Laural followed closely behind her companion. Nick's long-legged stride quickly out-distanced her but she did her best to keep up. Her excitement escalated as they drew closer to the excavation site. For over a week Nick's students had been diligently digging deeper into the grounds surrounding Penbrook Castle. Every day she waited expectantly for the news that the team had made a discovery that would prove relevant to her cause. So far they hadn't turned up anything. Laural wasn't sure whether to be relieved or disappointed. Her lips curved as Nick paused for her to catch up.

Grinning sheepishly he said, "Sorry, I'm just eager to show you what we've accomplished."

"That's alright," she responded as she walked up next to him. "I admire your enthusiasm."

As they moved forward together she watched him out of the corner of her eye. Even though she wasn't sure how she felt about strangers digging up part of her estate, she had no such ambivalence about her daily meetings with Nick. They had developed a habit of getting together in her study at the end of each day. A combination of eager anticipation and nervous tension had her looking forward to their daily session. Over a pot of tea he would regale her with the day's exploits. Occasionally Robert, his graduate assistant, or some of the other students would join in but the times she enjoyed most were when they were alone. Despite the lack of any real breakthroughs the ritual was quickly becoming an important part of her routine.

One I'm becoming too emotionally dependent upon.

Attempting to distract herself from her disconcerting thoughts and his handsome profile, she looked around the cordoned-off sections of land. Originally she had assumed the professor and his students were going to be using the entire grounds for their excavation. That was a misconception Nick had quickly corrected. Her lands were too vast to cover in one summer, so he had mapped out the most probable location for the artifacts his research had led him to believe were buried on the estate.

Laural was disappointed and troubled by this information. Since the idea behind allowing the class access to her property had been to unobtrusively discover the remains of Arthur Gabriel and his journals this left her with a serious dilemma. What if her ancestor wasn't buried in the area the archeologist had predicted? Then the problem of how to search the rest of the estate without raising Loyalist suspicions would still need to be resolved.

Laying her concerns aside for the moment, she allowed herself to be caught up in the excitement. What if they actually did discover the remains of the legendary King Arthur on Penbrook property? Laural was still straining to assimilate all the implications, but it was becoming more difficult for her to deny the possibility that Arthur Pendragon might very well turn out to be her own grandfather.

From earlier discussions with the professor she understood that in order to verify the find the ancient monarch would have to have been buried with clues to his identity intact--indicators such as distinguishing jewelry, a coat of arms or anything bearing the person's actual name could be used, in conjunction with carbon dating and other techniques, to authenticate a claim. Hopefully one of the methods used to identify her grandfather's remains would not turn out to be his journals. However, all the anticipation made her even more eager for the discovery.

As she observed Nick interacting with his students, she couldn't help but be impressed by his zeal. Striding from one dig site to the next, he offered words of encouragement and nodded his approval toward the teams as they toiled. The students' faces were full of respect and interest as they listened attentively to his suggestions. When he passed the workers paused in their duties to wave or look up with a welcoming smile. Laural admired the easy rapport and camaraderie the instructor elicited.

Walking further down the line they eventually reached a small group chatting excitedly around a large, well-defined site. When they saw Ravensblood several called out greetings. Nick and Laural drew up alongside of the excavation area. Nick asked, his eyes beaming with pride. "What do you think?"

Laural was so caught up in admiring the way his eagerness made his eyes sparkle that it took several erratic heartbeats before she was able to focus on his question. The balmy breeze blew wisps of hair into her face as she turned full circle, examining the stretch of land they had just traversed. Pushing the errant strands firmly behind her shoulders she smiled. "Very impressive."

She could see how much the group had accomplished in only a short period of time. She observed how earnestly the teams were digging, brushing and sifting their way through the earth. "I hope they find something of interest. I'd hate to think they're doing all that work for nothing."

He pushed his hands into his trouser pockets while his eyes scanned the groups of students gathered around their various excavations. "I've never had a dig where we haven't uncovered at least one shard of pottery. But my expectations on this site are much higher. If my research pans out these students will be rewarded for their efforts by a lot more then just a few pottery fragments."

Smiling into his eyes she asked, "Can they spare you for a little while?"

He studied her thoughtfully and nodded.

"Then follow me," she insisted, grasping his hand. The gesture had been impulsive, but once his hand was placed firmly in hers, a feeling like a low-grade electric current sent a tingling all the way up her arm. Startled at the intensity of her physical response she almost dropped his hand. As if sensing her intention his grip tightened. Afraid of confronting what she would see reflected in his eyes she avoided looking at him as she started forward.

Chapter 24:
The Dark Place

After rounding the side of the house Laural tugged Nick toward the stables. Throwing open the door she ushered him inside. Nick's eyes grew wide at the sight of two of the finest examples of horseflesh he had ever seen. One was jet black, the other snow white. They were in opposite stalls facing each other across a wide aisle.

"Meet Thunder and Lightning," she announced proudly, Flourishing her arm toward the stalls. He remained speechless and she grinned. "Do you ride?"

He moved toward the nearest stall and began stroking the stallion's glossy black neck. The horse snorted and tossed its mane. "I love to ride."

"So do I. Maybe we can go riding sometime."

"How about now?"

They saddled up and rode out across the countryside. Heathered hills and green pastures stretched out before them. As they rode toward the coast the paths became narrower and steeper. The wild coastal gusts bit into her cheeks and blew her hair into her face as Laural paused on an outcrop of rocks overlooking the roaring surf. Mild dizziness and nausea overwhelmed her when she glanced down at the waves. Inhaling deeply she briefly closed her eyes.

"Are you alright?" Nick asked, pulling up beside her.

Opening her eyes, she smiled at him reassuringly. "Sometimes when I come out here I get so overwhelmed by the sheer barbaric beauty it takes my breath away."

Nick gave her a strange look and changed the subject. "How much of the land we just traveled is yours?"

They brought their mounts around to face the rugged cliffs. She pushed errant strands of hair behind her ears while scanning the countryside. The tall meadow grass was being bent backwards by the strong breeze. "All of it."

His eyes narrowed against the sting of the salt spray. "Including the tin mines?"

She nodded.

"They seem awfully far from the castle. In ancient times they would have been difficult to defend."

"Originally they belonged to a relative. The relative wasn't popular and was abusive toward his tenants, so he was eventually driven off the land. When that happened his estate became the property of the next male heir, who was an ancestor of mine. After that his land was joined to the rest of the Penbrook estate. By then the country was at peace so they didn't have to worry about defense."

A gush of foamy spray struck them. They both gasped and laughed. Nick leaned forward to pat his prancing jet-black stallion on the neck. When he straightened his eyes had taken on a faraway look. Scanning the horizon, he asked, "And the displaced relative or his descendants never tried to reclaim the land?"

She glanced at him sharply. His green eyes bored into hers. She probed, but sensed nothing more then natural curiosity. Biting her lip she again allowed her eyes to stray across the fields. "He achieved his vengeance against my fa--ancestor in other ways. Unfortunately his campaign of revenge was successful. He caused my family a lot of pain and misery before he was eventually killed."

Nick reached across the space separating them to gently close his hand over hers.

Startled her eyes snapped back to him.

"You seem distressed."

She swallowed past the lump in her throat. He was very perceptive for a diurnal. But still there was no way he could possibly understand how deeply distressed she actually was. Any time her uncle Craven Maxwell came to mind, it brought back an avalanche of memories she would rather leave buried.

Nick placed his hand under her chin and lifted her face. They stared at each other for a long moment before he leaned forward and kissed her lightly on the lips.

Her horse snorted and shied. Laural reined her in as she gave Nick a searching look. Her lips still tingled from where his mouth had pressed against hers.

He grinned. "Just trying to bring your mind back from the dark place it seemed to be headed."

She opened her mouth to protest, but before she could say anything he spun his stallion about and galloped toward the castle. "Race you back!" he shouted over his shoulder.

Laughing with delight, Laural gave chase as she allowed her dark memories to be whipped away by the wind.

Later that evening Nicholas Ravensblood sat hunched over his notebook in his tent at the excavation site.

If my calculations and long years of research are correct...

Pausing, he listened intently and laid down his pen. He managed to slip his notes into the secret compartment of his desk just as the tent flap was thrown open.

"I'm here," announced a strikingly beautiful brunette in a breathless voice.

"Yes, Linda, so you are," he responded, studying the tall slender student dispassionately. She was a poor substitute for the marchioness but she would serve his needs. He walked over to the cot at the far end of the tent.

"Come here," he commanded. When she complied he pushed her roughly onto the makeshift bed. Hooking his fingers into the v neckline of her linen dress he savagely tore it down the front. As instructed, she wore nothing underneath. Linda opened her mouth to protest, but one look at her professor and her eyes glazed over.

Nick glared down at the offering before him contemptuously. All his for the taking--and he was going to take all of it.

Just like shooting fish in a barrel.

He kicked off his shoes and trousers then roughly mounted the young student. Linda's back arched while he drove mercilessly into her; punishing her for what she could never be.

When he had driven her past the point of all reason he pulled the dagger from beneath the cot. In a dazed stupor the girl extended her arm while he ran the blade carefully across her wrist. Violently he exploded within her as he fastened his mouth onto her wrist and drank deeply of her blood.

Chapter 25:
The Maxwell Heir

Laural paced restlessly across the expanse of Turkish wool carpet decorating the floor of her bedroom. She paused by the large bay window to stare down at the rose garden. "Roses were always Mom's favorite," she acknowledged aloud, her hand lifting to unconsciously finger the small gold crucifix at her throat. Her gaze strayed further afield to encompass the excavation. Narrowing her eyes she watched the distant figures moving about on the dig site. According to Nick the students would be quitting for the week in a couple of hours. That was how long she had left to make up her mind.

Wandering over to her armoire, she placed her fingertips on the painted pattern and began to trace the roses her Mom had created on the doors. Over forty years had passed since Victory Parker-Gabriel had painted a rose garden across her daughter's furniture and thirty since she had been slain by Craven Maxwell. Laural's hand dropped to the ornately-carved door handle. Her grip tightened reflexively as she thought of her demented uncle and what he had done to her family. The door handle snapped off in her hand. She stared at the pieces for a long moment before placing them on her bedside table.

Reaching up to the top shelf of the closet she pulled down a bottle of PS4 along with a crystal goblet. After pouring the reddish-brown liquid, she gazed pensively into the cup for a long time, considering the details Jordan had provided about the supplement. Thinking about the history of PS4 brought her mind back to the reason for her dilemma.

Returning to the window she slowly sipped her drink while unobtrusively watching her guests. Earlier that morning Ben Fletcher, her assistant director and self- appointed body guard, had called to advise her that the rebuilding of the facility had advanced more quickly than anticipated. Progress was so far ahead of schedule that the crews were currently in the process of putting on the final touches.

Ben expected everything to be finished by the end of the week and operational by Monday.

Although pleased, Laural had been surprised. Since opening the foundation's doors on Monday morning was contingent upon her final walk-through and approval, she was needed on site much sooner then she had originally planned.

She sighed as her eyes fell on Nick's lithe form. Even from this distance she could see his well-developed back muscles flexing whenever he heaved a heap of dirt from one of the pits. As her gaze lingered, doubts continued to nag at her. Despite all the evidence to the contrary, he looked so much like a combination of Jordan and Craven she just couldn't shake the suspicion that he was actually Jordan's son.

And if that's true, he's also the grandson of Craven as well as the great-grandson of Raven Maxwell.

And in that case he would have to be eliminated. It was obvious that the Maxwell heir—whoever he turned out to be--was promoting the legacy of his ancestors and was now the focal point for the entire Loyalist rebellion. This renegade group of porphyrians, in spite of the demise of their former leader, remained loyal to the ideals of Craven Maxwell. Under no circumstances could they be allowed to continue their attempts to dominate the diurnals by infiltrating into their society.

The Penbrook line had always held a completely different belief. Her father, as well as her mom, Jordan, and Dana Maxwell, had embraced a philosophy of benign assimilation into the human communities. Peaceful co-existence was advocated rather than subjugation and domination. Her father had been convinced that was the only way for their species to survive. His lifelong concern had been that if the diurnals ever understood they had the equivalent of modern-day vampires walking among them, they would exterminate the entire porphyrian species out of fear and prejudice.

As a result, the Willow Grove Foundation for Continuing Education had been conceived. The Foundation served a dual purpose. It provided financial aid to impoverished students interested in secondary education. The other, more covert part of the operation involved aiding immigrants in procuring citizen status. Although diurnal immigrants were welcome into the program, the candidates were often porphyrians who were interested in becoming interactive members of society.

Unfortunately, the benevolent purpose of the agency had been corrupted. Only too late did Andrew Gabriel become aware that his facility was being used by Craven loyalists to infiltrate the communities, warping its intent and placing the society he was pledged to protect at risk. As he lay dying, her father's last request had been for her to make it right.

The scene outside her window blurred as tears slid slowly down her cheeks. Her hand again rose to clench the tiny cross, the points dug into her flesh. The necklace had belonged to her mom and since receiving it she had never taken it off. As she opened her palm to study this connection with the past, her mind slipped back thirty years to when she had first developed her porphyrian abilities, back to the day she had been riding home with her dad from the Foundation. Excitement had gripped her when she realized her abilities had finally manifested. Exhilaration had quickly turned to horror when her first telepathic experience had been to be linked with her mom while she was being murdered.

The trauma had been so severe she had been in a coma for several days. As soon as she had regained consciousness, she had been kidnapped and tortured by her Uncle Craven. Her father had eventually undone the damage his half-brother had inflicted, but, in a final act of revenge, Craven had tried to murder her. In the end Craven had been killed, but only after her father had died while saving her life.

Laural let the cross drop back onto her throat. She was certain her father would have been proud of the advancements she and Jordan had made for the cause. They had built on his ideals by expanding his dream of integration into Europe, but now the Loyalists had tried to destroy her father's hopes of peaceful co-existence by blowing up the London branch of the Foundation. Laural blinked back her tears. "Don't worry, Dad, I'll keep my promise." She would never let her dad's dreams die, and she would completely rebuild what her enemies had destroyed.

Her eyes glittered and lips tightened. She had also vowed revenge against those who would carry on the legacy of Craven Maxwell, and if necessary, that would include his heir.

She drained the contents of her glass and slammed it down hard on the sill. Through the window, she again searched out Nick working on the grounds. Despite her growing attraction to him, if he turned out to be the one, he would pay.

And if he wasn't?

She couldn't deny the facts in favor of him not being the heir. The most indisputable was that, according to the last update, Jordan was on his way back from Africa with his son. And no matter how deeply she probed Nick's thoughts, she found no reason for doubting his identity.

What if Tim's background check was accurate and Nick proved to be nothing more sinister then an archeology professor searching for an historical treasure trove?

Swallowing hard, she stared bleakly out the window as her hand unconsciously balled into a fist. Logic dictated she relinquish her doubts, but they still lingered. In light of her uncertainty, she didn't see how she could go to London and leave him with complete access to the estate. She needed an excuse to give Nick to get him off her land when she was gone, for she didn't dare leave him behind while the burial site of Arthur Gabriel was still undiscovered. If only she had planned for this contingency, but there had been no way to guess the foundation would be finished this far ahead of schedule. Had the re-building gone another few weeks as originally anticipated, the semester would have been over and the students gone.

Turning away from the window, she placed her empty glass on the dresser. She tried telepathically linking with her cousin. No response. Picking up the phone she dialed Jordan's number and listened with disappointment when she received the message advising her that the subscriber was out of the area. Uneasiness gripped her as she replaced the receiver. She chastised herself. Jordan was completely competent and he had Tim with him. Her shoulders slumped as she resigned herself to the fact that she wouldn't feel comfortable until Jordan was accessible again.

Again she stared thoughtfully out the window. Suddenly inspiration struck. Excitedly, she hurried down the hall and descended the stairs. Slowing, she paused by the oak door seconds before it was thrown open and the object of her thoughts rushed inside.

He stopped short, a wide grin spreading across his face.

"Come quick," Nick insisted while tugging her hand. "We've hit pay-dirt!"

Chapter 26:
The Discovery

The mid-day sun glinted off metal, momentarily blinding Laural when she knelt next to the open pit. Nick leaned forward, picked up an armor breastplate, gazed at it for a long moment, then held it out for her inspection. He grinned triumphantly as she brushed her hand lightly over the smooth surface of the metal.

Impressed, she looked up into his dancing jade green eyes. "It's incredible."

"Yes, it is," he agreed as he waved one of the students forward.

Laural stood and brushed off her hands as a young man in his mid-twenties moved toward the professor. She had seen him on several occasions but they had never had direct contact. He had reddish-brown hair, light brown eyes, and freckles periodically punctuating his angular face. Lanky and sporting a short-sleeve shirt and cut-off jeans, he had donned a pair of knee-pads which were now stained with dirt and debris. Glancing back and forth between the two men she waited while the teacher made the introductions.

"This is Joe Harding," stated Ravensblood. "He's the one who discovered this." He laid his hand reverently on the armor.

"Nice to meet you," she said, extending her hand.

Joe flushed, started to reach out, but stopped and wiped his hand on his shorts. Hesitantly, he extended his hand again. She clasped it firmly and bestowed a generous smile, before kneeling down again beside the armor.

"How old is it?" she asked while examining the tarnished and battered metal.

"Twelfth century," blurted out Joe. When they both looked at him he reddened. After an uncomfortable pause the student shot an inquisitive look at his instructor.

Laural also looked to Nick for confirmation.

He nodded approvingly at the student. Joe dropped his eyes, fidgeted for a few moments, then busied himself cleaning the remaining dirt and sediment from the armor.

"Joe is very unassuming, but his specific area of study is that particular time period. If he says twelfth century then you can be certain that's what it is. Several of the other students have been coming up with bits and fragments of metal all day, but this is the first complete piece of armor."

She observed the student carefully.

Unassuming is an understatement. I wonder why he's so shy?

"You and the students must be very excited," she responded enthusiastically while glancing from Joe to Nick. "Can you tell anything specific about this find?"

"Yes, it's a very significant discovery because it's in one piece and in good condition." Nick shrugged. "Each artifact has its own story. The entire tale of this excavation has yet to unfold. Some of the other fragments appear to be from armor, some from weapons. The implication is a major battle took place here sometime in the Middle Ages. According to my research this area was rife with conflict during that time: Petty lords continually fighting for territory and power with constantly shifting allegiances. We'll just have to wait and see how this one plays out before we can tell the entire tale."

She looked away as she recalled the story her uncle had told her about the battle he had had with her father. According to Craven it had been this conflict which had resulted in the loss of his land, the same land which now was annexed to the Penbrook estate. That battle, however, had taken place several hundred years later then the time frame Nick was describing. It had also happened on Maxwell territory which was several miles away, so apparently that wasn't the fight to which Nick was referring. Concentrating on trying to remember if there were any others, she couldn't recall any family history that would give credit to the implication. Although still attempting to rein in her eagerness, the timeline was almost too coincidental. She was beginning to seriously consider the idea that her grandfather was the legendary King Arthur.

Nick's voice intruded on her thoughts. "This has been a wonderful experience for the students. I really appreciate you allowing us to make use of your property." He was gazing at her steadily.

Laural dragged her thoughts back to the present. Their eyes met and held. Unable to tear her gaze from his, she was overcome by the suffusing warmth of the blush staining her cheeks. She swept her gaze back to Joe, who was still busily engaged in his task and showing no sign that he was paying them the slightest interest.

"Of course anything found is considered solely your property to do with as you see fit," stated Nick, reclaiming her attention. "But I would highly recommend this piece at least be donated to a museum. It's a nearly perfect artifact of medieval culture."

"I'll consider it." She agreed as her eyes continued to probe him. "In the meantime," she said impulsively, "I have to go to London for a couple of days to take care of some business. I was hoping you would come with me."

He gave her a long meaningful look. Erotic exhilaration enveloped her as her skin tingled everywhere his eyes lingered.

"I can't think of anywhere I would rather be," he replied huskily.

Chapter 27:
Cynthia's Revenge

"It's time," commanded the harsh voice over the phone.

"Everything's in place?" Cynthia asked breathlessly.

"Yes. How are things on your end?"

Cynthia eyed her captive. "Everything's going great. It appears our guest doesn't have any useful information to impart that we didn't already know. But I've decided to have some fun before eliminating him."

"Just make sure he doesn't escape," admonished Nick.

"Not much chance of that," she scoffed. "The tower's impenetrable and virtually intact. It seems to have suffered only minor damage during the battle between the Marquis of Penbrook and Craven Maxwell. The only way out is either through a five-inch-thick oak door or a three-hundred-foot drop from the window."

Eyeing the window, she intentionally omitted the nearby door built into the wall with steps leading down the side of the structure. No sense disclosing information which could lead to a reason for Nick to veto her plans. She peered through the doorway to scrutinize the unconscious figure.

It's not like the Earl of Rockford is in any condition to get up and walk down several hundred stone steps.

"By tomorrow everything will be in place," asserted her confident leader before breaking the connection.

Cynthia dropped the cell phone into her pocket then walked into the adjoining chamber.

How thoughtful of Craven to include such a wonderful torture chamber in his original design.

She admired the iron maiden, the stockade, and several sets of manacles still set into the walls. Hooks also protruded from the stone, where she was sure whips of all sizes had been displayed. Even the ceiling still bore evidence of the previous lord of the castle's intent with thick metal chains dangling in the center of the room.

Cynthia pivoted to face the cell's finest feature. The ancient wood and iron rack sat off to one side of the room, its latest victim held securely in its grasp. Glittering green eyes as keen as a cat's watched the barely discernable rise and fall of the Earl of Rockford's chest. His arms and legs were outstretched and pulled taut with barbed wire. Releasing the crank slowly she eased the tension slightly so he could recover just enough to continue.

It wouldn't do to kill him too quickly, especially since she had Craven's and Thomas' deaths to avenge. Hatred shot from her eyes as she studied her prisoner. He was splayed flat across the wooden surface of the rack. Her blood boiled as she recalled the part this man had played in the demise of her former leader and previous lover.

Why should he live while two of the greatest porphyrians who ever existed are dead?

Her eyes raked over the battered body. She laughed.

That wouldn't be a problem much longer. If only I could make him truly pay for the loss.

An idea struck.

Why not increase the fun with a little psychological torture? I wonder which image would be more taunting: the thought that he hadn't managed to kill Craven after all or a visit from his dead twin?

Jordan groaned. She leaned closer. "Laural," he rasped.

I wonder if the Marchioness of Penbrook has any idea of her precious cousin's true feelings?

Her frown changed into a malicious grin. She concentrated and focused all her psychic energy.

Jordan peered up through a haze of pain. "Laural," he rasped again.

His cousin's long blond hair trailed across his bare chest while her sapphire blue eyes stared down at him.

"Laural!" he screamed in agony as the wires inexorably pulled his joints from their sockets.

Chapter 28:
The Loyalist Threat

Laural stood in the center of the room, inspecting her new office. After examining the rosewood desk, antique furnishings, and plush carpet she turned to the workman and smiled. "Looks pretty much like my old office," she commented with approval. "I especially like the color scheme," she added while admiring the rosebud print in shades of pink and cream which decorated the upholstery of the desk chair and matching sofa. The wingback chairs stationed in front of her desk along with the carpet were done in a rich shade of rose while the walls were a soft ecru. She turned back to the decorator. "This is really wonderful and I appreciate your hard work and the extra effort it took to get it ready so fast. You did a great job."

The workman beamed as he left the room. A tall man of about thirty-five with pale skin and dark hair and eyes brushed past him in the doorway. Laural smiled warmly when Ben Fletcher stepped into the office.

As he closed the door behind the workman he asked, "What do you think?"

"I'm impressed." She walked around to sit behind her new desk. "I'm also very pleased with the efficiency the construction crew has shown in getting us up and running so quickly. I'm absolutely delighted with all this." She waved her hand at the room. "How did you do it?"

He grinned broadly and unbuttoned his jacket as he sat across from her. "I have my ways. I know how important it is for you to feel as cozy as possible while you're working."

She nodded. She did feel cozier in appealing surroundings when she had to stay late at the office. Ben, who had been one of the first porphyrians integrated through the London branch, had worked with her long enough to know her personal tastes and understand her needs. He was often able to anticipate what she wanted even before she was aware of it herself.

"How about a status update?" she asked while pulling out a bottle of PS4.

He leaned back in his chair. "I've had a full team working around the clock, scrutinizing every shred of evidence. We've been unable to come up with a single terrorist or political group to blame. I've been coordinating our efforts with Tim Cooper in Washington. We've finally come to the conclusion the Loyalists are the culprits."

She frowned, feeling deflated. If Ben was consulting with Tim, that meant Jordan was also back. It was odd her cousin had not contacted her immediately upon returning from his assignment. Usually they connected with each other after any covert operations. This standard ritual had been in place for so many years it had become second nature. She realized just how much she expected and relied on their normal procedure. Her frown deepened.

Jordan not checking in with me just doesn't make sense. He's too responsible to forego protocol. I'll call Washington as soon as I can.

Is anything wrong?" Ben asked, sensing her change in mood. His eyes darkened from deep grey to black as he studied her closely.

Laural refocused her attention on the conversation and shook her head. "I can understand how you came to that decision. I also jumped to the same conclusion originally, but recently I've been re-evaluating my impulsive responses." She paused while recalling Jordan's demonstration with the rapier. "After further consideration I've decided to be more open-minded and examine other possibilities."

Ben raised an eyebrow. "We've already pursued all other possibilities. Upon careful evaluation and investigation, we've eliminated them. The dragon pendant and dagger have been authenticated, which proves Maxwell involvement. After determining that, excluding other groups became pretty much a formality."

She shook her head. "Believe me, I'm eager to find the culprits, and I'd relish being able to wrap this up in a nice neat package to lay at the enemy's doorstep. But all the pieces aren't falling into place. We've been battling Loyalists for thirty years. Why would these heirlooms only show up now? I think it's at least possible that another organization is involved. We can't discount the fact that, throughout the ages, there have been many zealots and religious groups that have used the dragon as their emblem."

"Not with the authentic Maxwell family crest," he protested.

"There's always the possibility the heirlooms could have been sold or stolen."

He appeared doubtful and about to protest again, so she quickly continued, "If it was the Loyalists, they wouldn't have missed a perfect chance to kill me. Not only have I been steadily terminating them for the past several years, but I'm also the last Penbrook and the most powerful porphyrian on the planet. Slaying me while I was incapacitated would have been too good an opportunity to pass up. The ensuing chaos would have provided the perfect time to coordinate their efforts to destroy the D.C. office. Their next priority would be to get rid of Jordan since he's the closest blood kin to the House of Penbrook and the second most powerful porphyrian on the planet. It's been a long standing goal of the Loyalists to get rid of both of us and terminate the assimilation program. Only by obtaining those goals would they achieve their purpose."

"Not if their actual purpose was to upset you personally."

Startled, she sat back. "Well, if that was their purpose they certainly succeeded, however, I think it's a lot of trouble to go to just to 'upset' me."

Ben flinched. "Sorry," he said, holding up his hand. "I just meant that, because of the circumstances, Tim and I have concluded, contrary to our original belief, that the Loyalist threat is to you personally rather then the agency or even the earl. It also appears that whatever their purpose is, it isn't to kill you--at least not yet. For some reason they seem to be more interested in rattling you and keeping you off guard so you don't know what to expect next."

"Then how do you account for the murder of the mid-wife?" she asked, using the same argument Jordan had brought up several days earlier. "I'd say that was directly aimed at the earl."

"True," he agreed readily, "but there's a world of difference between Craven's supporters eliminating evidence that might lead to the discovery of the earl's son and a direct attack on you personally."

She leaned forward and propped her elbows on the desk. She wasn't sure she liked referring to Mrs. Berkley as evidence, but Ben's theory was a definite possibility. As a direct descendant of the Penbrook lineage, she was the acknowledged leader of her people. If simply eliminating her was their goal, then Jordan, as her successor, still should have been in the line of fire. On the other hand, if the renegades or their leader had been after her personally, maybe it made her even more responsible for Tami's death.

"I'm assuming the trust fund has been established?"

Ben was momentarily flustered by the change in subject but quickly recovered. "The child will be well provided for, and financial compensation and condolences have been extended to the other families as well."

"No pending litigation?"

"The families seem to be looking at the bombing as an unforeseen tragedy with no culpability on your part or the agency's. Both families considered the settlement you bestowed to be quite generous and had only positive comments about you and the Foundation."

Laural was relieved. Her family had always considered it a point of honor to care well for those in their service. The smear on her family's reputation was another score to settle with those responsible. "And no luck locating the boy's father?"

Ben shook his head. "There was no name on the birth certificate. And I can find no record that the mother ever filed for child support. Medical records only indicate blank spots where paternal information is requested. Friends and family claim they didn't know Tami was even dating anyone special, let alone that she had become pregnant and had a son."

She frowned. "Any problems with the adoption?"

"No. The closest relatives are second cousins who are elderly and have no interest in wanting to raise a toddler."

She nodded briskly, then her eyes softened. "And how is the boy settling into his new home?"

Ben smiled reassuringly. "The little guy is doing quite well, according to Mr. and Mrs. Smythe. They tell me he's a godsend and that he's the light of their life."

Laural nodded her approval.

"Speaking of the adoption, I'd like to get your opinion about something."

She raised her brows.

"It's about my relationship with Lindsay."

Laural looked doubtful. "You know I think the world of Lindsay, but I don't believe I'm the one to be asking about diurnal relationships.

The only one I was seriously involved in failed."

Ben held up a hand. "I'm looking for your feedback as a female."

Laural's lips curved. "I believe I'm qualified to give an opinion on that subject."

"If you were in love with someone enough to marry them, would their inability to have natural children keep you from going through with the wedding?"

She leaned back in her chair and considered her friend thoughtfully. The seconds ticked by while she carefully weighed her words. "If I loved someone enough to marry them, a natural extension of that love would be a desire to have my partner's children. If it happened that we were unable to have biological offspring, I'd consider other options."

"Such as?"

"First I would check into the possibility of fertilization techniques and clinics that specialize in those types of services. After those possibilities were exhausted, I'd consider it a very viable alternative to provide a loving home for a child in need."

"Thanks," he said gruffly, "you've given me hope."

"You're going to ask Lindsay to marry you?"

"As soon as the right moment presents itself."

It was on the tip of her tongue to warn of all the pitfalls of such a union, but she knew Ben was already aware of them.

And who was she to stand in the way of true love?

Her own father had been willing to risk everything for the sake of her mother when she had still been a diurnal.

Smiling, she said, "Good luck." Her mood shifted and her expression hardened. "What's the status on the hunt for the blood drinker?"

Ben glanced down at his notes before addressing her question. "The team's been working around the clock, but so far hasn't been able to come up with any definitive leads. Since the last case in Washington, there haven't been any more murders with the same MO."

Frustrated by her own impotence, she demanded, "I want the blood drinker and the conspirators found before another crime is committed. If it wasn't for my responsibilities here I'd be leading this mission myself."

Before Ben could respond a knock sounded at the door.

"Come in," she called.

Nick sauntered into the room, eyes sparkling with interest. "Quite a facility you have here," he complimented her while seating himself on the rosebud-print sofa.

Laural discreetly slipped the PS4 back into her cupboard while Ben eyed the other man speculatively. Laural studied Ben studying Nick. Abruptly she stood.

"If you'll excuse us, Ben, Professor Ravensblood and I were just about to go for lunch."

Ben did a double-take as the professor's name registered. He threw her a quizzical look. She didn't need to probe him to understand his query. "I know the name is almost too obvious, but Tim has already checked him out."

Ben's expression shifted from suspicion to speculation. Laural blushed at the assistant director's next silent query. Quickly she led Nick from the room.

Chapter 29:
Stolen Secrets

The moon shone dimly over the Cornish countryside. The castle stood on the side of the cliffs, alone and proud in the moonlight. Wisps of fog shrouded the landscape while shadows danced and played across the terrain. In the distance an owl hooted and a lone wolf bayed.

Outside the fortress walls the forest lay shadowed and silent. The cloaked and hooded forms stealthily climbed from the recently exhumed pit. Like a well-oiled machine, they hauled their burden from its resting place and gently laid it on the ground. They placed themselves in a protective semi-circle around the casket. Four of their group stepped forward while the others stood as guards.

Ancient hinges, stiff with rust, creaked as the heavy stone lid was forced back. No candle flickered, no flashlight beamed. The followers relied only on the iridescent lunar glow and their perfect night vision to penetrate the darkness. At last the contents of the casket lay revealed. As one they leaned forward to peer inside.

A skeleton lay exposed, bones bleached white by time. Tattered remnants of faded fabric clung stubbornly to the frame. A ring bearing the family crest still encircled the third bony finger of the right hand. Around the neck rested a small leather satchel.

Solemnly the group parted. Another figure swept forward, dark cape billowing in the sudden breeze. Reverently the others stood sentinel while the satchel was removed from around the skeleton's neck. Lifting the flap, the figure emptied the contents and inspected them. The moon reflected a pale glow off alabaster skin and platinum hair when the figure turned to leave.

Silent as wraiths, the followers lifted their heavy burden and lowered the casket back into the ground. After removing any evidence of their visit and recovering the artifact from the past, they faded back into the darkness.

Chapter 30:
The Edge of Ecstasy

"Why was that man looking at me as though I was a bug under a microscope?" Nick asked once they reached the lobby.

"Was he? I didn't notice."

He raised a brow but said nothing. As they pushed through the double glass doors and stepped onto the sidewalk, a stretch limousine glided neatly up to the curb.

He looked at the car, then back to her. "I see college professors with interests in tin mines are not the only ones with perks."

She laughed as the chauffeur opened the door.

"So," he asked after settling himself on the plush velvet seat, "what's the story behind the explosion?"

She glanced at him sharply.

"Not you too," he groaned. "Why is it every time I ask questions about the bombing, everyone clams up and gives me strange looks?"

"Don't take it personally, but we're still recovering from the trauma. Everyone is a little edgy right now."

He gazed steadily at her. "Should I retract the question?"

She stared back, trying to determine how much to say. "The Foundation, as you're probably aware from the news, was completely leveled from the explosion. Three people were killed and I was injured." His gaze sharpened. "Not seriously," she added hastily in order to head off any awkward questions. "There's an ongoing investigation but the authorities have not yet apprehended the culprits."

"Do they have any suspects?"

She tensed. Watching him closely, she offered, "I have reason to believe their investigation will be concluded soon. I'm not at liberty to discuss any details."

"I hope their investigation concludes by arresting whoever's responsible. I'd hate to have anything happen to you." He squeezed her hand.

The heat in his eyes spoke volumes. She relaxed and smiled at him. Leaning back in her seat she turned her head to gaze distractedly out the car window until the limo pulled up in front of her London townhouse. Laural tried to calm the butterflies fluttering in her stomach.

This is ridiculous. It's not the first time I've ever been attracted to a man. Of course, it's the first time in a long time, but still--.

Out of the corner of her eye she studied her companion. Reclining against the plush velvet seat, he was strikingly handsome with his chiseled features, muscular torso and long legs. His light-gauge knit sweater clung provocatively to his chest while his designer jeans emphasized his narrow hips and well-defined thighs. She swallowed hard against the lump in her throat while the butterfly wings beat faster.

Emerging onto the pavement, she stood, irresolute. Nick stepped out behind her, and clasped her hand. She stared down at their linked fingers for a long moment, then looked up into his face. He smiled. The tension drained from her body as his light squeeze of her hand reassured her.

He's not Jordan's son.

Jordan was, at that moment, retrieving his son from Africa. So despite his resemblance and her anxiety, she was free to pursue their mutual attraction.

She began to wonder if her discomfort stemmed from another source besides a suspicion that Nick was a Maxwell. Guilt nagged at her conscience but she couldn't identify the cause. Banishing her disquieting thoughts, she smiled into his questioning green eyes. Taking a steadying breath, she led him up the stairs, unlocked the door and led the way into the foyer.

Nick gently closed the door behind him. For several long moments they simply stood, devouring each other with their eyes. All her fears were forgotten and nothing else mattered but their mutual desire. He opened his arms and she stepped into his embrace.

Laural's heart raced when Nick's arms tightened around her. Their lips clung together like magnet to steel. As the kiss deepened, Laural felt her senses reeling. She hung suspended, finally connected, then shattered into a million fragments only to drown in her desire as the process started all over again.

He unbuttoned her silk blouse. She groaned as his hand slid across her skin to caress her breast then stroke her nipple. Another groan escaped her as the rosy peak hardened against his palm.

Tearing his mouth away he rasped, "The bedroom?"

For a moment she just stared, unable to transition from pure sensation to coherent thought requiring verbal communication. His hold on her breast tightened slightly, pushing her closer to the edge of ecstasy. She was lost in the jade green depths of his eyes, captivated by her arousal.

His eyes are so much like--

Suddenly she felt smothered and couldn't breathe.

Is this an anxiety attack?

Jerking out of his arms she took several steps back while her breath caught in her throat.

"Laural?" he asked uncertainly. Confusion, doubt, and pain spread across his features. He tried to mask his disappointment while he searched her face. His arms reached for her, hesitated, and then dropped to his sides.

Gazing back, she licked her dry lips, urgently trying to find the right words. She didn't know how to explain. She had wanted to make love with this man only seconds before, and now she felt as though she was under attack.

"I'm sorry," she began. "It's not you." She grabbed his hand. "I thought I was ready for this, but I guess I'm not. You see, it's been a long time since I allowed any romance into my life—"

She froze, her grip on his hand tightened spasmodically. An image of Jordan strapped to some sort of medieval torture device assaulted her brain. She barely managed to keep herself from gasping his name out loud.

"What's wrong?" Nick demanded, snapping her back to the present.

"I need to make a phone call." She dropped his hand, unconcerned about the impression she left behind. She strode to the living room, re-buttoning her blouse as she headed for the end table. Snatching up the phone she waited with trepidation while the overseas call went through. She frowned in confusion when Tim Cooper's voice came on the line. She was sure she had dialed Jordan's direct number. "Tim, I—"

He interrupted her. "Laural, I just got off the phone with Ben Fletcher. The Smythes have been murdered and the little boy is missing."

Chapter 31:

Crisis

Laural's mind reeled.

"Laural, are you still there?"

Her eyes flew to Nick. Warily she watched while he ventured into the library, and stood regarding her curiously from across the room. "I'm here."

"They left another dragon-handled dagger."

She closed her eyes and exhaled slowly.

What could my enemies possibly want with Tami's son?

"Where's Jordan?"

A long pause dragged out across the line. "Isn't he with you?"

She gripped the receiver so hard the casing cracked. "No, he was in Africa with you. I assumed that since you were back--"

Tim interrupted her. "Jordan never joined me in Africa. He left three days ago to meet you in Cornwall."

Her eyes followed Nick as he walked over to the sofa and seated himself. "I received an e-mail from Jordan at about that same time telling me that you'd asked him to come to Africa."

"That's not a good sign," mused Tim, understating his misgivings. Apprehension tinged his voice as he continued, "I read the message he received from you requesting he join you in England. Jordan never questioned its authenticity."

The color drained from her face. If Jordan had considered the message genuine, that meant their encryption code had been breached.

Jordan had been tricked, abducted and—

Her mind clamped closed on the thought. If her cousin had been slain surely she would have felt something. Steadying herself she began breathing again.

No. He isn't dead--at least not yet.

"Do you think the two incidents are related?"

"It seems too coincidental to actually be a coincidence, but I'm going to have to check into it further."

"What about Jordan's son?"

"What about him?"

"The message I received said you requested Jordan join you because you'd found his son."

Tim denied the claim. "The only thing our team found in Africa was an abandoned compound and uncooperative villagers."

She glanced at Nick again. "Obviously we need to talk. I'll call you later when I'm free."

Slowly, she replaced the receiver. Again, the image of Jordan being tortured in the room of a castle intruded. Just like the last time, the image faded before she could get a fix.

It's almost as though someone's blocking it.

She watched Nick closely while he reclined on the antique upholstered sofa waiting for an explanation. She had no idea what to tell him that would even make a modicum of sense.

"I'm sorry to do this, but I have to go back to Cornwall."

He raised his brows.

"I just received news that there are a couple of crises that demand my immediate attention. My cousin may be in trouble and I have reason to believe he may be waiting for me at the estate."

He gazed steadily back at her.

"If you're that concerned and he's at the estate, why not just call?"

Her color rose when she realized he wasn't buying her explanation. He knew as well as she did that there was another reason for her abrupt departure.

She started to speak, but he held up his hand.

"Don't bother," he said, standing. "It's obvious that you have some sort of genuine crisis," he glanced at the phone, "but there's the issue that came up between us before the phone rang. I understand that right now your mind is on your cousin and whatever else is going on, but, eventually we have to talk."

"I appreciate your understanding. I'm afraid I wouldn't be very good company while my mind is distracted."

He watched her as she paced across the wooden floor. "I can

appreciate your concern."

She eyed him doubtfully, knowing he couldn't really appreciate everything she was going through, and she couldn't explain. An involuntary shudder ran through her as her mind flashed onto the image of Jordan tied on a medieval torture rack in the room of a castle. Judging from the circular parameters of the chamber, it was a tower room. She shivered again.

I've never seen such a device at Penbrook Castle, but I haven't been up to the tower since—

Her mind recoiled.

Could someone have gained entrance while I was gone and be keeping Jordan prisoner there?

Laural tried to establish a telepathic link with her cousin. Her anxiety increased when she received no response. Just as her hand closed on the telephone receiver, it rang. Before lifting it, she gingerly sat down next to Nick. He placed his arm around her shoulders.

"Hello?"

"Hello, Laural. It's Ben."

"I just got off the phone with Tim Cooper."

"Then he filled you in?"

"I'm aware of the situation regarding the Smythes. But there's a second problem: Jordan's missing."

A sharp intake of breath hissed across the line. "Do you need me to come over?"

"No, I'm on it," she said quickly. "I'm headed back to the castle immediately."

Ben sighed heavily. "That pretty much echoes what Tim said Jordan's policy's been recently. He called me a few days ago to discuss concerns he has about security, especially where it pertains to your safety. As head of security on this side of the Atlantic, I'm letting you know that I'm in agreement with my Washington counterpart. Both you and Jordan have been taking too many risks without proper precautions--one of the most serious of which is not allowing your security guards to actually guard you."

She momentarily bristled but then relaxed. He had a point and he was only doing his job.

To drive home his point, Ben continued, "I would remind you that his lack of caution may have placed Jordan in peril. It's my duty to make sure the same thing doesn't happen to you."

Again, she stifled her annoyance. Ben spoke from genuine concern, and he was probably right. "I want to move on this right away. If I have any problem I'll let you know. Start an investigation into both cases. Let me know the second you find out anything about the baby. I'm going to follow up my own lead regarding Jordan. Meet me at the Cornwall estate." She eyed her visitor. There was only so much she could say out loud in front of Nick. Silently she projected her thoughts to Ben.

If someone's imprisoning and torturing Jordan, there will be hell to pay.

Chapter 32:
Demented Experiment

Anxiety and dread fought for supremacy as Laural searched the tower rooms of Penbrook Castle. Swearing in frustration, she frantically ran from one chamber to the next. Empty, all empty. She had been certain that the image she had received was from one of the tower rooms in her own fortress. Helplessness and confusion added to her emotional turmoil when she came to the end of the hall and had to finally admit defeat.

She slumped against the window frame and stared blankly out across the barren fields. Visions of all the atrocities which could be inflicted on the earl tortured her thoughts. Closing her eyes, she tried in vain to recall more details from the earlier image of her cousin. After a few moments she opened her eyes and rubbed her temples. All she was getting for her effort was a headache.

Absently, her eyes scanned the horizon while she tried to figure out her next move. Panic threatened to overwhelm her, but she firmly thrust it aside. It wouldn't do Jordan or young Bryan any good if she gave into her own fear.

Holding onto the windowsill for support, she fought for control. In the distance she could just make out the ruins of her uncle's long-abandoned stronghold. Someday she planned on tackling the task of demolishing what was left of the Maxwell estate so that something constructive could be done with the property.

Maybe a community center. She smiled slightly. *Her uncle would certainly be turning over in his grave if he knew the same property where he'd once terrorized his tenants would now be used for their benefit.*

She scanned the vicinity again, searching for anything that might connect with the images she had received. When her eyes dropped to the ground below the window she experienced the familiar vertigo.

With relief she turned away from the portal. No point in battling her fear of heights when there was no purpose.

Disconsolate, she descended the circular stone stairs, pausing at the bottom of the flight, still considering her predicament. Her eyes probed the solid rock interior for any clues. There were none. She blew out an exasperated breath. Try as she might she couldn't determine any indications of Jordan's whereabouts nor could she establish a telepathic connection with her cousin. That was a very serious concern since no porphyrian alive should be able to block her telepathic communication with Jordan--at least none they knew about.

In her study, she threw herself into the antique rosewood chair behind her desk. She pulled out the documents Ben had faxed her earlier regarding the Smythe case. Maybe if she channeled her frustration and fear into this problem, it would aid with the other. Despite not understanding how all the pieces fit together she was completely convinced they were related. Now that Jordan had been captured she had no remaining doubts about Loyalist involvement. Even though she had already read the report several times, she hoped she had overlooked something which would give her an indication of why the Loyalists had murdered the Smythes and abducted Tami's baby. She clung to the hope that solving the mystery surrounding Bryan would help in locating Jordan.

As she sifted through the pages she wondered what the Loyalists' interest could possibly be in the toddler. No matter how hard she tried she couldn't make the pieces fit. He wasn't even a healthy child, she noted, frowning as she re-read the documents. Born prematurely, he had several underdeveloped organs. This had already caused him to have two organ transplants and several blood transfusions. According to the doctor's reports they hadn't even expected him to live this long and his prognosis continued to be poor.

Laural sat back and swept her hand through her hair. She drummed her fingers against the paperwork as she wondered about the fate of Tami's son. His father had disappeared and presumably had no interest in being a part of Bryan's life. His mother had been killed before he had reached two. Now his adoptive parents had been murdered. And after she rescued the child from the Loyalists, what then? It was going to be difficult to find more suitable parents who would be willing to care for a child with so many medical problems.

Unless—

Her mind flashed back to her earlier conversation with Ben. Maybe he and Lindsay would consider--.

I suppose it's a bit premature to make plans for the baby's next adoption before I even have him back. I'd better focus on the problem at hand.

But what could the Loyalists want with such an unhealthy child? Both the baby's and Jordan's lives could depend on her ability to figure out the mystery. The most likely scenario was that they were using the toddler for some sort of demented experiment, but just what type she couldn't fathom. However, their reasoning wasn't her main concern at the moment. Her top priority was to locate them and stop them before they hurt Bryan and killed Jordan.

Laural reached for the phone. Initiating a conference call with Ben Fletcher and Tim Cooper so they could brainstorm with her might provide her with a fresh perspective. Maybe they'd have an update. But, even as she dialed she recognized the unlikelihood of that possibility: If either of her assistants had had any news they would have already contacted her.

Just then the front door crashed open. Laural dropped the phone. Spinning around she was confronted by a disheveled but ecstatic student.

"Lady Gabriel," he gasped, breathless, "the professor wants you to come to the site right away!"

She scanned her memory for his name as she continued to stare at the young man. His windswept auburn hair was in a tangled mass around his face and his clothing was in disarray. Eagerness and a hint of impatience sparkled from his eyes as he waited for her response.

He certainly seems to have overcome his shyness. "Joe, right?"

He nodded, watching her expectantly.

She bent to retrieve the receiver. "I'm sorry, but I was just about to make a very important phone call. Let Professor Ravensblood know I'll be down in a few minutes."

Joe stared back, obviously uncertain what could be classified as a higher priority then the excavation. "We found something important. The most exciting discovery since King Tut, maybe bigger."

Now he had her full attention. Despite the crisis her curiosity was piqued. "What is it?"

The young man vigorously shook his head, his auburn hair flying wildly as he spoke. "The prof said not to even hint. He wants you to see it for yourself."

Her heart raced.

Could they have stumbled onto my grandfather's grave? If they have, does that mean the secret of PS3 was exposed? What if Nick or any of the students read my grandfather's journals? How will I explain them?

"Has anyone gone through the find?" she snapped.

Impatient, he shook his head. "That's why I was sent. But the natives are getting restless, so to speak. After all their hard work they don't understand why we can't even look until you arrive."

Laural hesitated, glancing from the student to the phone still tightly clutched in her hand. At last she replaced the receiver. Having the PS3 documents fall into the wrong hands would be disastrous. She knew Jordan would insist she make that the top priority, **so** she followed Joe out the front entrance.

Hopefully, this discovery will help the other pieces of the puzzle fall into place.

Chapter 33:
The Skeleton and the Sword

Laural and Joe wound their way down the heather-strewn hill to a flat field. The sun burned brightly overhead and Laural wished she had had the foresight to bring a hat. With the sun shining this strongly she would only be able to stay in the direct line of the ultra-violet rays for a few minutes. Ahead, she could see all the students clustered around an excavation site. As she drew closer she inhaled sharply. A large stone casket lay near the opening.

Nick smiled at her. "I'm glad you're here. I was barely able to contain the mob."

She smiled slightly at his humor while she glanced around at the expectant faces. Her eyes finally came to rest on Nick for a long moment before sliding to the casket.

Could this coffin actually contain the remains of Arthur Gabriel and the secrets of PS3?

"Are you ready?" he asked placing one hand on the lid.

She hesitated, drew a deep breath then nodded.

He and two other students positioned themselves around the stone. Slowly but steadily they carefully lifted and pushed the lid down the length of the coffin. Ecstatic shouts and peels of laughter reverberated across the fields as the thrilled students back-slapped and high-fived each other. Turning toward her, Nick beckoned.

Stepping forward she looked down. Her eyes widened. Inside the casket lay a complete skeleton, remnants of tattered cloth still clinging to several areas, its arm bones folded across its chest. She recognized the Penbrook coat of arms on the ring encircling the third finger bone of the right hand. She scanned the interior once, then checked again--no sign of journals, diaries, or ledgers of any sort. There were no inscriptions of any kind.

Could the legends have been wrong? Maybe there really were no journals or maybe--

"May I?" Nick asked.

Distractedly, she glanced up at him. She thought she saw confusion and disappointment etched into his expression.

But it could just be my overactive imagination. I'm seeing enemies everywhere.

Nick's sudden intake of breath brought her up short. She glanced over at him. Standing transfixed, he was gazing at a sword he had pulled out from its position beneath the skeleton. Laural scanned the faces of the students to gauge their reaction. They too were mesmerized by the artifact the professor was holding.

Sensing only natural curiosity from the group she turned her attention back to Nick. She probed deep enough to ascertain the truth. She didn't like invading his mind but she had no choice. Both Jordan's and baby Bryan's lives were at risk and this man could hold the key.

She read him. His thoughts were full of images--his job, the current situation and even his feelings about her. Ashamed, she blushed as she delved even more deeply into his private thoughts, convinced this was the only way to determine conclusively whether he was a diurnal or porphyrian.

She shook her head and exhaled. He read clean. As she watched him studying the sword she refocused. "A sword?" she queried, wiping her hand across her forehead. Dried flakes of skin rubbed off on her fingertips and she surreptitiously brushed them away.

Reverently he laid the sword in its scabbard on top of the lid. He searched the eager faces of his students before turning back to her.

"Unless I'm very much mistaken," he said in a hoarse whisper, "we've just uncovered the skeleton of King Arthur and his sword Excalibur."

Chapter 34:
An Error in Judgment

Cynthia kept a solitary vigil at the window of the ruins of Craven Maxwell's long abandoned stronghold. Shadows spread across the ramparts as she watched the dusk fade into twilight. She sipped her glass of PS4 while contemplating her situation. Her mouth twisted in distaste when she swallowed the drink. Bestowing a disdainful look on her glass, she set it aside and then gazed out into the deepening shadows of the landscape.

Not long now.

The phone rang. Her footsteps echoed hollowly on the barren wooden floor as she crossed the chamber. "Hello?"

"How's our guest?"

"Miserable and in pain."

"Good. What have you discovered so far?"

She sighed. "That the Earl of Rockford is very stubborn."

He cursed.

Cynthia frowned. "I take it you weren't the one who removed the journals?"

"You know damn well it wasn't me. I would never have directed you to go to the trouble of removing the documents and replacing them with forgeries if I was going to remove them myself."

"Not even to test my loyalty?" she asked doubtfully.

"And risk our enemies capturing and interrogating you? You must think I'm a fool," he snapped and then paused. "We found Arthur Gabriel's remains but no journals, at least not yet. I'm betting that they're either embedded inside the casket, still somewhere else on the estate, or hidden away by the Gabriel bitch or your prisoner."

"I guess it's a good thing I took my time torturing the earl rather then killing him right away."

A protracted pause ensued. Cynthia had time to regret her rash statement, belatedly recalling it had been Nick's idea to immediately eliminate the earl. Knowing her leader, he wouldn't take kindly to being reminded of any error in judgment. His next words bore out her misgivings.

"For your sake, let's hope that keeping the earl alive provides more then just your personal amusement."

She drew in a steadying breath and tried to keep the frustration out of her voice. He was already angry; it wouldn't be wise for her to provoke his temper. "It is as I told you. There were no journals. Do you doubt I conducted a thorough search?"

"There are many things I'm beginning to doubt about you. Your loyalty is one of them and your competency is another. In this case you're fortunate your story is borne out by your accomplices. However, because of your failure to procure the journals, we'll need to make an alteration to our original plan."

"What kind of alteration?" she asked warily.

"I'll have to take time away from what I'm doing in order to conduct a thorough interrogation of our prisoner so that I can be certain he doesn't have any knowledge about the journals."

"I've already probed him–I can assure you he knows nothing about the documents."

"I'm not interested in your assurances and I've already told you what I think of how you've handled the situation so far."

Desperate, her mind searched for a way to shift the blame. "Are you sure it was the remains of Arthur Gabriel you found? Because, if not, that would explain--"

"Of course it was him," he interrupted furiously.

"I was just hoping there might be a chance--"

"A chance I was wrong?" he asked contemptuously. "You should know by now that I'm rarely wrong. When I am, I immediately and decisively rectify my mistakes."

His ominous tone made her uneasy.

"If it sets your little mind at ease," he sneered, "he was wearing the Penbrook coat of arms and had what seems to be the famed Excalibur by his side."

She gasped. "Then the legends are true."

"Apparently so," he agreed disinterestedly, "but that's not the point. More pressure needs to be put on the earl so that he'll tell us what we need to know."

"And if it turns out he doesn't have any useful information?"

"I'll be the one to decide if his confessions have any relevance. Once I determine his usefulness is over, he'll be eliminated."

She chuckled. "I like the way you think. But I hope you don't mind if I continue torturing him until you arrive. I owe that man a lot of pain."

"Just make sure your vengeance quest doesn't interfere with our plans. Our long-term goal is worth far more then your pound of flesh."

Goosebumps ran down her spine at the implied threat. She tried to quell her fear; he needed her--at least for the moment. "I was thinking. Maybe once we get our hands on the formula, we can test the PS3 on Jordan and see if it makes him more fertile. His power ranks pretty high, so it seems a shame to waste the potential to be gained by Rockford progeny."

"I think the world is only big enough for one Rockford progeny and the position is already filled."

"Yes," she agreed, sighing, "I see your point."

He chuckled. "You can still have more fun torturing him. Just make sure he's still coherent enough to tell me what I want to know."

"How long before you arrive?" she asked, relieved his good will seemed to be restored.

He slowly exhaled. "I can only distract the Marchioness of Penbrook for a little longer before her need to find her cousin takes over. I estimate I'll be at the castle within the week."

"I can't wait," she purred into the phone.

"Cynthia," he commanded sharply," the earl is your responsibility. I won't tolerate another failure. So, if you want to redeem yourself, I strongly suggest you get some useful information out of him by the time I arrive."

She swallowed hard. So she alone was going to be held culpable for the missing journals. She had to admit the idea of switching the documents as planned then copying the contents before handing them over had occurred to her. But she had stifled the impulse since she knew Nick had no scruples about accessing her thoughts any time he chose, making duplicity impossible.

Did he read my intentions? Does he think I might have found a way around him? I'd better tread warily and consider other options.

"And Cynthia," he added menacingly, "I'll be very displeased if the earl should expire or escape before I arrive to question him personally."

Chapter 35:
The Disloyal Loyalist

Cynthia stood staring at the phone for long seconds after replacing the receiver. Finally, she left the study and mounted the spiral staircase. She hadn't revealed to her prince that she had been conducting her own experiments and had already concocted a rough draft of the formula. She was a bit more knowledgeable in the area of chemistry then she had let on. A strong survival instinct warned her that it would be wise to keep some discretion when it came to dealing with Craven's heir.

It was only to be expected that the last descendant of Craven Maxwell wouldn't want to have any competition. However, she felt enough distrust in her leader's intentions toward her to develop her own insurance policy. She wasn't naive enough to believe he wouldn't try and rid himself of her after her usefulness was over. With her knowledge she presented too much of a threat. And if there was one thing she knew about the grandson of Craven Maxwell it was that he had no compunction about eliminating threats.

Standing outside the impenetrable iron door she inserted the skeleton key and pushed. It took all of her considerable porphyrian strength to open the partition even after it was unlocked.

Inside, her adversary lay bound to the rack. Walking over, she grabbed a fistful of his sweat-matted hair and jerked his head up. The Earl's eyes remained closed. She slapped his face several times. Red welts stood out against the pale cheeks as his eyes hesitantly fluttered open.

The green eyes sharpened as they focused on her. "Laural?"

"Yes," she responded gently. "I'm here to help."

He strained against the barbed wire at his wrists and ankles. Fresh blood began to ooze from recently healed wounds.

"Jordan, why do you fight against me? I'm hurt, I thought you loved me."

"Who are you and why are you doing this?" he demanded hoarsely.

She chuckled while running her hands down his naked body. Her fingertips stroked and fondled. She motioned and two of her hired henchmen grabbed the struggling prisoner. One guard forced open the Earl's jaw while the other poured reddish-brown fluid down his throat. Jordan gagged and some of the liquid spewed across his chest.

"I think three days should be long enough," she mused, gesturing for the guards to withdraw. With deliberate intent she began to undress. Jordan's eyes closed and his head lolled to the side but she knew he was aware.

"Tell me, Jordan," she prompted softly, "how many times have you imagined how I would look and feel? I know you want me," she insisted in a husky whisper while climbing on top of his prone body. He stiffened and she chuckled. She kissed him on the mouth, then sensually slid her way down his flesh.

Jordan groaned and his eyes opened to narrow slits. Fascinated, he watched as the porphyrian pretending to be his cousin covered his skin with her tongue and lips.

This isn't real. She isn't Laural.

Her long golden hair tickled his skin as her nails lightly raked across his most sensitive spots.

It's not Laural!

Her triumphant sapphire blue eyes met his when his traitorous body responded. Frantically, he struggled to twist as far as his restraints would allow in a vain effort to stop her caresses.

Jordan abruptly went still as he became aware of her intrusion inside his mind. His eyes opened wide when he felt her delving into and sharing his most intimate fantasies.

"Jordan," she murmured, continuing to stroke him, "I knew you wanted me but now I know *how* you want me."

He swore as the telltale flame of arousal ignited his body. The woman softly chuckled at his futile attempts to avoid her onslaught. Her eyes mocked him as her mouth descended. Jordan bucked violently. A groan escaped from between his clenched teeth as she slipped her lips and tongue over his erection.

He closed his eyes and cursed violently. Fresh sweat dampened his skin and his muscles went rigid as he fought to resist her. His body ignored his commands as his flesh surrendered to arousal. Sensing just when he was on the verge of release the woman straddled him. With several fluid movements she sent him spinning over the edge. A scream **of** part ecstasy and part despair, tore from Jordan's throat as he climaxed.

As his heartbeat slowed he opened his eyes. The image of his cousin hovered over him. She removed a dagger from beneath the table. He tensed as she ran the tip up the side of his torso.

"Do you know who this belonged to?"

He just stared.

"This dagger belonged to Craven. You remember Craven, our rightful leader who you and my father killed?"

I've got to hand it to her. Whoever she really is, she's doing a great job staying in character. Could she be another Maxwell relative?

He jerked his head away as she ran the blade down the side of this face and across his neck.

Or could our investigation have been compromised? The Loyalists, who are certainly aware I'm searching for my child, wouldn't hesitate to plant evidence to mislead us. In that case, this sadistic imposter might really be my child.

A new surge of revulsion coursed through him at the idea that he might have been raped by his own daughter.

Of course, that would be in keeping with the Maxwell tradition—

The woman ran the point of the dagger up his inner thigh to his groin. Jordan's eyes bulged as they followed the track of the dragon-handled hilt.

"Don't worry," she soothed, "I may still have need of that particular part of your anatomy, so I can't do away with it –at least not yet. However," she studied him thoughtfully, "we can still keep things interesting."

While grabbing and stretching his flaccid flesh taut with one hand, she used the other to drag the point of the dagger down the center of his penis. Jordan groaned as the shallow slash began to bleed. She extracted the blade and pulled a jar of salt from under the rack. Poring the grains into her hand, she rubbed her hands across the cut. "Nothing like poring salt into an open wound."

He writhed as his flesh immediately began to repair the injury, sealing the agony inside. Frantically, he tried to focus on coherent thoughts to distract himself from the blinding pain in his genitals. He struggled to read his assailant but her mental barrier was too strong.

If I could just manage to focus enough psychic energy, for just a few seconds, I should be able to--

She slapped him hard and he groaned. The blue eyes gazed maliciously down at him. "For a moment I thought I was losing your interest. Am I not entertaining you enough?"

His eyes darkened. "So far you seem to be the only one being entertained."

She chuckled. "Don't worry, my love," she said, stroking his sweat-dampened face. "I'd never leave you like this. Let me give you something to distract you from the pain." Pulling another jar from under the rack she opened the lid and sprinkled an army of red ants across his chest.

Jordan screamed as a million tiny fires were lit across his torso.

She admired her handiwork for a few moments, then, chuckling softly, left the room.

Chapter 36:
Ancestral Remains

"I can't allow the remains of my ancestor to be put on public display," stated Laural emphatically as she glared across the coffee table at her guest.

Nick held up a hand to stop her protest. "All I'm suggesting is you allow an expert from the British Museum to come out and verify the authenticity of the skeleton and sword," he argued, leaning forward on the sofa.

Laural glanced doubtfully through the entrance way and into the great room where the remains of her ancestor now rested in his coffin on a long marble table. The sword, inside its scabbard, was lying beside it. Her eyes narrowed as she swung her attention back to her companion. "I thought you were the expert."

He shook his head. "I'm the archeologist who made the discovery. And even though I have the necessary credentials to authenticate the find, it lends much more credibility in the scientific community if an objective professional validates the claim. That would require someone who's a specialist in this field."

Laural stood and walked over to the display. She stared pensively into the sarcophagus for several long moments. Her eyes traveled up and down the length of the skeleton until they came to rest on the third bony finger of the right hand. Carefully she examined the signet ring bearing the Penbrook coat of arms. Underneath the lion and lamb emblem were the initials of Arthur Gabriel engraved in gold. As she unconsciously twisted her own signet ring, there was no doubt in her mind these were the remains of her grandfather.

But where are the journals that Jordan had insisted were buried with him?

Her eyes drifted to the sword. She studied the scabbard closely. She wasn't a linguist or symbolist so couldn't decipher the meaning behind the symbols painted on the leather. Even though the design had faded with age she had no problem distinguishing the individual characters, but had no idea if they were relevant to her quest. The notion that Arthur Gabriel would have written her people's most valuable secrets on the sheath of a sword was almost too outrageous to consider, but, at this point, she couldn't afford to overlook any possibility.

What if the secret to PS3 is right in front of me and I just can't read it? Nick's right: I need an objective expert to understand the complete significance of this find as well as to translate the symbols on that sword.

Her gaze moved back to the skeleton. " I can hardly credit the idea that these bones will prove to be anything more interesting then a Penbrook ancestor."

Nick rose from the couch and joined her. They stood together in silence, each absorbed in their own thoughts. At last, Nick's hands moved to caress, then reverently lift the sword. His eyes glazed as his fingers purposefully traced the patterns etched into the sheath.

She clung to her skeptical attitude. She had to convince him--no matter what her personal conjectures--that this was not a momentous discovery. Otherwise her estate would be overrun by experts, media and the general public, all trying to get a glimpse of the skeleton and sword belonging to the famous King Arthur.

She examined the inside of the coffin surreptitiously, thinking there might be a hidden panel or secret compartment containing the documents. A thorough investigation would have to wait until she was alone. If only Jordan were here to aid in the quest.

The thought of her cousin caused Laural's brows to furrow. She wanted to be pursuing leads to Jordan's disappearance and solving the mystery behind the baby's abduction--not debating the significance of some old bones. But if Jordan's predictions were true, the safety of their entire race, as well as the diurnals, could be at stake.

Now, due to the latest conjectures about King Arthur, she would have to delay her departure even longer. She frowned as she realized there was really no help for it. She would have to allow the expert access to the estate. Of course, she could always send the remains to the museum. Her eyes narrowed as she considered the idea.

That might only make the situation worse. The expert would be studying my ancestor's skeleton without my supervision and could potentially discover something I don't want him—and the rest of the world-- to know. It's better to keep as much control over this rapidly disintegrating situation as possible.

After expelling a long breath she confronted the professor. Delaying her search for Jordan was not an option. She was convinced every passing moment left him in more peril. She had to grit her teeth to keep from screaming every time she failed to make a telepathic link with her cousin. But she recognized how devastating the consequences would be if she were to leave. It was imperative that the secret of PS3 not fall into the clutches of the Craven Loyalists.

She stole a glance at her companion.

In spite of all the proof to the contrary, what if Nick turns out to be involved with the Loyalists?

She had probed and he had come up clean. But she had only been checking to determine if he was a porphyrian.

He could still be connected. In which case leaving was not only imprudent but could prove to be disastrous.

Suddenly inspiration struck.

Was there a way to combine all three elements?

The seed of a plan took root and started to blossom.

"Hold on. I'd better consult Tim and Ben before I even think about implementing this plan. The idea has plenty of pitfalls, but if we could make it work--

"I know you think I'm insane," Nick said, recapturing her attention, "but hear me out."

"I'm listening, Nick." While she half-listened, she allowed her thoughts to roam. "First of all," he said intently, "there's the name. You said the marquis who was living at the time was named Arthur."

She rolled her eyes. "You're going to have to do a lot better then that. His name was Arthur Gabriel, not Pendragon."

How difficult will it be to get Ben and Tim on board with my idea?

He smiled. "I'm just getting started. Pendragon, by the way, is not such a far stretch from Penbrook."

She opened her mouth to protest but he held up a hand. "Then there's the fact that we're in Camelford, one of the controversial possibilities for Camelot's location."

"But most historians agree the more likely spot is Somerset."

Tim and Ben's most serious objection will be the safety risk. Still, if they could figure out a way. . . And of course it would mean a complete reversal of my earlier position."

"Yes, but even those same historians believe in the legend of this being the location of Slaughter Bridge where Arthur and Mordred his evil son fought their last battle."

Suddenly he had her undivided attention. Something he said was nagging at her. Arthur Gabriel had been killed, but not by his own son. His nephew Craven Maxwell had been responsible for the marquis's death. And, now that she thought about it, Craven did share the dark looks of the legendary Mordred. Pressing her lips together she glanced uneasily back at the skeleton. "All that is very circumstantial."

"Then there's this," he declared triumphantly, brandishing the sword.

Laural eyed the weapon warily as it passed within inches of her face.

Nick smiled sheepishly as he resheathed. "Sorry, I got carried away. The markings on this scabbard," he pointed out the symbols, "roughly translate to 'Whoever shall wield this sword is the rightful king of all Britain.' On the other side," he turned the artifact over, "are more druid symbols indicating that as long as the bearer of this scabbard wears this on his person into battle, he shall lose no blood and his injuries shall be healed."

Startled, she glanced from Nick to the sword and back. "You can translate the symbols?"

He shrugged. "Of course. I studied several ancient languages and am well-versed in symbology as well. I can't imagine anything more frustrating then making a truly significant discovery then being unable to get the entire story of what I've unearthed because I couldn't read the inscriptions or text."

Laural's thoughts whirled.

Could it be that my grandfather was King Arthur after all?

She had heard the myths of Arthur's imperviousness to fatal injury but had always chalked it up to fairy tales. Even her discussion with Jordan several weeks ago, when she had argued the possibility, had been designed to cajole him into allowing her plans rather then from real conviction. But now she was being presented with virtual proof of her own speculations. Only a porphyrian would have been able to withstand fatal injuries and have them miraculously heal while suffering very little blood loss.

Still, if my grandfather had been someone that important, wouldn't my father have told me? And what of their policy of non-interference? Certainly reigning over an entire country could be construed as nothing less than the antithesis of everything my family stood for.

She didn't really have any choice. To refuse an expert's evaluation of the artifacts would make it seem like she was trying to hide something. Besides, if her burgeoning plan was going to work, the more publicity the better. However, she realized it was also in her best interest to continue to appear skeptical and resistant. Too much enthusiasm too soon would tip her hand.

She gazed down at all that remained of her grandfather. She didn't much care about the sword but could she afford to let the skeleton be scrutinized? What if, despite her understanding to the contrary, there actually were skeletal differences between porphyrians and diurnals? There were going to be risks no matter how she played her cards. Without her cousin to consult, she was going to have to make the decision and just hope it was the right one.

"Alright," she capitulated. "You've convinced me that the historical significance outweighs whatever reservations I might have about my family's privacy being violated. However," she admonished sternly, "I want this handled discreetly. No media leaks until we have definitive proof."

Nick nodded, a smile playing on his lips.

She looked into his eyes, a no-nonsense expression on her face. "I mean it. If this turns into some kind of stunt for publicity, I pull the plug, send all of you packing and fight you tooth and nail every step of the way. And even if you win in the end, I could tie this up in the courts for years."

He let out a whoop of delight and snatched her off her feet. Twirling her around in a circle, he planted a kiss firmly on her lips before setting her down. "You won't regret this," he declared, and raced from the room.

Her lips continued to tingle as she stared after him. "I hope not."

Chapter 37:

Family Flaw

The crumbling stones and dilapidated walls lent an air of oppressive gloom to the long-abandoned fortress. Shimmering moonbeams cast distorted shadows across the neglected courtyards and haunted the empty rooms of the former Maxwell stronghold. A lone rat scuttled through the darkness in search of a midnight snack. Its whiskers twitched inquisitively as its claws clicked cautiously across the stones. A faint glow in one of the rooms at the end of the hall caught its attention. The rat sat up on its haunches, sniffed the air several times then spun about and scampered back into the shelter of the shadows.

Nick Ravensblood turned down the flame of the Bunsen burner in the old stone room he had converted into a laboratory. Squinting in the half-gloom he studied the contents of the test tube. Loosening the clamps he lifted the tube and peered more closely at the reddish-brown liquid. It looked almost identical to the supplement his people were used to ingesting, differing very slightly in color and thickness. If it hadn't been for his sharpened senses he was sure he wouldn't be able to tell the difference.

His lips twisted as he continued to scrutinize his most recent results. He hoped this time the formula would be right. It had to be; he was running out of patience, not to mention opportunity. He couldn't predict how much longer Laural would stay with him before deciding she had to go hunting for her cousin or the baby.

The child had been a source of deep disappointment. In retrospect he regretted his decision to allow Edwards to attempt the experiment. Of course if his mating with the diurnal had produced a healthy specimen, the benefits would have been immeasurable. But the failure had put them all in peril. He had taken a calculated risk that his plans would bear fruit before the marchioness or the earl discovered the truth. Certain that success was imminent he had decided the potential benefits far outweighed the danger.

Even the failure hadn't been a total loss. He had gained a great deal in terms of raw data. And he had to be grateful to the marchioness for eliminating Edwards. She had saved him the trouble since he had never had any intention of letting the surrogate survive past his usefulness to the cause.

Shrugging he laid the concoction aside. By the time his opponents figured out what was really going on, the earl at least would no longer be an issue. And if Laural's part in his plans bore fruit, she would have to add her own pregnancy to her growing list of worries. He grinned wolfishly at the thought of being responsible for so much of his enemy's pain and suffering.

He tilted his head back and raised the tube to his lips. He hesitated while doubts pricked at him.

If the ingredients still aren't right, I don't want to risk the side effects.

Perhaps it would be better to do as Cynthia had suggested and try this batch out on the earl. If he impregnated Cynthia without deteriorating into a bloodthirsty demon, he could kill both of them.

And if my father does degenerate into a monster, I could always turn him loose on Cynthia and watch him tear her to shreds. Now that would be extremely entertaining.

With a bitter smile, he reconsidered. His time table was too short. Laural was becoming more suspicious by the moment. If he was going to have an opportunity it would be soon and he had to be prepared.

To the future.

He downed the contents. Setting the test tube aside, he turned the heat back up on the Bunsen burner. Holding his lab notes over the flame, he watched with satisfaction while the papers blackened and quickly turned to ash.

"What are you doing?" gasped Cynthia from behind him.

He backhanded her as he whipped around to confront her startled green gaze. "Spying is not your strong suit. I've been aware of your presence for the past several minutes."

Her eyes fastened on the ashes while her hand lifted to rub her cheek. The blow had stung slightly, but she knew there would be no mark to mar her flawless complexion. "Why?" she challenged.

"I don't want the results of any of my findings to fall into the wrong hands, hands that might use its potential to plot against me." He laughed. "Don't worry, I have it all committed to memory." He tapped his temple. "This way only those whom I choose will share the ability to become fertile."

She laughed lightly as she tried to temper his mood by wrapping her arms around his waist. "Providing you got it right this time."

He shoved her hard against the wall. "You sound as though you doubt my ability to succeed," he shouted in her face, defensive because she had echoed his own concerns. "Or," he towered over her with menace in his face and voice, "as though you'd rather I fail."

She laid a placating hand on his arm. "I don't doubt your abilities at anything and I'm as completely committed to the cause as you are. I just think it would be best to have the original formula."

He was in agreement, but he'd be damned if he was going to let her know. He still wasn't sure why the original journals of Arthur Gabriel hadn't been in the coffin with his remains. He was certain the skeleton and sword were authentic. Could the porphyrian legend have been wrong? Maybe there were no ancient formulas after all. Or maybe… his eyes narrowed as he scrutinized his companion.

"So you're not taking any chances?"

He focused on what she was saying. "From what you told me about my grandfather, it seems he was in the habit of keeping documents that could be used against him. It appears to be a family flaw." He glanced down at the small pile of ashes. "One which I will not repeat."

"Wise as always, Nick."

He grows more paranoid by the moment. I wonder how long it will be before he becomes a narcissistic megalomaniac like his grandfather?"

His eyes narrowed and she worried that he might be reading her thoughts. She wouldn't put it past him since he had no scruples.

"I think," she said hastily, changing the subject, "that the Earl of Rockford is due for another round of torture."

"How is our houseguest?"

"He's been given the penthouse suite and is making the most of his special accommodations."

He chuckled and she relaxed. She started to leave.

"Cynthia," he called after her.

She paused, one delicately arched brow raised.

"Make sure Rockford doesn't escape. I don't mind you having some sport with him, but if your entertainment causes me a problem, you'll be joining him in the penthouse to enjoy the same special accommodations."

Chapter 38:
Top Priority

"I need every available porphyrian who isn't necessary for the running of our facilities to get on this," Laural said with finality into the receiver. She paused to listen while Tim Cooper outlined other projects they were already involved in. "I don't care about the other projects. Pull everyone who isn't vital off their other assignments and get them working on locating both Jordan and Tami's baby. I've already advised Ben that finding them is the top priority. He'll be contacting you to coordinate your efforts."

"What about the special-ops team?" asked Tim. "They're still out in the field hunting for the blood drinker."

Laural hesitated for a long moment. She could hear the erratic beating of her own heart as she weighed the consequences of her decision. Her eyes lifted to a large framed photograph of herself and Jordan hanging on the wall above the mantle. They were smiling joyfully while they sat in her London office toasting the success of the Willow Grove Foundation's first overseas extension. With a pang she recalled how certain they had been of a bright future that would fulfill their hopes and dreams.

"Reassign them," she said firmly. Feeling as though she had finally made her point, she hung up. Before she could lift her hand from the receiver the phone rang again. Heart pounding, she grabbed it eagerly, unrealistically hoping for news. "Hello?"

"Hello," said a deep male voice. "May I speak to Lady Laural Gabriel?"

Her heartbeat accelerated as she frowned into the receiver. "This is Lady Gabriel."

"This is Dr. Ford from the British Museum. I understand you have some medieval artifacts you'd like examined."

She stifled her disappointment as her eyes flew to the table where the coffin and sword rested, a little surprised to be contacted so quickly.

"Yes, a skeleton and a sword.

" *It's just as well to get this started so I can put my plan into action. And the publicity might help flush out news about Jordan or the baby.*

"So, Dr. Ford, how soon can you send someone?"

"I can be out tomorrow."

"You're coming yourself?"

"I am the resident expert on medieval studies here at the Museum. Dr. Ravensblood has been very convincing in his assertion that this find is quite remarkable."

"Just how much has he told you?" she asked guardedly.

"Just enough to catch my interest."

"So you're coming out here based solely on his word?" she asked, a little incredulous.

"Lady Gabriel, I'm not sure if you realize it, but you have one of the world's most renowned authorities of medieval artifacts on your premises. If Nicholas Ravensblood says the find is worth my time, I believe him."

Minutes later Laural stepped out of the front door and headed toward the makeshift camp site. As she neared the main tent she paused.

Am I certain about doing this?

Before she could lose her nerve she lifted the tent flap and pushed it aside.

"Good evening, Lady Gabriel," called a cheery voice.

Laural hesitated. "Hello, Linda," she replied to the striking brunette who was heading in her direction. "Please call me Laural. Were you on your way in to see Professor Ravensblood?"

The other woman started to nod but at that moment Nick emerged from the tent followed by his graduate assistant, Robert Campbell. The two men looked from Laural to Linda.

Laural felt a blush staining her cheeks when everyone seemed to be waiting for her to speak.

"I'm sorry," she began awkwardly, reconsidering her impulse. "I didn't mean to intrude. If you're busy I'll come back later." Her eyes strayed from Robert to Linda.

"No problem," said Robert good-naturedly. "The professor and I are finished." Turning to Ravensblood, he continued, "I'll get team two set up first thing in the morning." To Laural and Linda he said, "If you ladies will excuse me, I'm going to call it an early night," he finished then headed off down the line of tents.

Laural watched him stride away for a moment then returned her attention to Linda. The young woman appeared freshly groomed in her clean white shirt and crisp khaki trousers. The scent of honeysuckle perfume permeated the air and Laural wondered if she had interrupted more than just a teacher-student consultation.

Nick studied her face for several long heartbeats before smiling warmly. "Linda and I can talk shop later."

Laural's misgivings began to recede until she glanced at the other woman.

She looks very disappointed for someone who was just going to talk shop with her professor.

At that moment the student lifted her hand to brush back some hair from her face and Laural caught a brief glimpse of gauze protruding from under her sleeve. Distracted by Linda's injury, Laural barely registered the look that passed between teacher and student. After a moment Linda seemed to get herself back under control.

"Yes, of course," she murmured, and, with a cheery wave she set off.

Laural continued to watch her for a few seconds. Several feet down the path she was joined by Joe and a couple of other students whose names she couldn't remember. Joe clasped Linda's hand. Linda adroitly extricated herself and the group moved off, laughing and chatting. Thoroughly confused by the episode she turned back to Nick.

His eyes delved into hers and it took many long seconds for her to remember what she had come to say. "I came to let you know that the expert from the British Museum contacted me. He's coming out tomorrow to examine the relics."

He continued to stare steadily into her eyes. "That's great news. But is that all you came to tell me?"

She swallowed hard. "I also wanted to invite you for dinner, but if this is a bad time..." she trailed off as her eyes again drifted to follow Linda's retreat down the path.

He smiled disarmingly at her. "I think your timing is perfect," he insisted, regaining her attention. "Ever since we returned from London I've had the feeling you've avoided being alone with me."

It was on the tip of her tongue to deny the allegation, but he was right. "Since I don't have a reasonable explanation for what happened I was keeping my distance. All I can do is apologize and assure you it won't happen again. But if you feel having dinner alone with me would be too awkward, I'll understand."

In response he took her hand and started back up the path toward the castle.

"Are you and Linda involved in a relationship?" she blurted.

He stopped and turned to face her. "Only in the same way I am with all my students."

"I noticed her bandaged wrist," she offered, watching him closely.

For a moment his brows drew together, then his face cleared. "She accidentally injured herself cleaning a metal fragment early this morning."

"I hope she wasn't badly hurt. I take injuries suffered on my estate very seriously. Maybe I should contact a doctor."

He waved his hand. "It was a superficial scratch, so minor that it completely slipped my mind. Unfortunately, as with most surface cuts, it bled a lot. It's been completely taken care of and I can assure you she's suffered no adverse reaction from the incident. I also take my responsibilities very seriously, and, if it had been warranted, Linda would have already seen a doctor."

"Still," Laural persisted, returning to the original subject, "I couldn't help feeling like I was interrupting something."

"Not a thing." He brushed his fingertips across her cheek. "She may have a crush on me, but as far as I'm concerned our association is purely academic."

After dinner they went for a walk in the garden. Laural inhaled the aroma of the roses deeply, bringing her mother to mind as she gazed toward the heavens. The starry sky radiated tiny bursts of light.

Nick pulled her into his arms. His eyes mirrored the sparks of passion smoldering in her own. By mutual consent they paused in their stroll across the garden and stood gazing at each other. Laural felt as though every nerve-ending in her body was vibrating when Nick took her hand and headed back into the castle.

"I think this is long overdue," he murmured huskily into her ear when they passed through the doorway. "I certainly hope you've resolved whatever your reservations were in London."

She responded by lightly kissing him on the lips then nodding her acquiescence as the light from the hall sconces played across his handsome features. His expression changed from relief to passion as she felt the insistent tug of her own arousal. Ever since they had met, this conclusion had been inevitable. She led the way upstairs to her bedroom, pausing outside the door as her mind tried to reassert control. But even though her intuition was still screaming to proceed with caution, the flames of desire burning through her body smothered her reservations.

Nick's lips came down hard on hers, disintegrating her last coherent thoughts in the chaos of erotic emotions. Opening the door she flicked the light switch. The room was instantly bathed in the glow of several dimmed wall lamps. Nick swept her into his arms and carried her to the bed. Lowering her gently he lay down next to her.

"Are you alright with this?" he whispered against her neck as he stroked her hair.

She gazed deeply into his probing jade eyes, and nodded. Despite the remaining doubts about his identity, the primal force drawing them together was stronger then her misgivings.

With deliberate slowness they peeled the clothing off each other's bodies and sank into the plush four-poster bed. They reveled in the feel of soft skin and hard muscles while exploring each other's sensitive spots, giving and receiving until they ascended to a level where nothing mattered but pure sensation. Laural was lost to the power of the moment, all her passion unleashed and unrestrained. She reveled in her arousal as she drowned in the depths of Nick's deep green eyes. No matter what the future held, at this point in time, she and her lover were bound to each other beyond any worldly constraints.

Chapter 39:
The Mistake

Jordan lay naked and spread-eagled on the ancient torture device. With his arms and legs stretched taut by the pulleys, he was completely exposed and vulnerable. Dazed, he shook his head slowly back and forth. If he had only been tied with rope instead of barbed wire he would have been free by now. Of course his porphyrian tormentor was well aware of that fact. Mercilessly she manipulated the restraints and administered intravenous sedatives in order to keep him subdued. Whoever she might really be under the guise of Laural's face, she was undoubtedly a Loyalist.

Obviously one with a score to settle.

In vain he tried to recall any of his kind who would have the level of animosity he felt emanating from this woman, but all his worst enemies had been destroyed long ago –hadn't they?

What if she's really my daughter? What kind of imagined sins could she have been harboring against me all these years?

A slight movement interrupted his thoughts. The earl's senses sharpened. A figure crept out of the darkness, step by step drawing closer. Within seconds the shape loomed over him, silently studying him as he lay bound and helpless on the rack.

A glint of steel flashed. Jordan's eyes bulged as they caught sight of the blade slashing down toward him. Again the arm raised and the knife lashed out allowing the figure to vent the full force of its fury.

Laural bolted upright in her bed, fragments of the nightmare still clinging to her consciousness. Almost immediately she realized she wasn't in the throes of a dream but in the middle of a telepathic link with her cousin.

She watched helplessly as the arm wielding the deadly dagger slashed in a downward arc straight toward Jordan's exposed flesh. Urgently she hurled a direct mental assault at the attacker but it was as though her mind was moving through quicksand. Frantically she unleashed the full force of her psychic power, but again the dagger plunged.

How can that be? No diurnal or porphyrian should be strong enough to resist my direct mental commands.

Switching tactics she probed the attacker. Maybe if she knew who the figure under the cloak really was she would be able to determine a way to stop them. But, despite her best efforts, the figure's mind remained blocked.

Perspiration dampened her skin as she fell back, shaking against the pillow, realizing there was nothing she could do. The knife drove into its target again and again. Blood and torn flesh filled her vision. Yells of terror and pain filled her ears. She screamed just as blackness claimed her.

Groggily, she sat up. Momentarily disoriented she swiftly scanned her surroundings. She was in her own room—her own bed—not in a torture chamber watching Jordan die. Gulping several steadying breaths of air she tried to calm herself while leaning back against the pillows.

Had it been only a nightmare after all?

She attempted a mental connection with Jordan. Nothing. Her eyes strayed across the bed to the man lying next to her. Nick remained sound asleep, unaware of her inner turmoil. She continued to watch him while her mind strayed back to the dream. Nick's smooth features became confused with Jordan's broken, bloody body. Shivering she drew the blankets closer around her.

It had seemed so real, as though I was there—but that wasn't quite it. More like I was living the experience through Jordan's eyes.

As she shuddered again her eyes refocused on Nick. He was very attractive and one hell of a bed partner. A warm glow at the memory of their lovemaking suffused her body.

But the only reason you're with him is because he reminds you of—

She went rigid with shock.

Where had that thought come from?

The idea hadn't been her own; it had dropped straight into her mind like a bomb. Frowning thoughtfully, she considered the implication. Slowly her frown lifted to be replaced by a grin of dawning comprehension.

I can't believe all this time I didn't realize . . .

Her grin faded as she recalled how intrusive the thought had felt.

But who had planted that thought-- and why?

Glancing at the man next to her, she began to regret her impulsiveness.

A few hours later Nick entered the study to find Laural gazing into the sarcophagus. Hearing him enter she looked up. She smiled, but the intimacy was gone from her eyes. He positioned himself on the other side of the sarcophagus and waited.

Unconsciously smoothing down the front of her blouse, she said, "I'm leaving for Washington this afternoon."

He looked at her, a question in his eyes.

"Last night was a mistake."

He nodded slightly, expecting as much. "Not for me."

She studied him. His black hair, still damp from his shower, curled at the ends and framed his face. His skin glowed and he smelled of soap and after-shave. His eyes were bright and intense with emotion as he gazed steadily back at her.

"I'm in love with someone else," she announced with a slight shrug. "I'm sorry, I didn't mean to lead you on, but I only just realized it. Feeling the way I do, I don't think it would be fair to you to continue."

"Does this someone else return your feelings?"

Her eyes clouded. "I don't know."

"Is he aware of how you feel?"

She shook her head.

"Are you going to Washington to be with him?"

Laural felt her patience slipping. Just because they had spent one night together didn't give him the right to interrogate her. "I really don't want to talk about it."

His fists clenched at his sides and fury shot from his eyes, but all he said was "I see."

Laural's irritation dissipated. She almost wished he would express his anger so she could cleanse some of her own guilt. If he turned out to be connected with the Loyalists, he had been using her, but if he was really who he professed to be, she had just hurt a really nice person. She wished she could be sure. If her plan worked she would know the truth soon enough.

"What about the project?"

She searched his face for any signs of duplicity. He seemed genuinely concerned.

Is his anxiety that of a college professor worried about the find of his career or as a porphyrian Loyalist interested in getting his hands on my grandfather's formulas?

"I've already contacted Dr. Ford to reschedule the appointment. He's agreed to come out to authenticate the find later this week. I don't have any intention of prematurely terminating the excavation, Nick. I wouldn't do that to you or the students."

He nodded curtly, turned and left. A moment later the front door crashed shut. Laural slumped down in a chair, laid her face in her hands and wept.

Chapter 40:
Raven's Blood

Later that evening Nicholas Ravensblood stood alone on the castle balcony of his grandfather's former estate. Although long abandoned and mostly in ruins, the tower section was still intact and stood as one of the twin sentinels proclaiming the previous glory of the Maxwells. While staring into the darkness he lifted the goblet of reddish-brown liquid to his lips.

He would avenge his grandfather's death and the demise of his plans by achieving a goal more grand and diabolical than Craven had ever conceived. He relished the idea of how proud his grandfather would have been if he had lived. Together they could have taken his plans of domination through infiltration to a whole new level. Upending the goblet he drained the contents in a silent toast to Craven.

He turned his thoughts to the present and future. He had sensed Laural's suspicion of him at their last meeting. Not that it mattered. Even now the heiress of Penbrook Castle could be carrying his child. In that case she had approximately nine months to live. He shrugged with a sardonic smile on his face.

Either way her days are numbered. And I finally have the only two remaining obstacles to regaining my rightful inheritance under my control.

Thoughtfully he stared into the cup, studying the reddish-brown liquid. Nine months felt like a long time to wait in order to determine the proof of his plans. Raising his eyes he surveyed the landscape spread out before him. He desperately needed to reassert ownership of his birthright, but he knew he was being impatient.

After all, what's nine months to a creature who will live hundreds of years?

If his conjectures were right, by this time next year, he would be in complete control of his people's destiny. Once his competition was eliminated he would inherit the position of leader of his race. As the closest relative, he would receive all the titles and property from both the Maxwell and Penbrook lines. He would also have two children: one from Laural and the other from his diurnal student, Linda, the idiot who thought he was in love with her. He would show her how much he cared right after she gave him proof that his alterations to the PS4 formula allowed porphyrians to fertilize diurnals. In the meantime, she was serving his needs as both a source of nutrition and an incubator.

He smiled. Supplementing the formula with ingredients enabling porphyrians to cross-breed had been a stroke of genius. His chemistry degree had stood him in good stead. If his re-working of the supplement was successful, not only would his species be able to more efficiently procreate with each other but with diurnals as well. Once he had the proof of his formula's success he would be selectively providing the Loyalists with his own version of the supplement: Raven's Blood.

With only the Loyalists given the formula which would allow them to cross-breed, it wouldn't be long before his people dominated the planet. Then they would see who took to skulking in the shadows and avoiding detection in order to survive. A smug smile curved his lips at the thought of superseding Arthur Gabriel's benign intentions for the supplement with his own brilliant scheme. From this point forward he, not Arthur Gabriel, would be forever remembered as the forefather of their race.

His eyes narrowed as he continued to think about the marquis. He tried to determine what use he could make of the remains. He couldn't fathom what had become of the journals reported to be buried with their former leader. He needed those books desperately. For even though he knew he was on the right track, his formulas still lacked the correct combination of ingredients for complete success.

Could he count on the information his mysterious visitor from a few hours ago had provided? A cynical smirk curved his lips as he recalled the interesting yet unexpected meeting. Even if the cloaked figure's revelations proved inaccurate the Penbrook estate would be left essentially unguarded while its mistress was in Washington. Since he was convinced the journals were not with the remains he could use the opportunity as an ideal time to examine the grounds.

His brows furrowed. He hadn't liked the idea of not knowing who was behind the mask of his mysterious benefactor. This deception had kept him from completely crediting the information provided. However, the figure had insisted that because of his highly-trusted position with the house of Penbrook, giving his identity would have immediate and disastrous effects. Nick couldn't have cared less about the consequences for the Gabriels, but decided it would be to his advantage to have a highly-placed spy.

Of course he could have probed the visitor and determined his identity, but, assuming the spy turned out to be a porphyrian, he would detect the mental intrusion and become less cooperative. Nick could have forced his guest's compliance easily enough but preferred to see what plans the "trusted" Penbrook servant had in place. So he had overtly allowed the stranger to keep his anonymity—and sent one of his guards to follow him.

Scowling into his drink he thought about all the possible mistakes inherent in the mixture of chemicals he had used, mistakes which could cause all kinds of complications, from miscarriages to birth defects.

Once I have the original formulas in my possession, I can outline the proper procedure, bypass the pitfalls and expedite the process.

Taking another sip, he reflected on his last mistake. John Edwards's son had turned out to be a disappointment and more trouble than he was worth. The only reason the child had been allowed to live this long was because of the hope that the puny infant would eventually develop into a pure porphyrian. Instead he had become a weak, pathetic cross-breed whose continued existence was a constant reminder of his failure.

He stilled his thoughts as he became aware of approaching footsteps. The movement was so light as to be almost imperceptible, except by someone with the well-honed instincts of a predator. He waited until she was almost upon him, then with a swift jerk, he grabbed and pulled her roughly around in front of him.

Cynthia laughed. "You caught me."

Her laugh was shrill with a nervous edge. Obviously she was up to something. "When are you going to learn you can never catch me unaware?"

Green eyes glittered as she slipped her arms around his neck. "But the possibility that I might is well worth the cost."

"Is it?" he wondered as his arms encircled her waist. "Is that why the earl is still alive?"

Her eyes closed briefly. *What kind of game is he playing?*

"I thought you wanted him kept alive until you finished interrogating him."

"Alive, but not quite as lively as you've been keeping him."

She shifted nervously and pouted. "I only wanted to have a little fun while I waited for you to join me. You know I would have been bored without the entertainment of torturing him. Now that you're here we can kill him together."

"So," he drawled, entangling his hand in her coil of long red hair, "you used him only as a diversion while I was gone? Tell me about your idea of entertainment, because I don't find your disobedience of my orders very amusing. Especially when his extended torture gives him time to send a message to Laural."

She blinked in surprise and gasped as his grip tightened in her hair. "Your sex scenes also left much to be desired. Did you think you could keep what you were doing from me? Did you think I'd allow another rival to be born? Did you think to hold it over me or use the child against me?" He shook her so violently that her teeth snapped together and cut into her lower lip.

A trickle of blood ran down her chin as fear filled her emerald green eyes. "I did it for us, for our plan. If Laural's pregnancy doesn't take, we still need another way to tell if your formula will work."

"So you did it all for us, Cynthia?" he sneered. "When are you going to realize-- there is no us?" He grabbed her upper arm, twisting it a little. "Now tell me the truth--did you steal the journals and use them to try and outmaneuver me?" His eyes bore into her. "No, I can see you didn't, but still your loyalty leaves much to be desired."

A servant appeared, hovering nervously in the doorway. Shoving Cynthia aside, he glared at the intruder. "Yes?" he snapped.

The man looked at Cynthia, licked his dry lips, and then faced his leader. "The prisoner has escaped."

Chapter 41:

Escape

"That's impossible!" Cynthia shrieked.

Rage radiated from Nick, smashing into her like a physical blow.

Wincing, she rushed to explain. "I swear he was bound and unconscious. He's been kept sedated ever since…"

Her voice trailed off but he knew what she had been about to say and it hung heavily in the air between them: Ever since she had used him as a surrogate sex partner. The earl, of course, would have had to be at least conscious enough to participate. She had made a miscalculation and somehow Rockford had taken advantage of her lapse in judgment and escaped.

Reading his intention, Cynthia began to back away. If she could just reach the window she could jump. It was a long drop to the cobblestone courtyard and she would certainly be seriously injured, but better that than to deal with the threat in Nick's eyes.

He dove for her. She turned and ran. Fingers grasped at the back of her shirt. Jerking free she leapt the final few feet to the window. A crash sounded behind her but she didn't dare look back. Glass shattered and a volley of curses followed.

She winced.

Had he hit the table and ruined the ingredients of his most recent creation right after he had destroyed the notes?

More anxiety ripped through her as she realized he would blame her for that too.

The crash gave her an extra second or two to determine a different strategy. She glanced up: No handholds and nowhere to go on the smooth surface of the circular tower.

She shifted her balance on the sill **as** her eyes dropped to study the pavement. She bit her lower lip. Three hundred feet.

Can I make it? What if I jumped and broke both of my legs? Of course I'd heal--but not before Nick came down into the courtyard after me.

The sound of running feet and heavy breathing behind her made up her mind. She sprung away from the ledge to embrace the cobblestones three hundred feet below.

A sharp jerk on her hair cut her fall short, almost snapping her head from her body. Nick had caught her by the long red gold mane and was pulling her back into the room. Twisting and turning violently she tried to break free but it was no use. She raked her long nails over his hands and arms, cutting deep, but still he continued to drag her back over the windowsill. Her back and legs were scraped raw by the sharp stone and she could feel blood from the abrasions running down her calves. With one final yank she was jerked over the ledge to land hard against his chest.

Nick slid the dagger out from the inner compartment of his jacket. "I warned you what would happen if the earl escaped," he snarled.

Cynthia screamed, "Nick, wait! Let me explain--

"I don't give a damn about your explanation," he spat furiously.

"Nick, please don't do this—what about all our plans? You need m—"

He jerked her head back and slit her throat. Still enraged, he drove the blade in deeper. He felt a glimmer of satisfaction as he watched the light fade from her eyes. "That's how much I need you, you stupid bitch." Using his grasp on her hair to stretch her neck back, he continued to slowly slice through flesh and bone until her head was completely severed.

Gratified, he watched while the decapitated neck spurted a fountain of blood. Quickly he snatched his goblet from the windowsill and held it up to catch the crimson liquid. He drained the contents in one swallow and grimaced. Her blood was weak, nothing like the hearty viscous fluid he craved. Disappointed and disgusted he let the body drop with a dull thud onto the balcony floor. Tossing the head on top of the corpse he removed a carved gold cigarette lighter from his pocket. Pleasure coursed through his veins as Cynthia's head and body were incinerated.

Turning his back on the smoldering pile of ashes, he strode out of the room and down the hall. He rapidly climbed the tower steps. Making his way to the partially open heavy oak door he pushed it wide. Stepping inside he paused to study the empty torture chamber. He approached the rack to examine the place where the Earl of Rockford had been imprisoned for the past several days. He picked up the barbed wire which had been used to bind the earl. Heedless of the sharp edges slicing into his skin he began to slowly twirl it between his fingers.

Who would have the power to enter, rescue Jordan Rush, and escape undetected? Who even knew he was here? And what effect will my father's freedom have on my plans?

Deadly rage darkened his eyes as he considered the possibility that he had been deceived by a traitor.

Chapter 42:
Clues

"There has to be a clue somewhere in this office." Laural insisted as she yanked open desk drawers and tossed papers onto Jordan's desk.

Tim sighed as he gathered another handful of notes from the accumulating pile and began to read. "If there is, it has to be in his personal documents because he didn't give any explanation. All he would tell the staff was that he was leaving for a few days and he'd be in touch. He told me that he was in a hurry and he seemed distracted."

"And you let him go alone?" accused Laural as she switched on the computer.

Tim glanced up as he pushed the papers aside to pull in a new batch. "In case you forgot, I wasn't given a choice."

I must be losing it. Of course he's right.

She rubbed her eyes. Too little sleep and too much worrying was taking its toll. Ever since the nightmare last night--or had it been two nights ago-she hadn't been able to think clearly. Her hasty hiding of the artifacts and her mad dash trip to the States hadn't helped matters either. She didn't know what she had expected to find but whatever it was it didn't appear to be here. So far all she had for her trouble was jet lag.

"You know," Tim continued, "Jordan's only slightly less obstinate then you are, and even though I'm the assistant director, he's still the boss. He tells me and the staff what to do, not the other way around."

Avoiding his accusatory gaze she looked out the window at the busy D.C. streets. "Still, as head of security, you should have insisted he not go alone." She turned back to the computer to scroll down his appointment calendar.

"I have, many times," he replied hotly. "Just as I'm sure your bodyguard protested you coming here without security."

Laural glanced up sharply.

Tim slammed the pile of papers he was holding down on the desk.

She jumped, startled at the demonstration of anger from the normally placid giant. She knew he could be tough, otherwise he would never have been selected as head of security, but until now she had never been on the receiving end of a demonstration of his temper.

They stared at each other. After several tense seconds, Tim exhaled. "I apologize for my outburst, but you have no appreciation for how hard it is to guard two of the most important porphyrians on the planet when they are both hellbent on their own destruction. Neither one of you will take my or Ben's advice when it comes to your protection, even though that's one of the main reasons you hired us. Jordan specifically refused to let me or any other security personnel accompany him. The only choice I had was to wait and wonder if he was going to return safely. Then something like this comes up and I'm left with the blame." His flushed face bespoke his anger but his eyes belied his concern.

"I didn't mean to come across as though I'm blaming you. I'm worried and edgy. I agree that no one could have changed Jordan's mind once he had it made up. But you're right. What we've been doing is unfair to both you and Ben. It's seriously impairing your ability to do your job. I promise from now on we'll keep you informed."

They took each other's measure for a long moment. He nodded. "Let me take a look at the computer. Even if Jordan deleted his messages I can probably retrieve them."

She hesitated before moving aside. Tim pulled up a chair next to hers. He frowned as he scanned the appointment schedule. "Nothing here appears to be missing." He clicked on the file holding Jordan's e-mail messages.

Laural peered over his shoulder. She could see the in-box was empty. Tim clicked to the deleted messages. Nothing. He moved to the recycle bin. The last deleted message had Laural's private e-mail address.

As Tim brought up the message the phone rang. Laural snatched up the receiver. "Hello," she said, still trying to see the computer screen.

"Jordan and the blood drinker are at Camborne Castle."

Laural gasped, projecting a command for Tim to pick up on the line. "Who is this?" she demanded.

Tim raced to the extension but the line had already gone dead.

Slowly she replaced the receiver.

"Who was it?"

Her eyes took on a haunted expression. "I don't know."

"Was it a man or woman?"

She shook her head. "I couldn't tell."

"What did they say?"

"The voice said that both Jordan and the blood drinker were at Camborne Castle."

He looked at her, confused. "So, if the anonymous voice is to be believed, then the blood drinker has Jordan. But I've never heard of Camborne Castle. Does that mean anything to you?" he asked, reseating himself at the computer.

" Camborne Castle was, at one time, the Maxwell family stronghold. But that was before my father took over the land from Craven two hundred years ago. Last I knew there was nothing there but a couple of decaying towers and a lot of rubble."

"Do you think it's a hoax?"

Something besides the ominous message had disturbed her about the call but she couldn't quite put her finger on it. "Could be, it seems highly unlikely. It sounds more like someone's trying to send me on a wild-goose chase, but it's the only lead we have. The vision of Jordan as she had seen him in her nightmare eclipsed her thoughts and she stiffened.

"Unless," she mused as her conviction grew, "the tower room from my dream wasn't at Penbrook Castle but at Camborne." She turned to face Tim. "I have to be back by Friday to meet with the head of medieval antiquities from the British Museum. At this point I can't afford to ignore any possibility, so I'll go over to the ruins then and take a look."

Frowning, he said, "Maybe there's more to it. Look at this."

She walked over to the computer. She read the message, sat down hard on her chair, and read it again. "But I never sent that."

"But Jordan thought you did. He obviously thought you needed him at Penbrook Castle. He showed me this message right before he left, but I wanted to check to be sure it was the entire message and that there weren't others."

His accusing glare spoke volumes. She shifted uncomfortably but her gaze into his eyes never wavered. "I understand you think Jordan and I have been keeping things from you, and you're right. But we can't always be completely open about our activities."

"This is very similar to the discussion I had with Jordan just before he disappeared," he replied, emphasizing the last word. "I'm not interested in all your activities, only the ones that might lead to a breech in security or compromise your safety."

She considered his words, then nodded. A premonition of doom settled over her as she reread the message. Whoever had sent it had used her and Jordan's encrypted code. "But that just brings us back to our original premise. We already knew he was heading to England to meet with me."

Tim gave her a level look. "I wasn't entirely sure."

For a moment she was perplexed before comprehension dawned. "You thought Jordan had told you he was going to meet me when he really had another destination?"

He shrugged. "He was acting so secretively, I couldn't be sure."

She studied the screen for a long moment. "The code is authentic. If Jordan received this, he wouldn't have any reason to doubt it came from me." She paused to think. "The ruins of Camborne Castle aren't far from my estate. Maybe he really is being held there."

"And maybe it's really a trap."

Her eyes shot to his.

"I was with Jordan shortly after he received this e-mail. I'm aware the two of you send coded messages. If someone has breeched your security, it could be the same person behind the phone call. Since they didn't identify themselves, I'd have to assume they could be behind all of this and are probably Loyalists. Since someone's gone to the trouble of kidnapping and possibly killing the earl, we have to assume that phone call was a ploy to put you at risk too."

She blanched.

"I know you don't want to think about it, but it's been several days since Jordan was abducted. If he was being held for ransom, the kidnappers would have contacted us by now. His abductors were almost certainly Loyalists--which means he's probably dead. It's my job to make sure you don't follow in his footsteps. We must consider the probability that whoever's behind this knows both of you well enough to know how to push your buttons. They knew sending a plea to Jordan to meet you would cause him to come running. They know calling you with a message that Jordan is at risk would put you right where they want you."

He saw her jaw set in that stubborn way of hers. "Think, Laural," he implored. "Don't play into their hands."

Chapter 43:
The Cross-Breed

Tears threatened, but Laural hastily blinked them away while considering Tim's words. As much as she hated to admit it he was probably right. Since the last telepathic contact with her cousin at Penbrook Castle, she hadn't been able to sense him. Choking back her fears, she asked, "Any update on the baby?"

Tim searched her face then walked over to the desk. Sifting through his notes, he pulled out several sheets and handed them to Laural. Crossing the room to the cabinet, he extracted a bottle of PS4. He filled two glasses then handed one to her. Sitting down on the couch, he watched her over the rim of his glass. Noting the change of expression he realized she had finished reading even before her confused sapphire eyes raised to confront him.

Laural looked back and forth between Tim and the papers several times. Her hand shook as she lifted her glass. She took several long gulps. "How is this possible?"

He shrugged. "I don't even know if the conjectures are valid. The only way to tell for sure is to have the child examined. Although the medical reports look pretty conclusive, it's obvious that the diurnal doctors didn't understand what they were reading."

Thank goodness they didn't. She gazed pensively into her drink for a long moment. When she looked up doubt and concern shadowed her eyes. "Finding that child is imperative."

"I understand."

She stood and started to pace. "This can't be happening. First Jordan, now this." She paced a few more steps. "Cross-breeding is impossible." She whirled to face him. "I may have spent only a few minutes with Tami, but I assure you she wasn't a porphyrian." Her eyes narrowed. "We need to find out the identity of that baby's father."

"We already have. The father was," he corrected, "John

Edwards."

The color drained from her face. "John Edwards," she gasped. "The Loyalist I killed a few months ago."

Overwhelmed by the news she sank back into her chair. Her mind reeled at all the implications, but finally the pieces started to fall into place. Dawning comprehension stole over her as she considered the possibility that at least part of the reason for the bombing of the building had been to insure the death of the baby's mother. It had provided the perfect opportunity to obscure the murder. Destroying the Willow Grove Foundation with her in it might have simply been a fringe benefit.

"Whoever did it will pay," she said hoarsely.

Tim nodded. "I agree, and would like nothing better than to get my hands on those murderers myself. But, for right now, I think the baby's safe since he's obviously part of some Loyalist experiment, and, therefore, probably important. Our first priority is to find out what's happened to Jordan and how to best protect you from potential assassination attempts."

Slowly she nodded her head in agreement. "What's the next step?"

"First, let's try and decide who specifically would have the most to gain from the two of you being dead."

"The Loyalists—but more specifically Dana Maxwell and Jordan's son. If Jordan and I were dead then Dana inherits the position of leader of our people, as well as all our family assets. But, according to the e-mail I received from Jordan, she's dead." Her face brightened. "Unless--"

Tim interrupted. "Unfortunately, that part's true. Dana's dead."

She drew in a long breath and slowly exhaled.

"I felt I should tell Jordan first. I informed him the day he left." When he noticed her expression, he continued, "Sorry, but with everything else I forgot to mention it. But we can definitely rule her out as a co-conspirator."

For a moment Laural had hoped the message she had received had been some sort of Loyalist trick. Despite the part Dana had played in Laural's own abduction all those years ago and her complicity in depriving Jordan of his son, she still felt a pang of regret.

However, now that she thought about it she hadn't felt Dana's presence in quite some time. Focusing, she discovered only a void. She should have checked when she first received the news but with all the distractions…

"That news was in the message I was allegedly sent by Jordan. The message said her remains were found in Africa."

"It seems she was murdered. Her body was found in a remote African village—completely incinerated except for her head," he confirmed.

"Then the only one who would benefit directly by our deaths would be Jordan's son." Her eyes shifted back to the screen in order to avoid his gaze. With every piece of the puzzle that fell into place, she became more convinced Nick was really Jordan's son. If that was true, she had literally been sleeping with the enemy.

Her stomach churned as a thought struck her. "When Craven kidnapped me, he was injecting Dana with diurnal blood. His goal was to create a baby with dependence on human hemoglobin and start a race of porphyrians who would become superior in their abilities by feeding off humans."

Her face flushed. It was difficult even now to speak of that horrific experience.

She walked to the window, staring out blindly at the city skyline for several seconds. When she turned back to Tim, she spoke calmly. "Since it's become obvious Craven's experiment was successful, do you think it resulted in a porphyrian with such enhanced abilities he would be able to block even me or Jordan from reading him?"

Tim considered the idea for a moment. "To the best of my knowledge, there's no precedent to draw from. I can try to do some research, but I think that would be a unique situation. My best guess would have to be based on your experience, since you're the closest we've come to a living porphyrian who was supplemented with human blood."

She blanched but forced herself to speak. "My physical strength increased dramatically and my senses were enhanced exponentially, but my mental faculties deteriorated until I was operating on pure instinct, like an animal driven only by the need to feed."

"Yes, but you were exposed rapidly without much adjustment time. Who knows what could be accomplished by a steady diet of human blood started prenatally."

She pondered the picture he presented. A porphyrian with enhanced abilities and a profound mental imbalance didn't bode well for the future of either species. She looked back at Tim again, trying not to let him know how deeply disturbed she really was. "The image I had was of Jordan being held in a tower," she said, changing the subject. "Originally I thought it was one of ours, but my intuition tells me Camborne feels right."

He nodded and stood. "How long will it take for you to get ready?"

She looked at him, puzzled.

"I'm going with you."

Chapter 44:
The Earl's Son

The Earl of Rockford hunched below the thick wall of shrubbery, casting a cautious eye through a small opening to carefully inspect his surroundings. Summoning the last vestiges of his strength he stealthily dodged across the final few yards of open terrain leading into the Penbrook stronghold. Wearily he stumbled into the courtyard. Shallow gasps tore from his throat as he collapsed against the stone wall of the inner keep.

He probed outward. Laural wasn't here, but, thank goodness, neither was Ravensblood. Of course, that didn't mean he was safe. For all he knew the "students" could be Loyalist spies.

And if Ravensblood's claims are valid, his ability to mentally barricade himself would prevent him from being detected.

Jordan was still unsure how many of Nick's boasts about his enhanced abilities were exaggerated, but until he knew for sure he couldn't be certain whether the bastard was here or not.

Warily he peered around the corner. Spying nothing out of the ordinary he drew back. As he leaned heavily against the wall, the sharp edges of the uneven stone bit into his scalp and skin, but he was too exhausted to care. Heavy with fatigue, his eyelids drifted closed. Every bone in his body ached and his joints shrieked with agony each time he moved.

Should I alert someone that I'm here, or should I wait here until nightfall?

His blood ran cold as he recalled the last confrontation with Nick. He hovered on the brink of awareness while the memory of the encounter replayed through his mind. A violent shudder gripped his body when he remembered how he had been bound and drugged, kept trapped and helpless in the tower at Camborne Castle. But even his state of semi-consciousness hadn't been able to keep him from sensing the malignant presence.

"I'm going to kill you--Father." Nicholas Ravensblood announced as he leaned over the battered and bruised body of the Earl of Rockford.

"So," Jordan managed to say through his dry, swollen lips, "you really are my son."

Nick smiled smugly as he stared down at his prisoner. "You know, Cynthia didn't do a half-bad job torturing you," he stated, admiring the barbed wire tied tautly to the pullies. "If I didn't have so many other demands on my time I might be persuaded to have a go at it myself."

So it had been Cynthia masquerading behind the face of his cousin. If he had known that she had survived the explosion of the crematorium he might have guessed. He stared directly into his son's eyes. "I've never caused you any harm. Why do you want me dead?"

The question brought a deep chuckle as Nick's gaze roamed over the broken battered body before him. He was pleased that the earl no longer resembled the sophisticated aristocrat of several days before. Mockingly he patted the bruised and swollen face, smiling with perverted pleasure as the Earl winced. "Don't take it personally, Dad. I have it in for both you and Laural."

At the mention of his cousin a burst of energy surged through him. Jordan struggled violently against his bonds. He couldn't let his monstrous son get his hands on Laural. The barbed wire cut deeply into his skin. Rivers of blood ran down his arms and puddled onto the wooden surface. He could feel the sharp ends cutting through his skin and down into his tendons. Unable to sustain the effort he eventually slumped, swearing and panting, back onto the rack.

Perspiration soaked his skin as he lay exhausted from his exertions. Studying his son he considered his options. Brute strength hadn't worked but maybe he could pull off some mental manipulation of his own. Focusing he projected his desire. Suddenly a burst of white hot pain tore through his skull.

Ravensblood snickered. "Nice try, Dad. I would wish you better luck next time, but there won't be one—at least not for you."

"Why are you doing this?" he groaned weakly. The drugs they were giving him were making it extremely difficult for him to stay alert or focus. But he had to try; he had to find out what this bastard son of his was up to. He had to get out of here and protect Laural.

"I'm doing this because you and Laural are in my way. By the way, my real name is Raven Rush. Nicholas is my middle name but the surname was made up. It has quite a ring to it, don't you think?"

"So, we were right. Even though your thoughts proclaimed your innocence, we still intuited that you were my son." He raised his swollen lids. "Why can't I probe you?"

Nick eyed him disdainfully. "Because of the human blood I've been ingesting since before I was born. The undiluted hemoglobin has given me powers which make every other porphyrian's abilities seem pathetic by comparison. I'm stronger, faster, have keener senses and am completely light-tolerant. And I have superior mental faculties. I can manipulate porphyrians and diurnals at will, as well as read them even when they're blocking. I also have the ability to cloak my own thoughts so completely they can never be discerned. As far as you're concerned it's all academic now," he proclaimed, pulling the dagger from inside his jacket. The ruby eyes of the dragon-encrusted handle winked in the light as he held the weapon aloft.

Jordan's eyes remained closed.

"Are you falling asleep?" the green eyes glittered dangerously as he grabbed a fist full of Jordan's hair and yanked his head back. "If you don't stay awake, you'll miss all the fun."

Jordan's eyes dragged open to see a double image of twin daggers poised at his throat. He blinked several times to clear his vision while trying to focus on the voice of his captor.

"Here's something that might pique your interest. I killed her."

Jordan's lids fluttered. Confused, he asked, "Cynthia?"

Nick laughed. "No--at least not yet."

Anguish clutched his heart. "Laural," he whispered hoarsely. *If she's dead, I might as well die too.*

"Wrong again, three strikes and you're out," he said, drawing the dagger lightly across Jordan's throat.

He felt the warm trickle of blood as it dripped down his neck. He probed and this time received a response.

"Dana! You killed your own mother!" he cried in a strangled whisper as horrific images flooded his mind.

"Yes, just like your bodyguard reported. By the way," he said amicably, "you might want to find someone else to fill that position. Tim Cooper doesn't seem to be guarding your body very well. As for my mother," he shrugged, "I'm allowing you access to my thoughts so you can see exactly what happens to those who get in my way. She tried to restrain me, tried to instill a sense of morality and conscience. She even attempted to get me to live peacefully with inferior diurnals. And all the time she was trying to stay one step ahead of you," he spat contemptuously. "She wasted our whole life together worrying that someday you would find us and feel obligated to kill me. I grew up despising the secret life we were forced to lead, until, at last, my power became so great from a lifetime of drinking blood that I could no longer be contained."

Jordan squeezed his eyes shut, but the images were being firmly imprinted in his mind, vivid telepathic pictures of how Dana had been mentally and physically abused by the Loyalists before finally being allowed to die. The bile rose in his throat as he continued to watch the spectacle unfold: bloodletting by leeches, ongoing mutilations and being seared by white-hot pokers had continued nonstop until the Maxwell heiress had finally expired.

Jordan couldn't understand why she had allowed it. The answer came in a flash of insight from his son. Nick's mother had allowed herself to be brutalized rather than overpowering her captors because she had been under the impression that fighting back would endanger her son. Jordan's repulsion for this child he and Dana had created sank to new depths when he realized Dana could have saved herself if only she had known that instead of being held prisoner by the Loyalists, Nick was actually leading them.

Jordan shuddered as despair overwhelmed him. He couldn't let himself give in to the emotional knife this bastard was twisting into his heart. He couldn't give up. He had to fight back for Laural, for the diurnals, and for his own race.

As if sensing his father's weakening spirit, he drove the emotional dagger in deeper. "For someone who was supposed to have cared so much for my mother, you haven't shown the slightest interest in the details of her life since she left you. Would you like to know?" He tightened his grip on Jordan's hair and yanked his head back further until their eyes locked. "She never completely recovered from childbirth. She was weak and wistful regarding the past she had shared with you. I believe she tried to instill in me the character traits that would have made you proud. She had you so far up on a pedestal there was never any hope of coming close to your pristine image. Eventually I grew weary of being compared to you and coming up short.

"And Mom made one fatal mistake. She was so focused on turning me into another Jordan Rush that she forgot the blood of her ancestors also runs through my veins."

A predatory grin spread across Nick's face. "As far as your precious Laural is concerned, she's living on borrowed time. I'm delaying her death until I determine the results of my experiment. Once I find out that she's carrying my child, I can kill her. I need to know if my experiment was successful, but I don't want any competition for my rightful inheritance. I've been cheated all these years out of both my worldly goods and my position as leader of our people--two oversights which I'm now ready to rectify.

"By the way, there's also a pregnant diurnal, who is poised to prove the second part of my theory." He began to smirk. "I have every reason to believe the improvements I've made in the supplement will enable porphyrians to impregnate diurnals. Within a few decades, our enhanced ability to procreate, along with our longevity, will allow us to take our rightful place as the dominant species on the planet."

"You're mad."

He shrugged. "So I've been told. Tell me, Father, how does it feel to die knowing you failed both the woman you love and the people you were sworn to protect? I wonder how Andrew Gabriel would feel now about having entrusted his daughter and his life's dream to you?" He grinned maliciously as he noted the pain in the jade green eyes. Perverted pleasure consumed him when he plunged the dagger further into his father's throat.

Jordan flinched but there was nowhere to go. He could feel the blade slicing into his skin, tissues, muscles, and still his son drove the dagger deeper. Blood poured in rivulets, but still he strained against the wires digging into his flesh. He couldn't allow this blood-drinking fiend to do to Laural what he had done to Dana.

A commotion sounded at the door. Ravensblood cursed as he turned his head to glare at the guard in the doorway.

"There's a visitor downstairs insisting on seeing you."

Nick scowled. No one even knew they were there, not even his most loyal supporters. He had intentionally planned it that way so the glorious termination of his enemy could be completed without annoying interruptions. "Who is it?"

The guard took a step back. "I don't know, he wouldn't say. He just kept insisting he had important news regarding some documents you were interested in."

Jordan groaned weakly and Nick watched him for a moment.

Could this reaction from my dear father be something about the missing journals?

He wavered then probed.

Yes!

He was able to glean the truth before his father was able to block his thoughts. He did have some information about the journals. How much and what kind Nick didn't know yet, but it was only a matter of time. He gave the earl one more disparaging look. He would have all the time he needed to secure the details after he dealt with the visitor.

But who is this stranger and could he really have pertinent information? If he is just wasting my time, he'll die.

Nick gave a rueful laugh.

Of course, he'll die whether he has information for me or not.

After wiping the bloody dagger on Jordan's chest, he slipped it back into his jacket. Striding from the room, he called back over his shoulder, "Watch him. If he gives any sign of becoming fully conscious, give him another injection."

The last rays of the setting sun shadowed Jordan's set features as he reopened his eyes. His subsequent memories had been a semi-conscious haze. He vaguely recalled a cloaked figure hovering over him with a dagger. He had lost all sense of time and had no idea if it was only minutes, hours or days later.

At first he had thought the figure was his son coming back to complete his task of patricide. But the figure never spoke, and Jordan couldn't imagine Nick killing him without taking the opportunity to gloat.

To his amazement the figure had slashed through the barbed wire instead of his throat. His liberator had then half-carried, half-dragged him out of the dilapidated fortress and into the woods.

Again he had lost track of time, but eventually had awakened to find himself buried beneath a dense thicket of bushes. His considerate liberator had also left some clothing and a flask containing PS4. Obviously, his rescuer had been a porphyrian—but who?

Jordan shrugged as he pushed away from the wall. Determining the identity of his rescuer wasn't his top priority right now. He had to get to Laural before she became Ravensblood's next victim.

Chapter 45:
The Tower's Secret

"There it is," announced Laural, drawing up her mount as they cleared the protective cover of the woods. When Tim drew alongside she gestured toward a dilapidated castle with walls crumbling from decay and disrepair. The inner courtyard was in ruins and the entire structure had the look of dank despair.

"It doesn't seem very habitable." Tim eyed the remains skeptically while patting his bay gelding on the neck. "What makes you think Jordan or anyone else is in there?"

She studied the structure for a long time before responding. Hesitantly, she inclined her head in the direction of the two towers. Despite the collapse of the rest of the castle the towers still appeared to be intact. "Now that we're this close I can feel his presence. The barrier that was blocking our telepathic link has lifted."

"Then why don't you just contact him and let him know we're here?"

Spurring her mount, she plunged headlong toward the remains of the Maxwell estate. "Jordan has himself blocked off, which means he's probably still in danger," she called back over her shoulder.

Tim galloped hard in pursuit, wishing again he had brought more back-up. But due to the extremely sensitive nature of the mission he considered himself lucky to get his boss to even bring him along. She had agreed only after he had pressed the point of their recent discussion about not impeding his job as head of security. Eventually she had capitulated, but allowing him to join her had been the only concession.

Not that she could have kept him from her side. He had never had any intention of allowing her to go into the lion's den unprotected. She had almost been killed due to his negligence once and he wouldn't make that mistake again. If it had come down to it, he had been prepared to wait until she left before discreetly following. In the end he had been relieved not to have to force the issue. However he still intended to impress upon Laural the importance of letting Ben in on their plans. He checked the thought. Before bringing Ben up to date, he had to have some idea of what was going on himself.

Pounding hoof beats tore up the ground as they rapidly bore down on the entrance. Tim continued to examine what remained of the castle.

At one time this place must have been quite a fortress.

It still retained the remnants of a partially-rotted drawbridge, moat, and portions of retention walls. On the opposite side of the drawbridge, the gate gaped open like an empty mouth, complete with jagged teeth, just waiting to swallow them whole.

Laural leapt from her mount while the stallion was still at a full gallop. Hitting the
ground hard, she rolled, scrambled to her feet, and raced across the bridge. Heedless of the risk she brazenly brandished her gun in front of her while rushing through the opening.

Reaching the drawbridge Tim jerked hard on the reins, causing his horse to rear up in protest. He jumped from the saddle and followed Laural discreetly while watching warily for any sign of attack.

"Damn it!" Laural obviously wasn't going to wait for him. Advancing more rapidly, he moved to catch up with his charge.

With a loud crack his right foot broke through the rotted wood. Cursing again, he yanked it out and hurried forward. He continued to visually and mentally scan the area. Pulling his gun out with one hand, he caught hold of Laural's arm with the other.

Jerking to a halt she stared at him in vexation.

"If I'm going to be your bodyguard at least let me guard."

She flourished her arm, gesturing for him to take the lead. He pulled her behind him and frowned sternly when she looked ready to protest. Laural remained silent but he could tell she wasn't happy about the arrangement.

"Can you sense any other porphyrians?" he asked next to her ear.

She shook her head.

He gave a mental sigh of relief but kept his guard up as he slowly entered the castle. After searching the darkened hall, he waved her forward. "It's a good thing we don't require much light to see or we'd be lost. Those stairs," he pointed at the twin set of branching moss-covered, spiral, stone steps with his gun, "am I correct in assuming they lead to the towers?"

She shrugged. "I've never been inside before, but the layout seems to be similar to Penbrook. You take that one," she said, gesturing to the left, "and I'll take the other."

His expression hardened. "I think we should stay together."

She shook her head. "Jordan could be in imminent peril. We can cover the area twice as fast if we split up. Every second we delay could cost his life. I'm not willing to risk it. Besides," she said more gently, "I've been on many missions like this before, and I'm probably better equipped to deal with whatever comes up than you are."

Clamping his jaw shut he swallowed his retort and raced up his flight. Halfway up the slimy stone steps he slipped. "Damn!" A shaft of pain pierced his knee. After pulling himself up he glanced toward the opposite stairwell. Laural was taking her stairs two at a time. Ignoring his injury he gritted his teeth and quickened his pace, determined to finish the inspection of his side and regroup with her as soon as possible.

Laural hesitated at the top of the stairs. Closing her eyes for a moment, she allowed instinct to guide her. Opening her eyes, she strode confidently toward a huge oak door reinforced with iron bands.

This door looks as if it was recently installed.

She tried the handle. Locked. She paused, certain that this last obstacle represented the end of her quest. She projected her thoughts beyond the barrier and frowned.

Strange, why isn't Jordan responding? And why can't I feel his presence?

She considered calling out but decided that the door was most likely too thick for her to be heard. There was also the distinct possibility that Jordan was unresponsive because he was unconscious. Still, if he was in the room just behind the door, she should be able to sense him.

Yet, her instincts had guided her here. She squatted in order to squint through the skeleton keyhole opening. The other side appeared to be blocked with the key. Standing she took a deep breath and kicked. Wood splintered but the door was thick. She kicked again, again, and again. At last she broke a hole wide enough to slip her hand through the door. Ignoring the splinters biting into her skin, she twisted her wrist until she reached the key. She turned it until the door clicked. Grasping the handle, she swung it open and stepped through.

Laural gasped and raced across the room.

Just like in my dream. It's some kind of medieval torture device.

Her brain couldn't fully accept what her eyes beheld: A long white sheet was half-draped over the top of what appeared to be a long wooden table, with four posts, two at each end set, to hold its victim in place. Grimacing she studied the wires, cranks and pullies. She fingered the neatly severed barbed wires dangling from the side of the table.

The sheet hung off the table, but fully covered a mount at its center. She hesitantly laid her hand on the corner of the sheet. Something was dreadfully wrong.

For a moment she was propelled back to the time when Craven Maxwell had kidnapped then held her prisoner; bound to a table while he conducted hideous experiments   just like…

Deliberately she shook herself free from the past and refocused on the structure in front of her.

The lump in the middle of the table was too small to be Jordan. Unless . . .

She briefly closed her eyes, swallowed hard and yanked.

Chapter 46:
Murder in the Tower

Tim raced back down the tower steps. Several feet shy of the landing he jumped. He hit the uneven stone pavement and winced. His knee had already begun to mend but a fresh wave of pain protested this renewed assault.

Since his side of the tower had contained nothing but empty rooms, Laural probably needed his help.

What if she had run into an ambush? She said she hadn't sensed any porphyrians, but she could have been wrong. Maybe ingesting human blood could cause one of their kind to become so powerful he could shield his presence, and Laural wouldn't realize she was headed into a trap.

Tim was aware that ordinarily she would have considered all the options, but he was concerned that her overwhelming fear for Jordan was making her reckless. He barreled toward the opposite staircase.

I wonder if the two of them have realized they're in love with each other yet.

Tim's lips tightened as he continued to consider the potential dangers. He should never have allowed himself to be separated from her.

Laural could have found the earl, and now they could both be hostages. Or she could have discovered the earl's dead body, and, even now, be engaged in a life-and-death battle with the Maxwell heir. I need to be there to cover her back.

He vaulted up the adjacent staircase.

He projected his thoughts as he ascended.

Why wasn't she responding?

Anxiety and dread kept pace with him as he continued to climb. He probed again—nothing. Frustrated, he wished he had the same mental power Laural and Jordan possessed. He could have circumvented the distance between them by locating her telepathically. Unfortunately, his ability to read thoughts was limited by proximity, so he had to find her the hard way.

Within seconds he passed the spot where he had last seen his charge. As he raced up the steps two at a time, he again cursed the design of the castle that had not provided a cross-over passage from the other side. At the top of the stairs he paused. Directly across was a thick wooden door boasting several feet of wooden splinters. The door had been left ajar. Drawing his gun, he approached warily. He wasn't sure what he was going to find on the other side of the splintered door, but he was certain he wouldn't like it.

A scream of protest exploded. He nearly dropped his gun as he instinctively covered his ears. It didn't help. The crescendo continued to build in intensity. Almost immediately he realized why: the mind numbing wail was internal. His eyes squinted in pain as he realized the barrage was coming from Laural, who was inside the room he had been about to enter.

Fear overcame caution as he charged through the doorway. He surveyed the space visually while sweeping the area with his gun. He stopped short. Ahead of him, Laural was holding the decapitated body of a male toddler. His eyes dropped to the rest of the grizzly remains and spatters of dried blood left on the wooden surface of a device he couldn't name. One look at the baby's head told him the story.

He approached and gently removed the body from Laural's arms. After placing it next to the rest of the corpse, he turned back to her and held out his arms. She collapsed against him, sobbing.

As he held her, he studied the grotesque spectacle, his fury gaining momentum with each passing moment. Eventually, she quieted, pulled herself together and stepped back. They stared silently at each other for several long heartbeats while they both tried to assimilate the implications.

"We'll need to take the body back for a complete analysis," Tim said softly. "If it turns out he's a porphyrian, it will be definitive proof that the Loyalists have found a way to reproduce with diurnals."

Laural nodded her silent agreement as she studied the child. "Whoever did this will wish they hadn't," she vowed. "But why destroy the evidence of their own success?"

Tim shrugged as he retrieved the crumpled sheet from the floor.

He carefully lifted the head and body, placing them on the sheet. After rolling the bundle tightly, he looked up to meet her outraged gaze. "My guess is that whoever did this was more interested in making a statement then keeping the evidence of their success. Since the baby himself was proof enough, once he was born, there was no real need to keep him alive. Besides," he continued as he hefted the bundle, "he was kind of a rough first draft, certainly an achievement but you read the reports—he was a medical mess. Knowing the Loyalists, I'm sure the goal is to have a perfect specimen. As far as they're concerned, he would have already outlived his purpose."

Nodding thoughtfully she considered what he had said. Now that the first wave of shock and outrage had subsided she was starting to think more clearly. Tim's theory sounded plausible, but she felt there was more. She believed this was meant as a private vendetta against her. The personal attention Bryan had received from the Foundation certainly would have alerted the Loyalists to her interest in the toddler.

To take out revenge on a helpless innocent was an act of pure evil--but why now? What had infuriated whoever had committed this atrocity to the point where they would take out their fury on a baby?

Laural straightened up, and carefully studied her surroundings.

This setting is an exact duplicate of my nightmare. This torture chamber wasn't designed for a baby, but for a full-grown adult.

The pieces began to slip into place as she picked up the barbed wire and examined the severed ends. Glancing up sharply she met Tim's questioning gaze. "I think Jordan was here, but somehow managed to get away. My intuition tells me that his captor was so enraged at the escape that he took his wrath out on…"

Her eyes dropped to the bundle in his arms and her throat ached.

About to turn away, she stopped short, and brought her hand to rest on the sheet, her fingers unsteadily picked up a single strand of ebony hair. She clutched it tightly in an iron grip.

This is Nick's hair. The bastard has deceived me and used me for the last time.

Voice quaking with fury, she said, "If Jordan did escape and he's not here, he'd most likely try to get to my estate. Not only is it the nearest safe haven, but he'd want to warn me. We have to get to him before his abductor does."

Chapter 47:

Avenging Angel

Laural descended upon the excavation site like an avenging angel. Her cape billowed out behind her as she strode rapidly through the maze of scattered equipment, artifacts and students. She stalked up to the main tent, oblivious to the curious stares following her as she passed. Without pausing, she grabbed the flap and threw aside the heavy canvas. Intent on her confrontation with the professor, it took her several moments to take in the scene.

Robert, Professor Ravensblood's graduate assistant, was sitting hunched over a makeshift desk writing in a large notebook. She fought to regain her composure, disappointed to be cheated of her prey. She scanned the interior, probing every shadow and exploring every corner. Consternation gripped her as she cleared her throat in order to gain the young man's attention.

Robert started at the interruption, glanced over his shoulder, and put down his pen. He stood and extended his hand. "Lady Gabriel, what can I do for you?"

Her grip was firm but brief. "Where's Professor Ravensblood?" she demanded of the lanky fair-haired student.

The hard edge in her voice caused him to glance around nervously, as though he could somehow summon his instructor from the shadows. Shifting uncomfortably under her scrutiny, he again wondered at the professors' sudden departure. Now he was concerned that the professor might have offended their host. If so it didn't bode well for the project. It was probably a good thing the semester was almost over.

"Professor Ravensblood had to leave unexpectedly due to a family emergency. He requested that I extend his regrets that he couldn't inform you in person, but his need to depart was urgent."

I'll bet, she thought suspiciously. Aloud she asked, "Which tent is Linda's?"

He looked down at the ground for a moment. There was a menacing attitude coming from the marchioness that he had never sensed before. He knew she wasn't going to like what he had to say, and wished again that his professor were there to handle the situation. "She was staying in the third one down on the left, but she left yesterday."

"Why?" she snapped.

He shrugged, trying to regain his composure. "It's the end of the semester and the students are starting to head home. Most won't be leaving for several more days but a few are leaving a little early."

"Isn't it a little odd to leave prior to the end of the semester?"

"Not in the slightest. Some of the students are on tight schedules and need to go back early so they can be ready for the next semester. Some want to have time for a little break in between classes. I didn't ask Linda specifically, but I presume she had good reason for cutting out a few days early. In the meantime," he smiled pleasantly, "I'll be wrapping things up here. If there's something I can--"

His smile dissolved into a worried frown as, without another word, Lady Gabriel turned on her heel and stormed from the tent.

Maybe we should work on wrapping things up sooner rather then later, he decided, staring after the retreating figure.

Judging from the look on her face, he was glad he wasn't in Ravensblood's shoes. He shook his head regretfully. Mixing business with pleasure never worked out well. Personally he never combined the two, and felt a flicker of irritation at his professor for causing the most promising expedition he had ever been on to end on a bad note.

Laural threw open the door and swept into her bedroom at Penbrook Castle. She dropped wearily into the rose chintz chair in front of her bay window and gazed forlornly at the scenery spread out before her. Usually the view of her mom's rose garden beneath her window and the heathered hills beyond provided comfort and solace—but not today.

She propped one foot on the windowsill and began tugging off her riding boot. She had been positive she and Tim would find Jordan on route between Camborne and Camelford. Several times she had thought she had sensed his presence but they had found no sign of him. At one point the feeling had been so strong that she was positive they had located him, only to be disappointed by an empty thicket of overgrown brush. She and Tim had scoured the area but had only come up with an empty flask for their trouble.

She propped her other leg on the sill and worked off the mud-encrusted boot. Her hopes had remained high until they had come within sight of their own stronghold. At that point she had had to face the fact that Jordan had either not survived or had been recaptured.

And, to top it all off, she had been deprived of her anticipated confrontation with Nick. She grimaced.

What did I expect? If he was behind all this, he wouldn't be waiting to discuss the murder of the baby and Jordan's kidnapping over a cup of tea. And what about Linda's coincidental departure? In spite of Robert's reasonable explanation, I think there must be a connection.

Her mind flashed onto the image of Linda the last time she had seen her.

What if the bandaged wrist hadn't come from an accidental injury but an intentional attack? If only I hadn't allowed my physical attraction to him to override my instincts, I could have saved her instead of letting her become Ravensblood's latest victim.

She stood and stole one more glance out the window before retrieving her boots. Flakes of dried mud fell to the floor from the filthy boots.

They definitely need a good cleaning, but I just don't have the energy to deal with something inconsequential like that right now.

The shock of finding the murdered baby coupled with the disappointment of not being able to locate Jordan had brought on an overwhelming apathy. The anger which had been sustaining her had evaporated when she had been cheated of the anticipated reckoning with Nick. Now she didn't feel like doing much of anything. Miserably she headed toward the armoire.

Of course, the enemy wants me to feel this way--hopeless and helpless. Then I'd be a much easier target for them to destroy.

Squaring her shoulders she opened the closet door.

I'll be damned if I'm going to provide them with an easy target. The Loyalists will pay for what they've done to poor little Bryan. And if they've killed Jordan . . .

Her eyes glittered dangerously as she pushed her boots into the corner. The only thing she could do at the moment was to go ahead with her plan. She would call Ben and have him come to the estate. Then she would go over her strategy to trap the Loyalists with both

Ben and Tim before Dr. Ford from the British Museum arrived to authenticate the find.

Her brows lowered as she wondered what the expert would think about the fact that Professor Ravensblood wasn't on hand to work with him on the project. After all, the find had been his, and even though she didn't know much about the field, Laural was sure it was unusual for an archeologist not to bask in the glory of his own discovery. She would have found it odd herself if she hadn't been convinced of Nick's duplicity.

Nick was goading me by leaving that strand of ebony hair at the murder scene. And when his graduate assistant said Nick had left abruptly, it only confirmed my suspicions.

Any lingering doubts were eliminated when Laural had returned from the site and called both Nick's home and office numbers. She had been confronted by an out-of-service recording at his home and the news of an untimely resignation from the university. Her failure to connect had been complete when she tried to obtain Linda's phone number and address from the school only to be told they could not provide student information.

She frowned in confusion as she pushed her boots more firmly into the back of the closet, but something was blocking that space. Peering into the darkness, she tried to determine the cause of the obstruction. She didn't remember putting anything else in that spot. No, she was sure there had been nothing in the way when she had taken the boots out this morning. She looked more closely. Several riding habits and other items of apparel blocked her view.

She sighed. She had been meaning to get this space more organized for a long time. It was no wonder some of the over-worked hangers had protested by dropping their burdens onto the floor. She leaned further into the closet and was rearranging the items closest to the corner when her arm was seized and she was yanked forward. A startled cry escaped her lips just before her mouth was covered by a large strong hand.

Chapter 48:
Captive in the Closet

Laural struggled but her captor was strong.

Is it another porphyrian? A Loyalist? Nick?

A deep male voice whispered huskily in her ear, "I was certain I'd never see you again."

Laural gasped but the sound was smothered as the hand covering her mouth was lifted only long enough to be replaced by demanding lips. Surrendering to her own pent-up passion, she gave way to the fierce onslaught of his kiss. She slid her arms around his neck, her pulse quickening when he groaned against her hungry mouth.

He pulled back reluctantly. "I've been imagining doing that for days. It was the only thing that got me through."

Her face was glowing as she smiled up into Jordan's jade green eyes. "I was so worried. Tim and I just returned from Camborne Castle. I sensed that you were nearby, but when we couldn't find you I became frantic. Are you alright?"

He probed her for a long moment. She gazed back at him steadily, allowing him to access her feelings. At last the tension drained from his face and he grinned down at her. "No, but I'll heal."

Laural didn't like the sound of that. It would help if they moved out of the closet and into the bedroom where she could maneuver better. She started to step toward the door but he yanked her back hard into his embrace. Having her pinned against his chest caused an unexpected reaction and his breath caught. Aware of his arousal, she lifted her eyes to meet his and stroked his cheek. He winced and, confused, she let her hand drop. "My face--along with the rest of me-- hasn't had a chance to completely heal," he explained, answering her unspoken question. Sensing she was about to ask more, he pressed a finger to her lips. "I'm actually in here for another reason besides just to admire your wardrobe," he whispered.

"Why are you hiding out in my closet? Certainly you knew once you got here you'd be safe."

He hesitated, staring long and hard into her upturned face. "I wanted to be sure you were alone."

By degrees her expression shifted from confusion to consternation as her cheeks flushed.

How much does he know about my relationship with Nick?

Jordan said softly, "While he was torturing me, Ravensblood offered the information that he was waiting to see if you were pregnant with his child."

Her hand flew to her mouth as she dropped her eyes.

He cupped one hand under her chin while the other pulled hers away from her mouth. He traced her full bottom lip with his thumb until she looked at him. "We can discuss that later if you like, but right now that isn't the point. I knew even while we were still in Washington that you were attracted to him. I'm not judging you for it or holding it against you, and right now we've got bigger concerns. Is Ravensblood here?"

"No, he's disappeared."

The tension drained out of his body, leaving him limp. He swayed slightly and Laural responded by putting a steadying arm under his. Together they emerged from the armoire. Her breath hissed out between clenched teeth when she got the first clear look at his face. Her blood boiled and her hands balled into fists as she considered retribution.

"That can wait," replied Jordan, reading her thoughts. "Right now we need a plan."

She probed him for a long moment before she allowed herself to relax. Taking his hand, she led the way downstairs and into the study. Tim Cooper and Ben Fletcher were seated at a small conference table, conversing quietly. Ben was obviously saying something that the other head of security disagreed with since Tim was continually shaking his head.

Laural smiled, recognizing the stony look settling on Tim's face. Hearing their approach, both men stopped talking and glanced up.

"I took the liberty of calling Ben and asking him to come down," offered Tim. "I was assuming we'd want his help. He was already on …"

Their welcoming smiles froze when they saw the earl. Tim jumped to his feet, toppling his chair in his eagerness. He vigorously pumped

Jordan's arm while Ben stood on the other side, slapping him on the back.

"Boy, are you a sight for sore eyes!" Tim exclaimed as he continued to shake Jordan's hand.

"You sure gave us quite a scare," offered Ben, peering at him closely.

Jordan read the concern on his face. "It's bad," he agreed, "but no permanent damage was done, so I'll heal."

Ben was relieved and returned to his chair. Laural took the seat opposite. Jordan cocked an eyebrow at Tim until he finally released his grip. Slightly embarrassed, he stepped back.

Jordan clasped him on the shoulder. "I'm glad to see you too."

Jordan helped Tim straighten his chair. After the men were seated they all looked expectantly at Laural. Her eyes met and held Jordan's. He gazed longingly back, wishing they were still up in her bedroom instead of there in the study.

"Ben and Tim are already aware of what's been going on here, but I'll start by bringing you up to date. A few days ago the archeology students headed by Professor Ravensblood made a discovery here on the estate. They found a sarcophagus with an intact skeleton and an ancient sword in a sheath." She nodded in the direction of the great room. "The discoveries are all in there and everything is as it was found."

"What about the journals?" he asked tensely.

Ben and Tim looked at each other, perplexed.

She shook her head. "There were no journals."

"Ravensblood took them?"

Again she shook her head. "I have every reason to believe they weren't there when the coffin was opened. To be sure, I had his belongings searched as well as the students'--no journals, diaries, or any other documents turned up. So either he's much better at subterfuge then I am or the documents were never there."

Jordan was uneasy and unable to accept that conclusion.

I'm sure those journals were there—or at least had been. Could someone else have already taken them? Perhaps Cynthia? Although she had the ability to disguise her features, she'd been unable to completely hide her intention of double-crossing her leader.

"If Ben and Tim are going to be assisting us, I think it's time we told them the full scope of our problem." He provided them with an abbreviated synopsis of their dilemma and the details regarding his entrapment, imprisonment and release.

"Any idea who the cloaked figure was?" asked Tim while taking notes.

Jordan smiled. "No, but the help was certainly appreciated."

"You say Ravensblood admitted to being your son and to killing his own mother?" asked Ben, while also writing in his notebook.

Jordan nodded. "He didn't just admit it. He bragged about it along--with his scheme to produce a supplement that would enable porphyrians to become so prolific that they would even be able to cross-breed."

Laural appeared thoughtful as she stared steadily back at him. "Nick's disappeared, leaving behind all the artifacts. From what Jordan has told us about the mysterious visitor who came to see Nick at the castle, let's assume, for the moment, he doesn't have the journals yet but still wants them."

Ben insisted, "That's an awful big assumption."

"Maybe, but it's a chance we'll have to take if my plan is going to work."

Ben appeared unconvinced. "There's a possibility that he left so abruptly because he'd found what he was looking for."

Laural's eyes rested on the display of her grandfather's remains for a long moment. Eventually her gaze drifted back to Jordan and she smiled. "I think what happened is Nick got nervous after Jordan escaped. He knew his time masquerading as a college professor was over. I'm sure the idea of facing us together was more then he was ready to handle—at least for now. I think he's retreated in order to plan his next step."

Jordan nodded his agreement. "I got the distinct impression the last time Nick questioned me that he still didn't know the location of the journals."

"I don't think I like where this is heading," Tim mumbled under his breath.

Laural took a steadying breath before continuing. She knew the idea wasn't perfect, but no plan ever was. And this was a pretty good one, despite any flaws. She looked around at the expectant faces. "I think we should put on a medieval fair."

Chapter 49:
Setting the Trap

Stunned silence greeted the announcement as three sets of eyes stared blankly back at their leader. Seconds dragged by as the men glanced around the table at each other. Eventually their confused gazes came back to rest on Laural.

Hesitantly, Jordan spoke his doubts out loud. "I realize I'm still recovering from my ordeal and my mind may still be a little sluggish, but I don't understand how a medieval fair will help with our problem." He grasped her hand to take the sting out of his words.

Her glance slid from one serious face to the next. "I know how strange it sounds, but hear me out. I originally conceived the idea from desperation when both Jordan and the baby were still missing. I thought we could trick the Loyalists into believing that we had found Arthur Gabriel's journals and would be willing to give them up in exchange for the captives. But I knew I'd have to come up with something more innovative than just expecting Nick to knock at my door, victims in tow, ready to trade them for the documents."

She paused to gauge their expressions. Ben stared at her, brows lowered and lips pursed. Tim frowned as he hastily scribbled on his notepad. Her gaze shifted to Jordan. Bruises covered almost every inch of his face. The skin around his eyes was puffy and discolored. Both his upper and lower lips were cut and swollen. It must surely have hurt for him to kiss her the way he had in the closet.

"But it was sure worth it," he projected silently.

Faint color stained her cheeks as her eyes met his and were held captive by the jade green depths. He grinned, then winced. He was trying to make light of his injuries for her sake and her heart warmed even as her resolve hardened.

"I'll heal," he reminded her unnecessarily.

She nodded slightly in acknowledgment of the unspoken statement.

Of course he was right. Even in the short time since they had come downstairs the discoloration had lightened. She frowned.

Something's wrong. Jordan hasn't been tortured for several hours, so why isn't he much further along in the healing process?

He tried to shield her from the truth but she gleaned the information before he completely blocked it: The most recent damage had been inflicted on top of previous injuries which had never been allowed to heal.

Her eyes became twin slits of blue ice as the images broke through. Bombarded by Jordan's memories she relived the experience of how they had deliberately brutalized him every few hours so his natural healing ability would never have a chance to complete its cycle. Abruptly the mental pictures stopped. Her brain shrieked with outrage. Jordan had tried to shield her from the truth, but the reality had been so horrific some of the gruesome details had leaked like a backed-up sewage pipe.

He squeezed her hand. "It's all over now."

She let her eyes linger on his battered features for another moment then deliberately put aside thoughts of personal revenge so she could stay focused on the larger problem. Before Tim or Ben could start to wonder about their silent dialogue, she pushed on. "Knowing I would need a more complex plan was what prompted me to come up with the idea of a medieval fair. The event would be advertised and give the local community a chance to see the artifacts we found. At the same time, the festivities would allow the Loyalists to camouflage themselves by blending in with the crowd. In an event like that they would feel less conspicuous and more apt to come in greater numbers. It would provide the ideal opportunity to obtain the journals while ridding themselves of the biggest threat to their existence at the same time."

Tim and Ben exchanged glances, sure that they had missed something, but still no one interrupted.

"Since the baby is dead and Jordan has escaped, the need for a trade no longer exists, but that doesn't mean we can't still use the ploy."

"In order to do what exactly?" questioned Ben, still straining to get his mind around the concept.

She smiled to instill a sense of confidence she was far from feeling.

"Purely for the sake of drawing out the Loyalists. If we let it leak that we've just found some ancient documents that are connected to the recently-discovered artifacts, that should provide enough bait to set the trap."

They still needed to be convinced, so she continued outlining the plan.

"Nick needs my grandfather's notes in order for his schemes to work. Arthur Gabriel's discarded formulas still represent the only data on a successful supplement that will allow porphyrians to drastically increase their rate of reproduction and produce healthy offspring. And even though the Loyalists were able to come up with a substitute formula which allowed them to cross-breed, the result was a child who had numerous medical problems. I'm sure Nick would prefer to bypass all the time it would take for trial-and-error by obtaining the original documents."

"Depends on your definition of success," Ben offered. "In my book giving up your sanity to procreate is not exactly a fair exchange."

"I'm sure once Nick gets his hands on the formulas he'll make adjustments."

"Then why would he need Arthur Gabriel's notes?" asked Tim. "Why not just continue to adjust the formulas he's already been creating until he succeeds?"

Three sets of eyes turned to Jordan, who nodded. "For several days I was forced to endure a noxious concoction. I'm not sure about the fertility aspect, but the taste could definitely stand improvement."

"I'm sure that Nick would continue his attempts to invent a substitute if that was his only option, but I'm banking on the fact that he'd still prefer the original. And if he believes he can get the journals and kill us in the process, he won't be able to resist."

Jordan shook his head. "Even if we decided to go ahead with such an elaborate idea, your plan has several flaws. For one thing, Nick was here and saw for himself there were no journals."

Laural shrugged. "He could never be completely certain that I didn't somehow manage to outmaneuver him. That alone would drive him nuts."

"Alright, but what about the man who came to the castle and distracted Nick from killing me? The guard said he had information about the documents Nick had been searching for."

She shrugged again. "True, but I got the impression from what you said that it's much more likely that the stranger's purpose was to distract Nick while you were rescued. However, even if he was on the level and somehow managed to obtain knowledge about the journals and then decided to barter the information, Nick could never be sure that he possessed all the documents or that the stranger wasn't working for us and feeding him false information. Nick would remember that it was during the distraction the stranger provided that you escaped, and if rumors circulated that ancient papers had been found, Nick would be determined to take them. He would want to be certain that nothing was missing from the notes he had and make sure there weren't other mysteries to be plundered."

"I have a strange feeling about this mysterious benefactor of Jordan's," interjected Tim, instantly gaining everyone's attention. "Well," he continued glancing around the table, "it's all just too coincidental. We're supposed to believe that an unexpected visitor just happened to show up to distract Nick with the one thing he most wanted, right at the moment someone else was helping Jordan escape?"

he paused to let his statement sink in.

"I believe it's much more likely that either Jordan's rescuer and the mysterious visitor were the same person or there were two people working together. Either way, it appears the main purpose was to free Jordan. Since it would be much more cumbersome for this to be a one-man job, I think the alleged presentation of material was designed as a ploy to pull Nick away from Jordan so they would have an opportunity to free him without risking a direct confrontation."

"And speaking of confrontations," interjected Ben, "how did your rescuer manage to get you past the guards?"

Jordan shook his head. "I was drugged and unconscious for most of the time. I don't know much about the details, but Ben's viewpoint does give additional credence to the theory of this being a two-man operation. I doubt one man--even a porphyrian--could have gotten past all the guards as well as Nick."

"Not to mention Cynthia," Tim agreed. "You're right, it doesn't seem very likely."

"Cynthia's dead," stated Jordan flatly.

Tim and Ben were taken aback but Laural simply nodded. Finally,

Ben cleared his throat. "Are you sure you didn't recognize the stranger?"

"I didn't get a good look while he was freeing me, and afterwards I was so weak from exhaustion and pain I passed out."

"And you're sure there was only one person helping you escape?" asked Tim.

"I can't be sure of anything. As I said, I was drugged and unconscious most of the time. When I finally regained consciousness I was in the woods—alone."

"Whether it was one man or two," Laural asserted, "it seems most likely that whoever released Jordan used the promise of providing documents as a ruse to distract Nick. So it would appear the Loyalists are still very much interested in obtaining the original formulas."

"I seriously doubt we can count on all of the Loyalists returning to steal the documents," insisted Ben, "no matter how important they are."

"True," agreed Laural, "but if we manage to eliminate their leader and several of his key followers, the survivors will probably disband."

"Or choose another leader."

Laural and Jordan exchanged glances. "If the Maxwells are eliminated, there are no others of our kind with the ability to go up against Jordan or myself. Since porphyrians are generally solitary figures who prefer to remain out of the mainstream, my best bet is that they'll fade back into the shadows."

She scanned their faces. She could tell they were considering the opportunities her plan presented. "The fact that my grandfather's remains were undiscovered until a few days ago could lend credence to the possibility that the journals are still here."

"You sound doubtful," Jordan prompted.

She shrugged. "It doesn't matter what I believe as long as the Loyalists credit the story. However, I'm beginning to think that the journals are merely a myth."

"Like the myth of King Arthur?"

Her eyes roamed over her cousin's features and her heart beat a little faster when he smiled at her. "Even if the mystery man knows about the journals, I doubt he would have freed you if his intention was to aid Nick. If the journals do exist they're still at large."

"Which brings up the third problem. What happens when Nick checks with his good friend Dr. Ford and finds out no documents were presented to him?"

Laural shot him an exasperated look. "Nick wouldn't expect me to hand over, or even make known, the existence of such sensitive documents. If Dr. Ford doesn't have knowledge of them, that could actually arouse suspicion that we really do have the journals."

Tim's lips pressed together in a tight line as he tapped his pen against his pad. "I don't like it. Since Ravensblood's quite aware of the whole picture, he'll be able **to** figure out exactly what you're trying to do."

She nodded her agreement. "That's why I'm counting on you and Ben to keep ahead of him every step of the way. Look," she continued earnestly, "this is the best chance we've ever had to draw out the Loyalists instead of having to search them out one at a time, and the only opportunity we've ever had to get a shot at their leader."

"What makes you think he'll come?" asked Ben.

Laural and Jordan shared a long look. "Oh, he'll come," asserted Laural confidently. "He won't be able to resist it when we've got everything he wants all in one spot."

Jordan squeezed her hand as he stared into her sapphire eyes. "Yes, to kill both of us and avenge his family by using the Penbrook legacy to destroy the diurnals."

Chapter 50:
The Expert

Late the following evening Dr. Malcolm Ford sat in the library of his small Mayfair townhouse. Hunched over his writing desk he earnestly detailed his notes describing his experience at Penbrook Castle. After a few minutes he lifted the pen thoughtfully to his lips, and studied what he had written.

How can I possibly describe one of the most important finds since the discovery of Tutankhamen?

During the long hours spent examining the artifacts he had become convinced that the remains of the legendary King Arthur had been found on the Penbrook estate.

Of course more tests would need to be conducted and carbon-dating established, but still--

The shrill ring of the telephone interrupted his thoughts. Removing his spectacles, he rubbed his eyes and reached for the receiver. "Hello?"

"Malcolm?"

"Yes."

"It's Nick Ravensblood."

"Nick!" exclaimed the curator. His eyes swung from the phone back to his notes. "How are you?"

"Fine, and yourself?"

"Fine." He leaned back in his chair. "As a matter of fact, I was just writing up my notes on the find out at Penbrook Castle."

"Really?"

"Yes, actually, Nick, I was surprised that you weren't there. I met a lot of your students, excellent group by the way, but when I enquired I was told you had left the site."

"I really wish I could have stayed to meet with you but I had a family emergency which required my immediate departure."

"Yes, so Lady Gabriel informed me. Nothing too serious, I hope."

"Fortunately, I was able to leave just in time to avert a major catastrophe."

And that's certainly a true statement. Who knows what would have happened if I'd still been there after Laural discovered my deceptions?

He smiled.

Of course, I could have handled her easily enough, but I prefer to deal with the situation on my own terms.

"Malcolm, what did you think of the find?"

The curator cleared his throat. "I concur with your hypothesis. I believe the artifacts could very well be genuine, pending further test, of course."

"I've been hearing rumors that there may have been an additional discovery made after I left," Nick said nonchalantly.

Ford frowned into the receiver. "Really? The only objects presented to me were the ones you mentioned. To what specifically are you referring?"

"I'd heard that there were some ancient parchments found, possibly within a secret panel inside the coffin."

Ford picked up his pen and began tapping it against the pad. "Now that you mention it," he said thoughtfully, "Lady Gabriel did make some enquiries about how to determine the authenticity and age of documents. However, I can assure you there were none actually presented. I put her questions down to her curiosity and enthusiasm. You know how it is, Nick, once the archeology bug bites it can become all-consuming--especially after as exciting a find as this one. It's not surprising that your host would be enthralled by the prospect of more discoveries."

Nick laughed. "Enthusiastic is not exactly the way I would describe Lady Gabriel's reaction to all of this. She's dead set against attracting attention."

The curator chuckled. "Well, let me assure you that is no longer the case. She's decided to have a grand display of the artifacts by throwing a medieval fair at her estate."

"Is that so?"

"Yes, she's come to the conclusion that the find should be shared with the locals before it's taken out of their shire and permanently removed to the museum. The possibility that the remains of the legendary King Arthur have been discovered has already provoked national and international media attention. As soon as I returned from my evaluation I was approached by several newspapers and two magazines. However, let me again reiterate in case you're concerned about the integrity of your discovery, there were no other artifacts presented while I was examining the skeleton and the sword. I assume you're going to write a paper on the subject?"

Of course," he agreed quickly. "And your reassurance sets my mind at ease."

"I'm surprised you, as the originator of the find, haven't been hounded by the press."

"I expect they'll be pounding down my door any minute."

Ford chuckled again. "I expect you're right. Well, if I can do anything else to help with the project let me know."

"Thanks, Malcolm, you've been a big help already." Nick rang off and sat unmoving, chaotic thoughts tossing and turning in his mind.

He sneered.

Obviously the idea of a medieval fair was the Marchioness of Penbrook's attempt to lure him into a trap. What a pathetically transparent scheme. I would have thought the Penbrook heiress and her consort could have put together a better plan.

However, the possibility of acquiring the information he needed while eliminating the competition for his inheritance was too good an opportunity to pass up. With the proper planning he could actually use their own idea against them. Even without the additional incentive of Arthur Gabriel's formulas, the potential to get rid of both his father and cousin in one strike was too good to miss.

He gazed out the window of his Miami mansion. The palm trees swayed gently in the tropical breeze under an inky sky dotted with pinpoints of light. A sliver of moon edged its way out from behind a cloud. As it cast an eerie illumination over the long expanse of lawn a shadow skirted the perimeter and scurried into the bushes. Nick's lips twisted as he watched the possum disappear.

The mansion had originally belonged to his family, and then his mother had sold it half a century ago. He had bought it back under one of his pseudonyms and was certain his adversaries would not be able to trace him. At this location he would be able to remain hidden until he was ready to make his move. He just wished he could be as certain of the rest of his plans.

The escape of his father from the tower had been unexpected and disconcerting. Equally disquieting was the unknown stranger who had obviously aided Jordan in his escape. Nick didn't like to think he had a traitor on his hands, especially one placed high enough to have inside knowledge. He would just have to determine a method of insuring security until he found the double agent. Retribution would be swift and merciless.

His lips twitched. At least he could discount Cynthia. With her penchant for duplicity she would have been his first guess. As her death replayed through his mind a cynical smirk curved his cruel lips. The grin soured. Her death would look like a picnic compared to his punishment of the dis-Loyalist.

Chapter 51:
The Medieval Fair

Dawn broke with splashes of bright orange and yellow on the day of the medieval fair. Within a few hours the sun was shining brilliantly and warming the grounds of the Penbrook estate. Gaily-colored tents festooned with brightly-painted pennants flapped in the breeze. Costumed servants traversed the grounds to insure the comfort of the guests. Booths of carnival games and refreshment stands dotted the lawns. Barkers called out loudly on their megaphones to entice small children to join in the fun. All across the courtyard people were munching hot dogs and cotton candy or drinking mugs of ale as they enjoyed the festivities.

Clad only in a nightgown and pajama bottoms, Laural and Jordan held each other close, bodies entwined as they snuggled together on the window seat in Laural's bedroom. They watched as the medieval-costumed workers casually mingled throughout the crowd. Laural pointed below. Jordan followed her direction and smiled when he caught sight of one of the performers acting as a mime. For a moment he watched, captivated by the show, but soon nudged Laural when his gaze strayed to the unicyclist.

Laural enjoyed his acrobatic antics for several moments before her gaze moved on to scan the rest of the crowd. She was gratified to see quite a few of her own staff and the extras she had hired playing their parts, interacting with the visitors, giving directions and providing impromptu entertainment. A bright grin lit her face as she recognized one of her own staff dressed as a jester juggling in front of a group containing two small children. The little boy's eyes were wide and the young girl giggled, both delighted by the jester's antics.

"So far I haven't seen anyone who looks out of place," she offered, her body resting lightly against Jordan's broad chest. Even though he was rapidly healing, mottled flesh still bore evidence of his torture.

Laural was careful not to press her full weight against him as she closed her eyes and briefly reveled in the feel of his warm skin against her cheek.

I wish I could stay this way forever and just let the world take care of itself.

Jordan leaned his chin on the top of her head. He rubbed his jaw across her silken tresses, luxuriating in the feel of her soft hair against his skin. The corners of his lips lifted as he nuzzled her. He didn't have to be a mind-reader to know what she was thinking and he felt the same way.

"Neither have I, but until recently my mind has been preoccupied with other things."

She tipped her head back in order to get a clear view of his face, and blushed when she saw the direction of his gaze. Jordan was staring intently at the four-poster bed they had recently vacated. The sheets and coverlet lay crumpled in a heap on the floor with the pillows haphazardly strewn across the mattress.

Due to the extent of Jordan's injuries, indulging in the full depth of their longing for each other had been delayed for several days. To pass the time they had indulged their feelings by flirting and teasing so intensely that once the earl had regained his strength all the built-up passion between them had quickly ignited then exploded. Their need to envelop themselves in their newfound feelings was the reason they had not yet gone down to join the festivities. Jordan's gaze swiveled from the bed to her face. The breath caught in her throat as she was seared by the heat of desire blazing in the depths of his jade green eyes.

"I know," he huskily replied to her unspoken thought before kissing her lingeringly on the lips. "I'm still amazed and exhilarated too."

"After all these years…" Her words trailed off as she was again lost in an onslaught of erotic thoughts.

"You're right," he agreed. "All those wasted years when we could have been having as much fun as we did last night," he said teasingly. Then he sobered. "Until recently I spent most of those years thinking of you as simply my younger cousin and the daughter of my best friend. Even after my feelings for you started to change, I wasn't sure if following my heart was the right thing to do."

"Why not?" she asked softly.

"There were several reasons. First of all, you're my cousin."

"Third cousin," she reminded him, "so that really doesn't count. Besides, with only about twenty-one-hundred of us on the planet, if we go back far enough, probably all porphyrians are related."

He chuckled. "You're probably right." Then he sobered. "But you're also the daughter of my best friend. And even though your dad's been dead for thirty years, I can't help wondering what he would think."

"I think," she smiled into his eyes, "Dad would want me to be happy, and I am."

"Really?" he asked with a gleam in his eyes. "Why don't you show me just how happy you are?"

Her body suffused by an erotic rush, Laural's cheeks turned bright pink. Shakily, she stood up from the window seat, shook out her cornflower-blue nightgown and moved to her armoire. Trying to reclaim some vestige of control over her rioting emotions, she opened the closet and pulled out her long medieval gown. Costumes had been Jordan's idea. He had made the case that being dressed in time-appropriate attire would separate them from the public and give them the advantage in distinguishing their own people from the Loyalists. Feeling as though she had finally regained her composure, she held up the beautiful flowing blue satin and lace confection, spinning around to face Jordan.

"Wearing this I'm going to feel more like a damsel in distress than the leader of this group. I hope I can maneuver when the time comes."

Jordan rose to join her. His copper hair was tousled and his green eyes were still heavily-lidded with arousal. His satisfied grin told her he knew the effect his half-naked body was having on her as he approached. Winking wickedly at her, he pulled his own outfit of tunic and hose from the closet. "That's why you have all of us big strong men to protect you."

Admiring the sensual movement of his body as he neared her, she grinned provocatively back at him. "Ha," she scoffed. "That's why I have pant legs in addition to layers of underskirts sewn into this get-up," she proclaimed, lifting the hem to reveal the trouser bottoms attached to the garment.

Minutes later they were downstairs in the crowded great room. Laural marveled at the number of locals who had gathered to glimpse the artifacts.

"I suppose they're in awe and rather proud to have the remains of what might prove to be King Arthur discovered in their domain," Jordan commented.

Laural could only shake her head at Jordan's understatement. As she glanced around the room her attention was drawn to a village woman who was pointing out details of the skeleton and sword while speaking animatedly to her two children. The children's eyes were filled with wonder as they gazed at the artifacts. On the other side of the woman stood a reporter busily engaged in taking notes as he plied the mom and kids with questions.

Laural shifted her view to encompass the rest of the room. Both the skeleton and sword were connected to a sophisticated alarm system and well-protected behind shatter-proof glass. Two of her staff hovered discretely nearby, diligently scanning the crowd. Despite all the precautions Laural was still tense and uneasy about the safety of her ancestor's remains.

She examined the room more thoroughly. Nothing seemed to be out of place. Everyone appeared to be enjoying the spectacle. The locals were taking advantage of the privilege of touring part of the castle. Her ancestral home had never been on display before and the residents of Camelford were making the most of the opportunity.

She massaged the back of her neck in a vain attempt to unknot her tense muscles. She noticed the local residents weren't the only ones taking advantage of the opportunity to inspect the inside of the castle. Two photographers were making the most of their chance to snap rare shots of her home. She grimaced, not completely comfortable with her privacy being invaded, even if it meant trapping the Loyalists.

One of the photographers spotted her. "Lady Gabriel," he called, "would you mind coming over so we can get a shot of you next to the display?"

As Laural groaned mentally, an unexpected clatter arose from the adjacent hallway. She swiftly moved to see what was going on. Three staff members dressed in medieval regalia were already converging on the scene.

Could this distraction be a ploy meant to take me off guard while the Loyalists try to steal the journals?

She glanced over her shoulder. The artifacts were still secure behind the glass.

She redirected her attention to the scene unfolding in front of her. Jordan glanced toward her as she joined the group gathered around the foyer. In the center of the circle of burly medieval security guards stood a young boy of about ten. He looked anxiously from one adult to the next. Confused, Laural turned to Tim for an explanation.

The big man grinned sheepishly as he rolled his eyes. "I guess we're all a little on edge," he explained, holding out his hand.

Laural glanced down into his open palm. A small bundle of grey fur sat hunched in the middle of his hand, whiskers twitching as its eyes shifted fearfully from one person to the next. Her brows raised. "We're having a security crisis over a mouse?"

Jordan took the small animal from Tim's palm and held it out to the boy. "Here you go, sonny. Run along, and please keep your pet outside."

After the child scampered off, they all just stood there. Jordan exhaled a long breath. "Okay, I'd say we're all a little uptight, but better to err on the side of caution."

Tim nodded. "Okay, folks, false alarm but good response. Please disperse back to your assigned posts."

After they had gone, Laural addressed Tim and Jordan. "Have either one of you noticed anything amiss?"

They both shook their heads. Tim scowled. "It's almost as though things are running too smoothly."

Laural checked her watch. "Well, it's about time for the jousting match. Come on, Jordan, we'll cover that. Tim, you're okay here?"

When he nodded they headed for the tournament field.

Chapter 52:
The Victorious Knight

Laural and Jordan walked toward the makeshift arena. Halting outside the ring they observed two of the combatants who were preparing for their first joust. Laural's eyes lifted to scan the area. Some of the spectators were standing around the perimeter of the ring while others sat on temporary bleachers in order to get a better view. Laural smiled as she tugged on Jordan's tunic sleeve. When he grinned warmly down into her upturned face her heart skipped a beat.

"You look completely captivating in that gown," he asserted as his eyes slid down the revealing bodice. He paused. "And if you don't stop looking at me like that we'll be watching the joust from your bedroom window."

She raised her brows. "If we go back to my bedroom we won't be watching anything but each other."

His grin broadened. "No, we won't–at least not for the next several hours."

She warmed at the thought. For a moment she considered his suggestion, but her sense of duty prevailed. To distract him, she pointed toward the two actors they had hired for the performance.

Jordan swung his eyes from the view offered by the low cut of her gown to the ring where two men in armor sat astride their steeds. "They certainly do look the part," he commented when the two jousters took up their positions at the opposite ends of the field.

Even though she knew they were only actors putting on a show, she couldn't help holding her breath as the knights barreled down the arena at break-neck speed. The first pass was clean and they wound up on opposite sides of the field unscathed. The crowd clapped and cheered.

"Stick it to him!" yelled one onlooker.

"Let's see some action!" demanded another.

Jordan laughed. "They sure are a bloodthirsty lot."

Their chargers pawed the ground while the armored actors made a show out of checking their lances. They nodded toward each other and started their second charge down the field. Gathering momentum and ever-increasing speed, they hurtled toward each other, lances outstretched. Laural tensed as the two came within striking distance. A loud crack sounded as one knight struck the other in the center of his breastplate. His opponent was hurled from his saddle, landing hard on his back in the center of the ring.

Laural relaxed as the triumphant knight completed his pass. The performance had gone off without a hitch. The crowd roared their approval. The victorious knight trotted his stallion around the perimeter of the ring to bask in the accolades. When he drew up in front of Laural and Jordan, he paused to offer a salute. Laural smiled brightly while Jordan offered his congratulations. The knight bowed from the saddle then beckoned to Laural.

She leaned toward him.

"A favor from my lady?" he requested, pointing to one of the bright blue ribbons decorating her gown.

Laughing delightedly at his impromptu addition to the performance, she made a show out of pulling off the ribbon and tying it around his wrist. The crowd roared again as the victorious knight lifted his arm to display his prize, spun his mount and rode off toward the tents.

Jordan looked from the retreating combatant to the fallen figure on the ground. Several extra stagehands had appeared right on cue to carry the loser out of the ring in order to preserve the authentic feel of the performance. But, instead of removing the knight, they stood clustered around the body looking baffled and shaking their heads. At last, one glanced up, noticed Laural and Jordan and waved his arm at them wildly.

The crowd was dispersing, and still the stage crew stood milling about, consulting with each other. They shook their heads while tossing anxious glances toward the man on the ground. The actor hadn't moved.

Is he taking his part that seriously or has he really been hurt? Jordan wondered, concerned.

The stagehand who had beckoned to Jordan earlier opened his mouth and started to shout something, but the earl quickly shook his head. Looking around, the man seemed to suddenly become aware of the crowd. He gave a nod and started toward them.

Jordan tugged Laural's hand as he edged forward. Once they were in the arena he hastily made his way to the fallen knight's side. Laural bent beside him, and together they looked for signs of movement. The fallen figure was as still as a statue.

The man who had beckoned spoke up. "He's completely unresponsive. I'd guess he's been seriously injured and is out cold."

Leaning close to the helmet, Jordan said, "The show's over. You've more than earned your pay for this performance."

No response.

Laural leaned forward from the other side and gently shook the knight's arm.

Still no response.

She raised her eyes to Jordan's.

He shook his head. "Not here," he projected silently. "We don't want to start a panic." To the gathered men he said, "I'll need you to help get him to one of the tents."

Laural looked at him, knowing Jordan was aware they could have easily carried the actor without the extra help. He threw a quick glance in her direction and she understood: They couldn't allow the diurnals to see them hefting such a heavy burden without aid. The man along with his armor would weigh at least three hundred pounds. If she hadn't been so distressed she would have realized the dilemma.

Together Jordan and two of the stagehands lifted the man. Laural moved to the side to let them pass, and followed as they half-carried, half-dragged him to the actors' tent. After lowering him onto a cot, they cautiously began removing his armor. Jordan dismissed the extras. One of the men appeared about to protest but a closer look at the earl's set features changed his mind.

Laural carefully pulled off the helmet. The knight's face was completely drained of color. She glanced at Jordan but he was preoccupied removing the man's breastplate. His eyes widened in alarm, and Laural's gaze dropped back to the knight.

"Oh my God!" she cried out when she saw the gash running straight through the actor's chest.

Chapter 53:
Tim's Revelation

Two hours later, Jordan, Laural and Tim gathered around the desk in the main study at Penbrook Castle. Tim glanced at the door, insuring it was secure before he spoke. "I can understand the position of the police given the information they have to go on, but, in terms of our own security, we can't assume this was a random accident. Until we know better we're going to have to treat it as though it is a Loyalist attack."

After seeing the injured actor off in an ambulance, Jordan and Laural had been questioned by the police. An extensive search for the other actor had been ordered but he couldn't be found. Despite the fact that the other performer had disappeared the authorities hadn't wanted to presume that his act was intentional. Upon request, Laural had provided the man's address from his records. Once they had taken their final statements the police had left the scene to pursue the lead.

Jordan's eyes sharpened. "Which, in all probability, is exactly what it was."

Tim didn't respond to Jordan's comment. "We're fortunate that the press had already left, otherwise they'd have been breathing down our necks this whole time and we'd be right in the middle of a publicity nightmare."

Jordan scowled. "How long do you think it will take for them to return?"

Tim sighed. "Since they're always monitoring police transmissions, they're certainly already headed in our direction."

"But what purpose would be served by intentionally injuring a diurnal actor?" asked Laural. "Surely the Loyalists would realize that would draw unwanted attention and put us on our guard."

"True," Jordan agreed. "Scheduling the media coverage of the event early in order to get them out of the way was great planning and works to the Loyalists' benefit as much as ours, so why make their first strike over something high-profile and completely unrelated to their goal?"

They both looked expectantly at Tim.

Tim was carefully considering how to phrase what he had to say. The next few minutes were going to be difficult. He really hated to have to disappoint these two, who were more like friends then employers, but he didn't have any choice.

"They could have done it to keep us off balance, to act as a distraction, just to upset us, or to show their disdain for the diurnals—take your pick. Personally, I'm not as concerned about why right now. I'm more worried about what they're going to do next. So, as a precaution, I've doubled security around the artifacts for the moment and cancelled all other shows until we can confirm whether this was really a random accident or the deliberate attack of a Loyalist infiltrator."

Jordan took Laural's hand when he saw the horrified expression on her face. "We knew there were going to be risks."

Her voice was shaky when she replied, "Yes, for us, but not for the innocent bystanders."

"As far as the Loyalists are concerned there is no such thing as an innocent bystander."

"You're right. I don't know why I was expecting them to play by the rules when it's obvious they don't have any. But the Loyalists are certainly aware that attacking a diurnal right out in the open, along with the subsequent investigation, will shine a direct spotlight on them and place our entire species in danger of exposure and extermination. No porphyrian in their right mind would risk that."

"Since when has Nicholas Ravensblood or his followers been in their right minds?"

Tim cleared his throat to regain their attention.

Jordan searched his head of security's anxious expression. "There's more to this, and judging from the look on your face, what you haven't said yet is even worse."

Tim nodded curtly but didn't respond directly. "I've alerted Ben to the need for heightened security and briefed him on the situation. Right now he's guarding our forefather in the great room. The relics should be pretty safe, but Jordan's right. We need to consider the danger to the public's safety. We should think about shutting down and sending everyone home."

Laural protested. "I understand and share your concern about the risk to our guests, but if the knight was really a Loyalist, our plan to draw them out is working. It would be a shame to pull the plug now. Do you think our security teams can protect the public for just a little bit longer while we ensnare the Loyalists?"

Tim glanced back and forth uneasily between his two employers. He knew they weren't going to like the rest of what he had to say.

Hell, I don't like it either, but all the evidence points to the same conclusion.

Jordan continued to watch Tim keenly. "Laural has a point," he interjected. "It would be a shame to stop just when we're this close. The fact that they're here means we've got a real chance of catching them."

"Or at least some of them," amended Laural. "I'm sure Nick is here somewhere."

"Do you sense him?" asked Jordan, redirecting his gaze away from Tim's tense features.

"No," she shook her head, "it seems the part he told you about being able to shield himself was true, but I'm sure he wouldn't allow the journals to be removed by anyone else. Besides he's the only Loyalist who has extensive knowledge of the grounds."

Tim raised his hand. "Everything you say makes sense, but there are two factors in addition to the imminent media scrutiny that overrule all other considerations." Noting he had their total attention, he went on. "First of all, I'm doubtful that my security team can protect the diurnals, the artifacts, or even us."

Jordan eyed the security director, intuiting what he was going to say even as Laural asked, "Why is that?"

"Because of my second concern: We have a traitor."

Chapter 54:
Damage Control

Jordan inhaled sharply and Laural looked thunderstruck.

"Think about it," insisted Tim. "Only a small group of us knew about the costumes and the decision was made, more or less, at the last minute. So, if the Loyalists were able to infiltrate our security dressed as one of our actors, my best guess is they're also moving about freely in costumes--just like the members of our staff."

Laural closed her eyes. She couldn't believe the scheme on how to distinguish her people from the enemy was now being used to camouflage them instead.

Why didn't I think of that possibility?

"Stop it!" Jordan reprimanded, pulling her from her dark thoughts. "There's no such thing as a foolproof plan. Since all the staff has been part of your household for years, screening them never occurred to any of us. Besides, I'm the one who thought up the part about dressing up in costumes and we all approved it."

Tim nodded his agreement. "But I think now we need to do damage control."

Laural stood. "You're right, of course," she agreed, trying to mask her disappointment. She had counted on this ploy as an excellent opportunity to draw out and potentially capture the most prominent Loyalists. It made her blood boil to think they had turned the tables on her by using one of her own people against her. She would really like a chance to trap the traitor along with the other renegades, but Tim was right: They simply couldn't take the chance of injuring their diurnal guests.

They headed toward the great room where the display of Arthur Penbrook and his sword were being guarded. Ben Fletcher was on guard, protecting the artifacts along with several other employees Laural had known for decades. Studying their faces, she couldn't help wondering if any of them was the traitor. Most she had hand-picked, but some of the staff members were from families who had been with the Penbrooks for generations. As her eyes traveled from one familiar face to the next, she recalled how and when each one had come into her employ. They had all served her loyally for years.

Or at least I thought they were loyal.

Heartsick at the prospect of being betrayed, she quickly turned away.

Ben looked in their direction, caught their serious expressions, and joined them. "You folks look like you've come to some definite decisions."

"We have," confirmed Laural, looking from Ben to her grandfather's remains then back. "We're going to shut down."

Ben nodded his agreement. "I really think that's best under the circumstances."

Laural silently projected that they were being betrayed.

He projected his answer back.

I know you're shocked because you trust your staff, but since there's a possibility of an in-house traitor, we need to round up the staff and question them individually. In the meantime, the project's become too dangerous to continue.

He turned to Tim and said, "How do we want to go about it?"

"I think we'll disperse security in teams of two each to all the main areas while you and I—"

He broke off as a flaming arrow sailed through the window and hit one of the security guards.

They all ran toward the man as he screamed in agony, each shouting out orders.

"Water!"

"Drop and roll!"

"Grab something to smother the flames!"

But they were too late. In only the short time it took for them to cover the distance separating them from the guard, most of his body was incinerated.

Chapter 55:
The Loyalist Attack

They all stood staring in shock at the pile of ashes which only moments before had been one of Penbrook's devoted servants. Chaos erupted when a woman near the fallen guard started to scream. Panicked people began running, banging and knocking each other over in their haste to flee. Parents grabbed their crying children by the hands or snatched them up and began frantically searching for the nearest exit. They lunged toward the doors and dove out the windows while more flaming arrows flew into the room. Several of the fiery missiles hit their marks, and three more of the Penbrook staff burst into flames. Laural watched helplessly as her family's servants disintegrated at her feet.

Horrified, the four porphyrians stood rooted to the spot, gaping at the spectacle. Never had they imagined anything like this. Ben glanced out the nearest window, and alerted the others to the astonishing sight he beheld.

The castle was surrounded by men dressed in medieval costumes on horseback. They each held a bow and at their feet stood another man dressed as a page with a quiver of arrows. Spellbound they watched as the pages, in unison, each took out an arrow, lit the end, and handed it to the men on horseback. The riders then drew back and released another volley of deadly missiles into the fortress.

"They look like the performers we hired for the shows," Laural mumbled to Jordan.

He nodded grimly. "I think that's part of the plan. They want it to appear as though they are part of the event so later you'll be blamed."

Ben and Tim were the first to recover. "You three help the victims out of this mess," ordered Ben. "I'll take my men and get the artifacts to safety."

Laural and Jordan looked at each other, then nodded. Jordan was on the verge of asking where they should meet up afterwards when a fresh surge of flaming arrows swept the room. One lodged in an ancient tapestry that had been in the Penbrook family for generations. Laural winced as part of her heritage went up in flames. Another arrow struck one of the sofas. Mesmerized, Jordan stared as the fire licked its way up the wood paneling behind the couch.

Now all the pieces finally fell into place. A Loyalist had injured the knight knowing the distraction would give the rest of his group the opportunity to set up their attack while, at the same time, driving them back to the castle for a meeting.

What better way to kill all the birds with one stone—or, in this case, flaming arrows? We'd better move or this room is going to become our funeral pyre.

"Once we get all the guests out--"

His voice trailed off when he turned to face Laural. An arrow had embedded itself in the hem of Laural's gown and the flames were blazing a fiery path up her dress. He immediately snatched the skirt and ripped the material away from Laural's body. Dropping the burning fabric to the floor, he stomped hard until the flames died out.

"Thanks," said Laural shakily." I-I didn't realize."

"Nor would you have unless you had eyes in the back of your head. Maybe wearing that gown isn't such a good idea."

She raised her brows. "I hardly think this is the time to change outfits. Besides," she added, noting his worried expression, "the extra layers will act as an additional buffer between the fire and my skin."

He grabbed her by the arms and pulled her tight against his body. "I love you," he said, giving her a quick kiss on the lips.

"I love you too," she replied and moved away to help a fallen woman regain her balance.

Jordan maneuvered himself through the crowd aiding people to safety. After a few minutes his brain began to clear and he was able to start thinking beyond the immediate crisis. Nagging doubts intruded.

Burning down the castle may destroy the Penbrook stronghold and kill all of us in the process, but what about the artifacts? If those journals were so important to Nicholas Ravensblood, he would never allow them to be placed at risk--no matter how much he wanted revenge.

A thick shroud of smoke billowed around him. He couldn't see more then a few feet in front of him.

I have to find Ben!

A spasm of coughing shook him as acrid smoke filled his nose and throat. He tripped over something and almost went down. Eyes burning and tearing, he peered down at the floor. Squinting through the smoke he recognized the boy they had searched earlier.

Reaching down, he scooped up the lad. "We need to get you out of here, sonny. Where are your parents?"

The boy's face crumpled and he began to cry. "I don't know," he wailed. "Greybeard got scared when all the people started screaming and he ran under the chair. Now I can't reach him."

"I'm sorry about your pet, but we've got to get you out of here."

The boy started thrashing about and screaming so violently that Jordan almost dropped him.

We'll never make it to the door if he keeps that up.

He placed the boy back on the ground. "Which chair?"

The boy pointed at an ornate low-seated chair a few feet away just as an arrow hit the back of the seat. The boy screamed when fingers of fire rapidly spread across the upholstery. Before Jordan could restrain him he flew at the seat and scrambled underneath. The earl rushed after him, grabbed the chair by one of its thick legs and heaved. The frightened ball of fur ran straight into the boy's open hands.

Standing, the boy turned around to thank the rescuer of his beloved pet.

"Mister," he yelled, "you're on fire!"

Chapter 56:
Chaos in the Castle

Urgently, Jordan swatted at the flames as they raced up his tunic. He winced and cursed under his breath when he felt the fire scorch his skin straight through to the bone. Ignoring the pain he briefly glanced at his hand. The skin shriveled, flaked and fell off. His lips tightened.

No time to worry about that now.

Despite the continued volley of arrows catapulting into the rooms people were still pushing their way out the doors and diving through the windows. He blanched as an arrow hit its mark and a woman's dress caught fire. Grabbing the boy's hand he rushed toward the woman. The flames were spreading quickly and he feared he wouldn't be able to get to her before she became a human torch.

The panic-stricken woman started to run towards the nearest exit. Holding the boy even more tightly, he shoved past the confused and frightened onlookers.

There are too many people! I'll never get to her in time.

Relief flooded through him as Laural rushed to the woman's aid. Grabbing hold of the fleeing female, she restrained her while using part of her own gown to smother the flames. Jordan scooped up the boy and managed to move in their direction through the throng of hysterical people.

A loud crack and snap sounded overhead. Jordan looked up as one of the wooden beams from the ceiling crashed down right in front of them. Sparks flew in every direction. He stumbled backward, colliding with the crowd still trying to surge forward. He held the boy tightly and shielded him from the falling debris. Sparks from the collapsed timber landed on his shirt sleeve. He would have to drop the boy in order to smother the flames. Suddenly cloth from his tunic was draped over the sparks and they died out. Jordan's head swung around to stare at the child in his arms. The boy grinned up at him and he grinned back.

A few feet away, another support beam came crashing to the floor. Jordan's lips tightened into a grim line as he realized the Loyalists were also shooting at the roof. The boy's grin faded and he buried his face in Jordan's shoulder. He could feel the little body quaking with fear. He squeezed the youngster reassuringly while urgently casting about for a safe exit. Noting the back entrance was still not blocked, he called for the people around him to follow and headed in that direction.

Guests streamed all around them as they pushed their way through the back door. The earl held the boy close to keep him from being jostled. If he dropped him the crowd might unwittingly trample the youngster in their rush to reach safety. Once they were outside and safely clear of the crowd, he placed the boy on the ground. "We're going to find your mom," he promised the boy in a reassuring tone.

The boy pointed, excited. "There she is over there!"

Relieved, Jordan watched as the boy ran toward a middle-aged woman with outstretched arms. Gathering the child to her she smothered him in a tight embrace. She was holding her son so close Jordan wondered if she would ever let him go.

Hopefully she won't squash Greybeard.

Just then a small furry head poked its way out of the boy's side pocket. The corners of Jordan's lips lifted as he watched the whiskers twitch. The mother gave him a teary smile as she mouthed her thanks. He nodded in return.

Turning away from the happy reunion, he steeled himself to confront the villains responsible for the catastrophe, but was taken off guard when he got his first clear look at the extent of the damage.

"Bloody hell!" he cursed under his breath. The ancestral home of the Penbrooks was going up in flames and there wasn't a damned thing he could do about it.

The brick and stone outer walls had withstood the devastation but the roof was being eaten away by the fire. Through the windows he could see the inside of the fortress was also being completely consumed by the flames. He raced toward the front of the building.

Laural will be heartbroken since this was her favorite of all her holdings. But this is no time for sentimentality.

Last time he had glimpsed Laural she had still been inside.

Has she made it out yet?

He doubted it since he couldn't reach her telepathically. Knowing her, she would be the last to leave, and then only after she had personally made sure everyone else was safe. Laural would risk her own life if she felt there was even a chance that someone else was still in harm's way. Her ability to sacrifice herself for others was one of the things he loved most about her. He resolved to tell her that as soon as she was safely back in his arms.

After he rounded the corner of the building he began anxiously scanning the surrounding area. From what he could tell most of the visitors had escaped the destruction relatively unscathed. Now that a substantial amount of people had exited the castle, the perpetrators had turned tail. Hands fisting with impotent fury, the earl watched helplessly as the villains rode off.

Obviously, their purpose had been to create chaos and destruction. Having accomplished their goal, they no longer felt the need to face their foes.

Jordan counted ten figures on horse back fleeing the scene. There would be no way to catch up with them before they escaped into the woods, and once there, the cover of the trees would conceal their movement.

He scanned the front lawn. The staff was engaged aiding the injured and helping people to safety. The guests milled about, bewildered and frightened as they watched the blaze. Aside from a few minor wounds no one seemed to be seriously injured.

Where's Tim?

Projecting his query outward he requested a status update from his head of security. Within moments he got a response from Tim that he was still inside, rescuing some guests barricaded behind a blocked door.

As Jordan looked toward the front of the house again he noticed several staff members coming around the side. Carrying buckets of water and equipped with a gardening hose, they tried valiantly to put out the blaze. His gaze swept further out and he caught the first glimpse of approaching fire engines.

His attention shifted back once more to the Loyalists. As he watched they veered off the road and into the trees.

Should I try to go after them myself?

He projected outward again.

Why would Ben be blocking? Is there trouble with the artifacts?

Tension mounting, he searched the crowd and surrounding area. There was no sign of Ben or the men who had gone with him. If the artifacts were at risk that had to be his top priority.

Desperately, he searched for a glimpse of his love. Laural was not among the last wave of people surging from the castle. He probed and this time caught the barest psychic vision of her inside the fortress before she had time to block him.

Apprehension flooded through him as he examined the castle engulfed in the inferno. Smoke billowed out the doorway and windows. It was impossible to see inside.

If Laural is intentionally blocking me from her thoughts, that means either she's putting herself at risk in order to rescue people who were trapped or--

Fear for his beloved chased all other thoughts from his mind. Clamping down on his anxiety he raced toward the entrance.

His frantic flight toward the burning building was abruptly cut short when he spotted Ben Fletcher and two of his men carrying the remains of Arthur Gabriel toward the rear of the castle. All his original concerns about protecting the secrets of PS3 came crashing back as he tried to determine their destination. There was nothing in that direction but an old service road. His stomach muscles clenched. Something didn't feel right. He hoped that his uneasiness was stemming from the fact that they had never made definitive plans of where to reunite. But he couldn't keep his mind from flashing back to Tim's warning about a traitor.

This is absurd. Tim's talk about a leak has me seeing spies everywhere.

He looked in the direction the Loyalists had taken. It was the opposite direction of where Ben and his men were heading, but still Jordan's uncertainty grew.

I have to make sure the remains are safe—no matter what.

The earl moved to intercept the men. He tried to calm his fears as he hurried toward Ben.

If I can just get Ben to let me know where they're going, Laural and I can meet up with him later, after we've insured the safety of the diurnals.

About to call out a greeting, he stopped. The men were carrying the casket toward a waiting horse-drawn cart.

Did Ben radio other staff to come and pick up the artifacts?

Squinting he tried to make out the features of the driver. He didn't recognize him as any of their normal staff, but they had hired several extras, so he could be one of them.

The man turned his head.

Jordan's eyes widened in shock as he recognized his son.

Chapter 57:

Interception

Jordan bolted toward the cart. Sensing his presence, Nick looked up. His lips twisted maliciously as he lifted his gun and fired. Jordan dropped to the ground just in time to dodge the bullet whining past his shoulder.

With his face pressed to the dirt, Jordan could hear Nick issuing orders to the other porphyrians even while he continued to fire. The earl risked a glance, lifting his head just in time to see the traitors give one final heave and hoist the coffin into the cart.

Alarmed, Jordan started to get up.

No matter what else happened, the secret of PS3 must not fall into Nick's depraved hands.

Another bullet plowed into the ground directly to his right.

Thank goodness Nick's such a lousy shot.

Again he flattened himself against the lawn and listened intently for several more moments until the firing stopped.

Cautiously he lifted his head and helplessly watched as the remains of Arthur Gabriel, with all his secrets, were secured in the wooden cart.

Nick hastened back to the driver's seat while Ben and the other henchmen ran to intercept the earl. Scrambling to his feet Jordan pulled the gun from his waistband as he ran. He fired two shots at the approaching men. The ground was uneven and his arm unsteady. His aim went wide of the mark; he struck one porphyrian in the shoulder and the other in the neck. Both reeled back from the blows but Jordan knew they wouldn't be out of action for long.

He spared a glance for his son before refocusing his attention on Ben. To his surprise, Nick was still sitting with the cart drawn to the side of the rode, watching the battle.

He must want to insure I'm dead before he moves on.

Ben lifted his gun.

Jordan took aim. "Don't make me shoot you, Ben. Put the gun down."

For a moment Ben hesitated. He glanced from the earl to Nick. Ravensblood stared back, his face hardened, and the other man's resolve returned.

"Why?" Jordan probed silently.

"You wouldn't understand," Ben projected. "I didn't mean for things to turn out this way but now I have to see it through. I don't have any choice."

Jordan detected regret warring with resignation as Ben tightened his grip on the trigger. His brain refused to accept that Ben was the traitor even as his eyes stared down his friend's gun barrel. For an instant he wondered if he should try to break Nick's hold over the other man. But even as the thought was forming he realized that would take more time then he had left.

Before he could fire, another shot rang out and Ben crumpled to the ground.

Casting a glance over his shoulder, he found Tim Cooper glaring hard at the corpse. Two more shots rang out in rapid succession. Jordan's head spun around just in time to see the other henchmen collapse. Tim again took aim as he started determinedly toward the cart. Nick glared back defiantly at his pursuer. Abruptly Tim froze in place.

Jordan cursed under his breath as he dashed toward the cart. Hopefully, even his son's enhanced abilities would have limits.

If I can just distract Nick's focus from Tim long enough.

He fired as he ran.

Nick started when a bullet whizzed past his face. Blazing hatred seared Jordan's brain as their eyes clashed. Nick's gaze swept back and forth between the two men before he turned around and snapped the reins.

Freed from his temporary paralysis, Tim started after the vehicle.

Jordan intercepted his thoughts. "Leave him to me."

Paying no attention, Tim lowered his head and pumped his arms as he sprinted forward. Like a linebacker running for the goal he doggedly pursued his quarry. "He can't use mental domination on both of us at the same time. If we double-team him then at least one of us stands a chance of success."

He understood his security chief's premise. He'd also picked up on the fact that Nick couldn't focus on both of them at once. Tim's idea of double-teaming was a good one and might even succeed—or it might get him killed.

"Tim stop! Damn!" he exclaimed, realizing Tim was intentionally blocking to prevent him from giving a direct order to desist. He could force the issue but didn't want to take the time or be distracted. "You're no match for him," Jordan insisted.

Tim's only response was to run faster, picking up speed and closing the gap more quickly with each step.

"Damn it," Jordan projected exasperatedly, "if you want to be a hero then put your efforts where they'll really help. Laural's still inside the castle."

Jordan inwardly sighed with relief as he realized he had finally caught the man's attention.

Tim jerked to a halt and turned to stare back at the castle. Dark smoke and deadly flames could be seen spewing from the doors and windows.

He hesitated uncertainly and projected, "Are you sure? I'm not getting a reading from her."

Pressing his advantage Jordan continued to distract the man from plunging headlong into peril by projecting his concern. "That's my point," he insisted as he raced after the cart. It was gaining momentum but if he could just--

He leapt the last few feet and landed hard on top of the casket. "If she were safe she'd let us know. She's either intentionally blocking so we won't know she's taking a foolhardy risk trying to help someone or she's trapped and doesn't want us endangering ourselves by coming in after her."

Tim looked indecisively back and forth between the burning castle and the cart bearing his friend farther and farther away.

"If she's trapped you could be her only hope. Go, now!"

Tim ran back the way he had come, plunging toward the blazing Penbrook Castle. Jordan looked after him for a long moment. Guilt tore at him as he wondered if he had literally saved his friend from leaping into the frying pan just to toss him into the fire.

Chapter 58:

The Search

Laural headed toward her study. This was the last room she needed to check for guests before she could feel free to leave. She briefly considered investigating the second floor, but that section had been cordoned off from the visitors. She didn't sense any porphyrians upstairs, and if anyone were up there now, they were sure to be Loyalist infiltrators intentionally blocking and she was inclined to leave them to deal with the consequences of the fire they had started.

Time was running out and she knew it would only be a matter of minutes before Tim, Jordan or Ben came back in after her. She had received both Jordan's and Tim's enquiries but had deliberately blocked them so they wouldn't know where she was or what she was doing. She knew Jordan would guess what was going on, but, by that time, she hoped to be able to contact both of them from outside the burning building. By then it would be safe to let them know she had just been doing a final sweep. She knew an ear-blistering lecture was on the agenda, but better that than allowing them to put their lives at risk.

About to cross the study threshold she froze. Two men in costume along with two visitors were gathered in the room. One porphyrian was holding a gun on a diurnal couple while the other ransacked her desk. So intent were they on their task they hadn't even noticed her approach. Of course they wouldn't have any reason to think a porphyrian would be insane enough to risk spontaneous combustion by intentionally remaining inside a burning building. They must be extremely loyal to chance it themselves--either that or completely dominated by their leader.

"Would you just waste them already?" the one at the desk demanded of his companion. "They don't know anything and I could use your help--or did you forget there's a fire blazing through this place?"

His partner raised his gun but hesitated. A wicked grin split his face. "I'm up for a little fun. This job doesn't have many perks, but torturing an occasional diurnal is one of them. And this time it's like getting a bonus because once their bodies are incinerated no one will know what happened before the fire got them."

"Well, whatever you're going to do, be quick about it," snapped the man at the desk as he rifled through another drawer.

"Let's see," mused the porphyrian with the gun, staring at the female, "shall I mentally manipulate your husband into killing you?"

The woman's eyes filled with tears, her face paled. Her husband turned a sickly shade of grey as he began backing away from his spouse.

The armed porphyrian laughed at their obvious distress. "That would be fun but it would take too long. Since we're pressed for time I'll just kill you outright," he said, aiming his weapon at the man's mid-section. "Since stomach wounds take a long time **to** bleed out she gets to watch you dying, screaming in pain. While you're writhing in agony I'll mutilate and terrorize your wife to death while you watch."

Laural's blood boiled as she listened to the threats. Reaching into the pocket of her skirt she withdrew her pistol. She took aim and fired. The Loyalist who had been covering the diurnals dropped to the floor. The woman shrieked as blood and brains splattered out from the man's head wound. The husband quickly dove for his wife and yanked her behind him as the other Loyalist snatched his gun off the desk.

Lightning-quick reflexes combined with years of combat training had Laural firing before the other porphyrian even had time to turn around. Advancing into the room she smiled reassuringly at the couple. Their faces remained pale as they silently watched her approach. "I'm terribly sorry you had to go through that," she murmured soothingly, looking from the husband to the wife who was visibly shaking. The man placed a protective arm around the woman as Laural continued, "Don't worry, there aren't any more of them."

I should have sensed those two. If I hadn't been so distracted trying to block myself from Tim and Jordan I would have been better prepared.

The couple embraced for a long moment before turning their eyes to Laural again.

"What were you still doing in here?" Laural asked.

The woman started to push past her spouse.

"Hey, where do you think you're going?" Laural demanded. "Stop her," she commanded the husband.

The woman ignored Laural, and, rather than stopping her, the husband followed her as she headed toward the stairs.

"The reason we were still here is because we're looking for our daughter." The woman choked back a sob as she continued toward the staircase. "In the chaos we were separated. We've already searched all the rooms downstairs and were headed to check upstairs when…"

She gestured toward the bodies lying in the study in spreading pools of blood.

Laural glanced at the dead porphyrians.

It's obvious what they were looking for. Unfortunately for them, they found bullets instead of formulas.

"I can't let you go up there," she insisted.

"We're not leaving without our daughter," the father shot back.

She hated to do it but she had no time to debate the issue. One life at risk was bad enough; she wasn't taking chances with three. Projecting her will, the couple appeared confused for a few seconds, then, without another word, they changed direction and went back through the house and out the rear door. Laural knew her influence would disintegrate in a matter of minutes.

That's how long I have to find their lost child.

Anxiety ripped through Tim as gunshots alerted him to the true nature of Laural's plight. He flew across the last few yards as though he had wings on his feet.

Wasn't Mercury the ancient god known for speed?

He tore up the remaining distance to the castle, preferring to focus on anything besides what might be happening inside.

Apparently Ravensblood wasn't completely convinced that the formulas were in the coffin so had left some of his men to search the burning building. The gun fire could only mean one thing: Laural must be engaged in a battle with his henchmen.

The disoriented couple hovering near the back entrance confirmed his suspicions. It was clear they were shaking off the last remnants of influence.

Laural's or the Loyalists'?

He paused just long enough to determine if they had any information that would prove useful when planning his strategy. The couple was terrified, screaming at the top of their lungs that their daughter was still inside. The only thing that kept them from reentering was the raging fire now blocking the back door.

Undaunted, Tim broke through one of the windows. He had several cuts and a bloody fist for his trouble, but he paid the already-healing injuries no notice as he began prowling the castle. Desperately he swept the halls and scoured the rooms for any sign of Laural. Entering the study he briefly examined the two dead porphyrians. His anxiety grew when he recognized one as a specially-trained member of Ben's security team. He would have to do a thorough sweep of the agency's personnel to clear out all the infiltrators—providing any of them survived long enough for it to matter.

But where's Laural?

Again he reached out—nothing. His jaw tightened in frustration. Suddenly a slight movement caught his attention and he turned to see a man dressed in a page costume aim a gun at his head. He dove around the corner as the shot smashed into the wall where his head had been only a split second before.

Darting back into the hallway he gave silent thanks to the Penbrook forefathers who had built a design which enabled him to sneak around the adjacent hallway and come up on the Loyalist from behind. Stealthily he approached until he was almost on top of the man. Sensing danger at the last moment the traitor whirled on his attacker, swinging his gun at Tim's head.

Tim fired point-blank into the center of the man's forehead. The page collapsed a few feet from his fellow conspirators. After glancing disgustedly at the traitors Tim stepped over the bodies and headed toward the stairs.

Chapter 59:
A Battle in the Stairwell

Laural rushed through the upper floor of the castle. She hurried by every bedroom, scanning each one swiftly but thoroughly as she passed. Just then she became aware of another Loyalist entering the castle from below. She knew she had to deal with this new threat but she couldn't leave without the missing child. Relief swept through her when she sensed Tim Cooper downstairs.

I can count on Tim to take care of the intruder.

At the final room of the east wing, she paused. A child sat in the far corner of the room with a toy chest propped open by her side. She was holding a doll in each of her small hands. Laural smiled for a moment at the picture she presented. Then she recalled the raging fire just waiting to swallow them in its deadly jaws. Her smile faded as she remembered how anxious the parents had been when explaining that their child was missing.

Striving to project calmness that she didn't feel, she approached the little girl. The girl was so engrossed in her activity she didn't even notice the intrusion. Laural was momentarily thrown back in time. For an instant she recalled her own childhood and the times she had spent happily playing with the same figures. "Hi," she said softly, squatting down next to the young girl.

The girl glanced up. "Have you come to play with us?" she asked, beaming at her new playmate.

She shook her head. "I've come to take you back to your parents. They're very worried about you."

That was an understatement. The child's parents had been willing to risk their own lives to search for her.

She cringed, remembering she'd had to use influence to get them to leave without their child. Even now her persuasion might be wearing off and it would only be a matter of minutes before they attempted to reenter the burning building.

I can't blame them. I'd also be willing to risk my life to protect a loved one or to save someone I felt responsible for.

A stubborn look settled on the girl's face. "All Mommy and Daddy do is yell at each other. I like playing with the dolls better. They never fight."

"Well, we have a problem because there's a fire downstairs and we need to leave. I need you to come with me right now."

The girl clutched the dolls protectively against her chest. "Can I bring them with me? I don't want them to get burned."

"Okay, you take one and I'll take one. Now I need you to hold my hand and not let go no matter what."

The girl's eyes grew round and she was silent as she handed Laural one of the dolls. Laural gave her hand a reassuring squeeze.

I think she finally understands that this is serious.

The acrid smoke attacked them when they entered the hall. Looking around, she silently cursed. The bottom portion of the stairway she had raced up only minutes before was now blocked by a wall of fire. Turning, she pulled the girl in the opposite direction and headed toward the back staircase.

It was clear, but as they rounded the last bend in the stairwell, they stopped short. Just ahead lay the back entrance and safety, but they weren't going to make it--at least not without a fight. Three men were heading up the stairs toward them. She didn't recognize them.

Loyalists! But what could possess them to head up to the second floor of a burning building? Maybe they were sent by their leader to make sure I'm dead and to try to find the journals.

Her hands itched to get hold of them.

But what about the little girl? I can't send her back and I can't imagine the Loyalists would let her pass unharmed.

"Get behind me and stay there, no matter what happens," she ordered the child, handing her the other doll.

At that moment, the men spotted her. The one in front was drawing his gun. Laural paled.

If they start shooting in such close quarters, one of the bullets is bound to ricochet off the curved walls and hit the girl.

The same problem occurred to them. Once the shooting began they wouldn't be able to guarantee they wouldn't wind up on the wrong side of their own bullets. The second man held back his companion while drawing his sword.

Laural slipped her hand into the side slits of the gown. She had engineered it specifically for this purpose. Her sword gleamed and flashed in the dim glow of the wall sconces as she moved to intercept her adversaries. She struck the first blow before the man even had a chance to draw. The severed head dropped to the stairs and rolled down several steps. The girl screamed and started crying. The other two paused in their attack. They had been so focused on Laural they hadn't realized the little girl was there. Recovering quickly, they charged in unison.

Laural steeled herself for the double onslaught. Fortunately, fighting outnumbered odds had been required training by her mentor. She smiled slightly as her mind turned to thoughts of the earl. She prayed he had made it out and was safe because, right then, she couldn't afford any distracting thoughts.

She sized up the remaining attackers as she maneuvered her body into position. Protecting her head was vital at all costs. If they had any training, the shorter and stockier of the two would try and get in under her guard while his companion relied on his longer reach.

Revising her strategy, she braced for the attack. They pounced. The first aimed high and she was ready. The ringing of steel clashing against steel echoed through the stairwell as she blocked his assault. The second aimed low. Laural spun out a roundhouse kick which sent him sprawling. She tried to follow up with a quick slice that would have ended his threat, but the first one was on her again. He slashed at her repeatedly. She blocked but this time he caught her by surprise. Aiming low instead of high he managed to slide his blade straight across her midsection. The gash wasn't deep enough to damage any vital organs but stung like hell.

Laural gasped in shock and pain.

Anger dulled the agony as she intensified her attack. The man was no match for her and lost ground quickly. Her ferocious assault drove him back against the wall. Striking swiftly she sliced off his sword arm and followed up with the death blow. Blood spewed from severed arteries as his head hit the stairs with a thump. Quickly she spun to confront her remaining assailant.

A strangled gasp tore from her throat as she realized her mistake.

Jordan had warned her that her anger would get the better of her someday and he had been right. While she had been completely focused on the porphyrian who had hurt her, his comrade had taken the opportunity to sneak behind her and snatch her charge. He held the little girl imprisoned in his deadly embrace, his sword pressed tightly against her throat.

Chapter 60:
The Getaway

Jordan hung suspended over the asphalt while the cart careened down the road. Perspiration drenched his skin as he clung precariously to the back of the vehicle. Searing pain shrieked through his still-healing arm sockets when he yanked his body back over the edge. With a grunt, he landed on the wooden planks.

Barely pausing to catch his breath he scrambled to his feet. Nick was still speeding down the service road, wildly veering from one side to the other.

Oh no, you don't! You won't get rid of me that easily.

Gripping the sides of the cart for balance, he inched closer to the driver's seat. Half-crawling and half-dragging himself over the sarcophagus, he continued determinedly toward his goal.

In the distance he could make out a black van with its engine running, whitish smoke puffing out the exhaust pipe. Although unable to identify the occupants inside the van, he assumed they were collaborators. As he watched the vehicle started rolling forward. Gravel crunched under the tires as it moved to intercept them.

Now he understood their plan. The Loyalists had decided that because of the festivities, stealing the artifacts by using the cart would go unobserved. If anyone noticed they would have paid little attention, assuming it to be part of the event. Once the thieves rode into the woods, some of their party had doubled-back to provide transportation in order to whisk themselves and their treasure away from the area.

The cart hit a particularly big pot-hole and Jordan was almost knocked out of the wagon, but he managed to hold on.

If I'm going to prevail, I'll have to get the upper hand before Nick joins with the reinforcements.

Even without the extra interference his chance for success was already severely compromised by Nick's enhanced abilities. Once the other Loyalists intervened he would be outnumbered, outmaneuvered and overwhelmed.

Steadying his balance, Jordan continued to move ever closer to the driver's seat. Dark thoughts ate at him as he considered how the Loyalists had been able to corrupt Ben Fletcher. He had been sincerely shocked and truly disappointed by the other man's duplicity. Ben had been a devoted and trusted member of their facility, and, even more than that, he had been a friend to Laural for years. She would be deeply wounded by his betrayal.

Maybe that had been the point. I wouldn't put it past someone as perverted as my son to gain sadistic satisfaction from eroding Ben's integrity and using him against the very person he was pledged to protect. We'll need to re-evaluate our entire staff--even those at the highest levels of authority--as potential traitors.

Clambering across the final few feet separating them he reached out to grab Nick's tunic. Before he could make contact the other man twisted around in his seat. Jordan was momentarily taken aback by the depth of hatred in the hard green eyes. Nick raised his whip and struck Jordan hard. The earl lifted his arm to block the blow, and, off balance, he staggered back, barely able to keep from falling over the edge.

He thrust his hand inside his pocket for his gun. Realizing his intention Nick struck his father again and ripped the gun from his hand.

Jordan staggered and began to topple over the side. Just as the ground was rushing up to meet him he made one final grab and caught hold of the other porphyrian.

Chapter 61:
The Hostage

"You know the drill," the Loyalist said coldly to Laural, eyeing her warily. "Drop your weapon."

Laural tried to get a reading on him. Of course, he was blocking her but from what she could tell he was serious. Should she try to overpower his will in order to mentally maneuver out of the situation? Her face hardened. Mental manipulation was always trickier on her own kind, with no guarantee of the outcome.

Still, if there was even a chance…

The girl whimpered. Laural's gaze flicked from the Loyalist's stony features to the girl's frightened face. Her eyes were enormous and her lower lip trembled. Laural could tell she was on the verge of crying out. She wasn't sure what effect the noise would have on the porphyrian, but considering their low regard for diurnals, she assumed he wouldn't have much tolerance. Even if she could use mental persuasion, there would be no way to completely insure the child's safety.

"Don't worry," she reassured the girl as she dropped her sword, "everything will be alright."

"Yes, it will," agreed the man in a malicious tone. "Now the gun."

Laural hesitated and his sword arm moved a fraction of an inch. The girl started to cry as a trickle of blood ran down her neck. Instinctively the girl dropped the dolls and reached to push the blade away. A sadistic grin split the man's face when the sword sliced into her hands and she yelped in pain.

Laural inwardly winced as she reached inside the inner pocket of her gown and withdrew her pistol. She looked at it regretfully for an instant before dropping it to the steps. The metal made a sharp clang as it hit the stone and tumbled several steps further down the stairwell.

While keeping a watchful eye on her, the porphyrian maneuvered himself to cut off any ability to retreat. "We're going to take this nice and slow." He kicked her gun and sword further down the stairs then deliberately stomped on one of the dolls. "You're going down first. Try anything and the girl dies."

Laural stared grimly at the smashed fragments of porcelin then up to confront the Loyalist. "How do I know you just won't kill us both once my back is turned?"

"I've got other plans for you. I'm taking you to someone who very much would like to get reacquainted. As for the girl," he shrugged, "once your back is turned you won't know—unless you'd prefer to go down backwards."

The mockery in his voice made her blood run hot, then cold. Tilting her chin defiantly she continued to face them while backing down to the next step.

He grinned when she took the bait but continued to eye her suspiciously. "Fine, but remember one false move and the kid gets skewered."

Laural's mind raced as she backed slowly down another step. It was obvious he was going to take her to Nick. Once the child had served her purpose as a hostage and Laural fulfilled whatever diabolical plan Nick had for her, he would have no compunction about killing both of them.

If the girl's going to have a chance to get away, it will have to be before we're in the Loyalist leader's clutches.

She eyed her adversary. He was prudently keeping enough steps between them to deprive her of any potential for an easy attack.

"Laural, where are you? Damn it, answer me!"

A burst of hope shot through her. In all the excitement she had forgotten about Tim. She kept her face a blank mask as she mentally responded to the silent query. "Tim, we're in the back stairwell."

"Well, it's about time you responded. Are you alright?"

She projected the details of her predicament to the security chief, being careful to block the message from her assailant. "Hurry!" she pleaded. "I don't know what this sick bastard might do."

Tim slipped stealthily around the corner leading to the back stairwell. The smoke seeping up from the lower level stuck in his throat and he almost coughed. Repressing the impulse, he peered around the edge of the entrance leading into the stairway. It was rather dark but his heightened senses allowed him to see well enough.

Laural was standing several feet further down the stairs, facing him. He knew she was aware of his presence, but she managed to keep from betraying him. A few steps above her stood a man holding a little girl of about eight. Tim's face reddened with anger as he realized the man was holding a sword to the girl's throat. His fury mounted when he watched the man, for no apparent reason, give a malicious yank on the girl's long brown hair.

Laural gasped as the girl yelped in pain. Tim immediately understood. The man was intentionally goading her. Tim inched closer, knowing he would only get one shot at the porphyrian before the man realized his peril. If he missed, he would place both the girl and Laural in jeopardy. Carefully he took his stance, stretched out his arms and aimed. Everything had to be timed perfectly. He waited, hardly daring to breath.

"Now!" commanded Laural.

He squeezed the trigger.

Laural dove for the man just as the gun blast echoed through the stairwell. The loyalist's hand convulsively tightened as the bullet struck, but Laural had already yanked his arm away and snatched the girl from his grasp. Thrusting the girl behind her, she kicked out and sent the man's blade sailing into the darkness. The porphyrian collapsed face down on the stones.

Laural pulled the sobbing child into her arms and held her while offering words of comfort. She heard Tim Cooper's steps ringing out on the cold stone floor as he rushed to join them.

"Watch out!" Tim yelled from several stairs above.

Laural looked up just in time to see the porphyrian, gun in hand, taking aim at her head.

Chapter 62:
The Death Blow

Time seemed to pass in slow motion as Laural watched the porphyrian pull the trigger. Instinctively she threw herself between the oncoming bullet and the girl.

So, this is how it all ends.

She was amazed that part of her mind could remain detached about her own imminent death. Regrets seized her at the thought of leaving Jordan and not being able to resurrect her family's heritage. The legacy of her ancestors would just have to continue through her cousin's lineage--assuming he survived his battle with his son.

For an instant she considered checking in to see how he was doing. To connect with him one last time was almost too much of a temptation to deny, but memories of being telepathically linked with her mom when she was dying strengthened her resolve. She would gladly forego the last moment of her own emotional comfort if it would spare Jordan that agony.

Time reasserted its grip on reality as the gun fired. For a split second she stared into the malicious smile of the Loyalist, then he vanished from view, replaced by the bulk of her bodyguard as he dove in front of her.

"No!" she screamed as Tim Cooper's body fell at her feet.

Tears blurred her vision but she hurriedly brushed them away as she knelt by the side of her loyal guardian and friend. The shot had embedded itself right in the center of Tim's forehead--the death blow for any porphyrian.

She lifted anguished eyes to confront those of Tim's killer. For the moment, the Loyalist appeared as stunned as she was by the unexpected intervention. Before he could recover, she snatched the fallen sword from the floor. Swept away by a tidal wave of rage and grief, she leapt across Tim's body to attack her enemy. Again he raised his gun. Laural slashed down. The gun fired. Searing pain ripped across her hairline. The Loyalist's severed head rolled down several stairs then stopped to glare accusingly up at her.

A tear-filled wail began to build in the back of her throat. She swallowed down the cry as she spied the girl, staring in shocked silence at the sight of the carnage. Sheathing the blade, she walked over, picked up the child and hurried down the stairs. A few feet further down, she stopped. She sensed other Loyalists in the castle and on the grounds. She needed to be as prepared as possible in case they encountered any more trouble before they reached safety. Setting the girl down, she searched for her gun.

"Look!" the girl cried out, drawing her attention. Following the child's gaze, she gasped. The fire which had started in the front of the building had had time to work its way to the back. Now their exit to the rear door was completely engulfed in flames.

Thinking fast, Laural hastily hoisted the girl up into her arms and tucked her face into her shoulder. She charged back the way they had come.

Our only chance of escaping is going to be through one of the upper-level windows.

Taking the stairs two at a time she soon passed the bodies of Tim Cooper and her assailants lying in a widening pool of blood. Skirting the carnage she felt another moment of overwhelming sadness but didn't dare look down. Her grief would have to wait. If she paused to view her friend's body one more time she might not be able to leave him behind.

Smoke burned her lungs and clouded her vision as she raced down the hallway. Flames licked their way down the passage as the greedy fire continued to feed off the hardwood floors and wooden support beams. Frantically, Laural dove into her bedroom. Hastily she dropped the girl on the bed and pulled open the large bay window.

Heart pounding and her breath catching in her throat, she stood motionless for what felt like a very long time, staring down at the ground. Nausea gripped her and a wave of dizziness caused her to sway slightly. Closing her eyes she prayed for it to pass.

A tug on her gown brought her back into focus. She glanced down. The terrified child was grabbing her skirt with one hand and pointing out the door with the other. The fire was at the bedroom door. Tongues of red yellow and orange were snaking their way up the walls and across the floor.

Galvanized into action, she snatched the sheets from her bed, knotted them together and tied the end to the bedpost nearest the window. Using all her strength, she gave a mighty heave and pushed the heavy wooden structure flush against the window seat. "Climb on my back, honey," she directed, squatting next to the girl, "and whatever you do don't let go."

The girl did as she was told. Laural climbed on the sill and immediately turned her back on the view. Holding tightly to the sheet rope, she inched her way out the window and began the descent.

Thirty feet shouldn't be a big deal. I've climbed structures much higher. And since I'm going down, every move brings me closer to the ground.

She descended steadily but cautiously. She made sure of her footing and handholds. With each shifting movement she compensated for the girl's additional weight.

The girl screamed, "Look!"

Laural glanced over her shoulder. The girl was pointing back in the direction they had come. She looked up to see the fire eating its way through their sheets. She quickly glanced down to gauge their distance. Vertigo enveloped her. She slipped and the sheet rope swayed wildly. The girl screamed as they hung suspended.

"It's okay." Laural gritted out between clenched teeth while she tried to get her racing heart under control. Spontaneously her mind flashed onto the image of her and her father dropping from this very castle thirty years before. It was a fall which had cost her father his life and initiated her acrophobia.

Firmly, she banished the memory. Regaining her grip on the sheets and her footing on the wall, she told the girl in a voice sounding much calmer then she felt, "We're going to jump down the rest of the way, and I need you to hold tight and not let go. Can you do that?"

The girl nodded against her back.

She carefully shifted her position so she was facing outward. Briefly she looked up. The fire had eaten almost entirely through the sheet rope. If she didn't do it now the decision would be made for her. Taking a deep breath, she used her legs to push outward away from the inferno, and jumped.

Chapter 63:
Leap of Faith

"Your dress is on fire!" shrieked the girl as they hit the ground.

Laural pulled the girl over her head and tossed her several feet away before rolling across the lawn. Over and over she spun, rotating back and forth until the flames were out. A scream of agony tore from her lips as the last of the flames were smothered by her skin. She lay on the ground, panting from her exertions, until the little girl came to stand over her.

They stared at each other for a long moment then the girl held out her hand. Laural's lips curved as she placed her hand in the much smaller one. Reaching into her pocket as she rose Laural tugged out the second doll and handed it to the girl.

"You did such a good job of saving her I think you should keep her."

The girl's eyes sparkled as she hugged the doll tightly to her chest. "I'm going to name her Laural," she announced happily.

You know something," she said hugging the girl and the doll, "I don't even know your name."

"Victoria," she responded still smiling, "but everyone calls me—"

"Tori, Tori!"

"Mommy!" she exclaimed excitedly as she spun about and ran toward the woman Laural had influenced earlier to leave the castle.

"Thank God, you're alright," she said breathlessly as she held the girl in her arms.

"Tori." The name rang in Laural's ears as a lump rose in her throat. For a moment she was captured then held prisoner by the past. Tears blurred her vision while she watched the happy reunion.

"Mommy, you have to meet Laural. She gave me this," she exclaimed while waving the doll, "and saved me from the fire and the bad men."

Smiling, the woman walked forward holding out her hand. "I don't believe we were ever actually introduced. I'm Sheila Johnson. Thank you so much for rescuing my daughter. I don't know what happened. One minute she was right beside me and the next she was gone. I'm sorry for all the trouble we caused earlier, but once the fire started and we couldn't find her, my husband and I were out of our minds with worry."

Laural blinked away her tears. "I'm Laural Gabriel." She shook the other woman's hand. "Your reaction was perfectly understandable. I'm just glad everything turned out the way it did and your little girl is safe."

They were approaching the front of the castle and Laural gasped when she caught her first complete view of the ruined structure. The roof was destroyed and all the wooden fixtures had been eaten away by the fire. Local authorities and the press had arrived in full force. The firefighters were focused on putting out the blaze while photographers and camera crews took shots of the ravaged castle. Laural skirted the crowd when she spied a reporter, microphone in hand, interviewing several onlookers.

Being hounded by the press is the last thing I need right now.

Peering past the maze of people and equipment she tried to examine her home. She couldn't get a clear view but from what she could glimpse of the inside she could tell her ancestral dwelling would not survive the damage.

"So am I," stated Mrs. Johnson emphatically as she trailed behind the marchioness. "I'm really sorry about your home," she offered, noting the direction of Laural's gaze.

"Mommy, you should have seen Laural when she chopped off the bad guys' heads," volunteered Tori, regaining both women's attention.

Laural winced as she considered how to explain the situation to Tori's mother.

Just then a man in his mid-forties rushed toward them.

"Tori! Thank God!" exclaimed the man as he reached down and lifted the girl off her feet.

"You remember Tori's dad," explained Sheila.

"Yes, I do" responded Laural with a smile.

"Tori has a very active imagination," explained her mother. After a beat, she added, "I'm just glad you did whatever was necessary to keep my daughter safe."

Laural nodded, relieved not to have to make excuses. Her eyes strayed toward the people clustered at the front of the castle. She searched the throng of onlookers. She picked out several staff members dressed in costumes. The Loyalists had disappeared, but her relief quickly shifted to concern.

Where's Jordan?

Noticing two EMTs carrying a stretcher, she excused herself and hurried toward the ambulance. Pausing by the side of the stretcher she stared down into the lifeless face of Ben Fletcher. Shock and pain twisted her heart when she realized she had lost both of her chiefs of security. These men hadn't just been staff members but also close friends. Grief threatened to overwhelm her, but she beat it down.

She stood rooted to the spot while her mind tried to fathom the implications.

If Ben's dead, it most likely means the Loyalists have the artifacts. And what about Jordan? If he was able to, he would have been actively seeking me out by now.

Her mind projected outward to search for the earl.

She caught an image of Jordan and Nick engaged in mortal combat by the side of one of the show carts. As her connection with Jordan deepened, she felt his anxiety when a sudden paralysis overtook him and he fell to the ground at Nick's feet.

At that moment, Jordan became aware of her presence. He blocked her from his thoughts--but not before she registered the surroundings.

Lifting the hem of her gown she began to run.

Chapter 64:
Family Secrets

Nick Ravensblood glared down at the Earl of Rockford's body lying in the dirt at his feet.

At last I'll have my revenge. Only the complete destruction of my enemy could compensate for the centuries of devastation suffered by the Maxwells.

He kicked Jordan in the ribs. His sire grunted in pain but remained motionless. Completely at his mercy, the other man could do nothing to prevent his abuse. This final triumph caused a broad grin to break out on Nick's face as he reveled in his enhanced powers.

"That much pride usually comes right before a fall."

Nick scowled down at his father. "The only one who appears to have fallen is you," he jeered, kicking him again.

Jordan grunted but said nothing.

Squatting next to the earl, Nick patted him down while holding a gun to his head. "Now," he said, standing, "You're going to tell me everything you know about PS3, starting with where the journals are actually located."

"I don't have the slightest idea. And even if I did I certainly wouldn't tell you."

The black van drew up alongside of them. Nick raked Jordan with one more disdainful glare then strode over to slide the side door open. The Loyalist in the front passenger seat started to get out.

"Don't bother," Nick commanded, "the earl's not in a position to cause us any trouble."

He returned to gloat over his father's prone body. "I'm sure you'll prove much more cooperative once we have more time for a private chat."

"The only thing I'd like to chat about," Jordan growled, "is what you did to Ben Fletcher to make him betray us."

Nick shrugged. "That's not the topic I would have chosen for our final father-son chat, but, to satisfy your curiosity, it seems everyone has their price--even those you think you can trust. You'd be surprised how many times self-interest will change your most loyal friends into the bitterest of enemies. In Ben Fletcher's case, I had something he cared about more then his loyalty to Laural, the mission or the foundation."

"I don't believe you." Jordan was adamant. "I think it's much more likely that you used mental domination to force Ben's compliance."

"If you actually believe that, you really are naive," Nick stated derisively. "Most people will do the right thing only until it smacks up against the hard wall of their own greed. Yes, I used influence on Ben Fletcher," he agreed, "but only after he started to regret the choice he made. Have no doubt, he came to me of his own free will."

"What would possibly have made him do that?"

"He did it because I had something that you, with all your ethics and integrity, couldn't provide."

"What could you have possibly offered Ben that would make him turn his back on everything he believed in?"

"The ability to procreate with a diurnal," explained Nick triumphantly.

Jordan's eyes filled with despair. Even though he had been interested in the reason behind Ben's betrayal, he had hoped the distraction would cause Nick to drop his guard long enough so he could free himself from the paralysis.

"Nice try," Nick commended, reading his father's thoughts, "but, as you can see, useless. Enough with the small talk. The brief reading I got from you while you were in the tower enabled me to determine that, before he died, Andrew Gabriel passed on the secret of the PS3 formula to you. He also provided you with the location of the documents. The marquis, however, must not have trusted you completely," Nick smirked, "because rather then letting you know outright, he embedded the information deeply in your subconscious. Then he erected a mental barrier to insure that only in the event of the last Penbrook dying without an heir would your memory be triggered."

Jordan closed his eyes trying to work through what he had just been told.

"So," he reasoned, opening his eyes to confront his son, "if I had the secret of PS3 all along, why the elaborate hoax that you were an archeology professor interested in the Penbrook estate? Unless," he mused, "you were just looking for a way to keep Laural distracted."

Nick shook his head. "You attach too much importance to your lover. I would never have gone to that much trouble just to keep the Gabriel bitch distracted." He grabbed hold of Jordan's arms and dragged him toward the van. "By the way," he asked, "how did you find her in bed? Quite a wild cat, isn't she? Tell me, Dad, did you make her scream and beg while you were inside her? Or maybe she wasn't quite as unrestrained with you?"

Jordan flushed as he felt the blood pounding in his head, but he ignored the taunts, knowing Nick was intentionally baiting him. Instead he focused on his son's revelations about the journals.

Could Andrew really have buried something so deeply inside my mind that I was completely unaware of it? If so, then he was more powerful than anyone had comprehended. But his plan was flawed: he never anticipated dying and leaving an heir who hadn't been endoctrinated.

"Hey, Nick," called the driver, "I think we should get moving before someone spots us."

Nick glared at the driver over his shoulder.

How dare he question my judgment?

The porphyrian paled as the full force of his leader's displeasure penetrated. Swallowing hard he turned his attention back to the road. If he was lucky his leader's involvement with the earl would distract him enough so he would forget the insubordination. He glanced sidelong at his partner in the opposite seat, but he was studiously avoiding being drawn into the conflict.

Certain that he had quelled any more interruptions, Nick refocused on his prisoner. Just then a fist connected with his jaw. He staggered back a step.

Damn it! He took advantage of the distraction provided by my idiot driver.

Jordan followed up with a quick kick to the stomach. Nick doubled over, the wind knocked out of him. Before the earl could take a step to flee, the Loyalist in the passenger seat tackled him from behind and they both fell to the ground.

The other man was no match for the earl and Jordan had him off his back in a split second—but that was all the time it took for Nick to regain his control.

Jordan's heart sank as the numbing paralysis enveloped him again.

Chapter 65:

Reunion

"Nice try," Nick said, walking over and waving the gun in Jordan's face, "but if you give me any more trouble, I'll project your location to Laural and happily shoot her right between the eyes when she comes to rescue you. Before you die you can have the burden of knowing you brought about her death." At his father's stricken look, he laughed. "By the way, your suppositions were correct," said Nick, responding to his earlier conjectures.

Jordan shuddered as he understood his thoughts were no longer his own. He hadn't been victimized by that kind of violation since Craven. "In that case it was never really the artifacts you were after."

"On the contrary. Since the legend was that the journals were buried with Arthur Gabriel, I originally thought I needed them in order to exploit the secret. It was only after my brief link with you in the tower that I understood the secret was already within my grasp."

Nick's eyes bored into Jordan's brain. Never breaking eye contact he delved further and penetrated deeper until he reached a spot Jordan didn't even know existed.

Jordan moaned and closed his eyes, in a vain attempt to ward Nick off, but it was no use.

I can't allow Ravensblood to get this knowledge. If he does it will mean the demise of both species.

Desperately, Jordan threw up a mental barrier, but Nick thrust past his defenses as easily as drawing aside a curtain then savagely ripped what he wanted right out of Jordan's brain. The flood gates abruptly opened and all the subconscious secrets came pouring out.

"You were right, Father," Nick said, hoisting Jordan up against the bumper of the van, "for all the good it does you now. It wasn't until you were imprisoned in the tower that I learned you, not these irrelevant objects, held the secret to PS3. Right before I was going to kill you, I gleaned the truth that you held the information that I needed. Since I realized it would require extra effort and involve a struggle to break through your mental barriers, I figured if the stranger who interrupted us could give me what I wanted without the hassle, then so much the better. I'm sure you can imagine my disappointment to discover the whole charade was just a hoax designed to lure me away while you were liberated."

"So sorry you were disappointed," Jordan said sarcastically.

Nick shrugged. "It doesn't matter, now that I've set things right. How ironic that it will be my own father that gives me what I need in order to realize my destiny. I knew all along taking the artifacts would cause either you or the Gabriel bitch to come running. Either way I'd win. If you came, I could get what I needed directly, and use you as a hostage to lure Laural into my trap. And the genius of my plan is it would have worked exactly the same in reverse. Too bad for Andrew Gabriel that his precaution didn't take into account the existence of a porphyrian who would be so powerful from a lifetime of ingesting human blood that he could penetrate his friend's mind on that deep of a level."

Now that Nick had everything he needed, the earl was completely expendable. His father's jade green eyes stared back at him, a mirror image of his own. He was so transparent that he didn't even need to read him to know what he was thinking.

"After I dispatch you," he informed the earl, "I'm going to take my time maiming and torturing Laural before I kill her. How long her torment lasts before I allow her to die depends on whether or not she's carrying my child. Once I have proof that my created supplement is a success, I'll truly be free of the curse of the Penbrooks. Then I, and only I, will be at the head of our race. The diurnals will never know what hit them. I predict that within three generations," he said, attaching the silencer before aiming the gun between Jordan's eyes, "we'll have procreated to such an extent we'll dominate the planet. Then we'll see which species has to skulk in the shadows in order to survive."

Jordan closed his eyes as he waited for the shot to come.

I've failed completely. I wasn't able to protect the Penbrook family secrets, the diurnals, Dana, or Laural.

His last regret would be never to see Laural again.

If there's an afterlife, I won't be able to hold my head up when I see my dear friend the Marquis of Penbrook with the weight of having left Laural to this bastard on my soul.

"Fortunately, that won't be a problem."

The gun went off but Jordan felt no pain.

Is this what it's like to be dead? A feeling of nothingness?

Then his mind registered what he had heard. His eyes snapped open to confront Andrew Gabriel, Marquis of Penbrook, standing over the corpse of Nicholas Ravensblood.

Reality tilted as Jordan looked from the lifeless body of his son to the man dressed in velvet tunic, striped hose and feathered cap with his gun still aimed at the Loyalist leader.

"Now I know I'm dead," he whispered hoarsely.

Andrew jerked Jordan away from the van just as the engine revved. Tires spun and kicked up dirt and gravel as the driver gunned the engine. Andrew leapt past Jordan and into the van. Taking aim he fired first into the head of the driver, then at the other henchman. Both porphyrians fell forward, dead.

The corners of the marquis's lips lifted as he held out his hand. Jordan's eyes traveled over the outstretched hand, up the length of Andrew's arm and finally rested on his friend's face. He stared for a long moment.

Andrew's been dead for over three decades. Maybe I've died and this is his spirit.

"I'm not a ghost and you're not dead."

He gazed deeply into the turquoise eyes, took the proffered hand and allowed himself to be helped up.

"Andrew, is it really you?" he asked, shaking off the last vestiges of the paralysis. Still reeling from the unexpected turn of events he watched as his lifelong companion ducked inside again to snap off the ignition then they both moved away from the vehicle.

Before the marquis could answer a loud shriek sounded from behind them. Both men turned just in time to watch Laural, from several feet away, catapult herself into her father's outstretched arms.

Epilogue

REFLECTIONS

Sun glinted off the windshield as the limosine pulled into the parking lot of Washington General Hospital. As she waited for the driver to park, Laural's thoughts rewound to review the extraordinary events of the past several days. She could hardly comprehend her father's miraculous survival. Although he had been their constant companion for the past several days, she still kept periodically touching him in order to reassure herself that he was real. Even now as her hand squeezed his she gave an inward sigh of relief when she felt the return pressure.

"I'm not a product of your imagination and I'm not going anywhere," he assured her again. He continued to grasp her hand tightly for a moment then released it just long enough to slip an arm around her shoulders.

"I can understand how she feels," asserted Jordan from the opposite seat. He eyed his friend as if he, too, expected the marquis to disappear as suddenly as he had reappeared several days ago. "This does take some getting used to since, for the past thirty years, we thought you were dead."

"And I'm still having a hard time getting my mind around the incredible story you told us," insisted Laural, shaking her head. "The idea that you spent most of the past three decades in some remote African village with no idea of who you were sounds like a story you'd read about in a novel."

Andrew closed his eyes as his daughter's words provoked an onslaught of memories:

The five-hundred-foot fall from his castle tower onto the Cornish cliffs, and the subsequent plunge into the Atlantic, should have killed him. Lord knew he'd wanted to die badly enough because without his beloved Victory he hadn't thought life was worth living.

When he opened his eyes a mist of unshed tears had dulled the turquoise depths. Pretending to be distracted by the scenery, he swung his head to look out at the parking ,lot. He was certain his heart had remembered he had a daughter--no matter how much his mind had wanted to give up. Because of his devotion to the child born out of his love for Victory, he had clung to life even after being batted about like a soggy rag doll on the ocean waves for he knew not how long. Somehow the salt water had aided in the healing process and he had still been alive when a fishing vessel had spied his body and retrieved him from his watery grave. He had slowly but steadily revived, only to discover he had amnesia.

He had never figured out whether the memory loss was due to the head injury, the emotional trauma, or a combination of the two. When the ship, which had been bound for Africa, put into port, he had disembarked. He wandered for months until he had come to a small village. Even though he had no idea why, the occupants were vaguely familiar. So he had remained there, hoping to recover his memory.

Eventually he became aware that there were captives being held within the village. Curiosity tinged with a disquieting sense that there was something he had in common with the captors and their prisoners drove him to covertly explore their compound.

The shock of finding Dana Maxwell's decapitated head had brought about spontaneous and complete memory recall.

"I still can't believe she's dead," said Jordan soberly.

Surprised, Andrew turned from the window to regard his friend. The look Jordan gave him made him aware he had been unintentionally projecting at least part of his thoughts. "I know," he agreed. "Regretfully that part of Nick's story was true."

The three of them sat silently while each reflected on their memories of Dana. At last Jordan spoke. "Dana's life was always so emotionally chaotic, maybe in death she's finally found peace."

"Let's hope so."

The limosine glided to a halt in front of the entrance, but no one made a move to get out. "What I can't get over," stated Laural, "is how you kept the fact you were alive from us even after you returned."

Andrew studied his daughter's lovely face which was so much like her mother's it made his heart ache. He understood her statement was an expression of her emotional distress rather than an accusation.

He reiterated what he had told her earlier. "I'm sorry for the pain I caused you, *ma petite*, but I was concerned that if you or Jordan discovered the truth, you wouldn't be able to keep it from Ravensblood. If he knew I was still alive and presented a real threat to his scheme, he'd have changed his plans accordingly. I thought that we'd have the best chance of maintaining the upper hand if I kept my participation a secret."

She nodded. Her mind understood but her heart still ached.

Gently cupping his hand under her chin, he lifted her face. "It was hard on me too," he assured her. "I wanted so badly to reach out to you and let you know I was here, but given the severity of the situation I had to do what I thought was best for everyone."

"I know now that you implanted the information about PS3 in my subconscious, but were there ever actually any journals?" asked Jordan, deliberately changing the subject. He knew Laural well enough to realize she was struggling for composure and needed an emotional break.

The Marquis of Penbrook looked at their expectant faces. He reached into the inner pocket of his jacket and withdrew three leather-bound notebooks.

THE PATIENT

Laural and Jordan stood staring at the closed hospital room door for a long moment. Laural tapped lightly. A muffled voice called a greeting. Jordan juggled the large bouquet of roses as he pushed the door open to admit his fiancée. There were already several other flower arrangements decorating the otherwise sterile area. Jordan placed their offring on a nearby table while Laural took a seat next to the bed.

The woman's eyes slowly traveled over their features, shifted to their flowers, and then settled back on the marchioness. For a moment her face took on a quizzical look. Then recognition dawned and she attempted a smile that did nothing to ease her haggard expression. "It was really nice of you to come, Lady Gabriel," she offered half-heartedly.

Laural smiled briefly as she squeezed the other woman's hand.

Linda was hardly recognizable as the perky and pretty graduate student she had known at the dig site. Her ordeal had permanently embedded lines in her face and deep shadows behind her eyes. "Considering the circumstances, I thought I should tell you in person about the fire and Nick's death."

"That was very considerate of you," she responded listlessly.

"This is my fiancé and business partner, Jordan Rush," she explained as Jordan extended his hand.

For a moment Linda stared deeply into the jade green eyes. Questions trembled on her lips as she lost herself in the earl's steady gaze. Her eyes became vacant then haunted and she remained silent for several more seconds.

"We were both truly sorry to hear about your loss," offered Jordan, stepping back.

His words seemed to break her morose trance. Linda smiled ruefully. "I'd really hoped to give Nick the child he so desperately wanted. He was so excited when he found out I was pregnant. I was certain the babies would entice him to stay with me. Then when even that didn't keep us together, I consoled myself with the thought that at least I would have the twins as a reminder of our relationship. Now all that's over."

Laural and Jordan exchanged glances. "Did you say twins?" Laural clarified.

Linda nodded her head drowsily. "Yes, If I hadn't miscarried I would have had twin boys."

Stunned, the two porphyrians stared at the woman, suddenly understanding. "This could have turned out worse then we even imagined," Jordan projected to Laural.

"Let's just be grateful that his attempt at cross-breeding didn't bear fruit," replied Laural silently.

Jordan reached out to place a comforting hand on Linda's arm. "You're still young and you'll have other children."

She stared back sadly. "But they won't be Nick's."

Laural nodded solemnly as she and Jordan looked at each other.

Linda's eyelids fluttered closed then dragged open again as the sedative a nurse had given her minutes earlier started to take hold. "It's such a shame that Nick died before he could become a father or famous. I read in the paper that the fire destroyed everything. I'm sorry you lost your home and your ancestor's remains."

"Thank you," replied Laural, briefly placing a hand on the other woman's arm, "I've already started plans to rebuild my ancestral home. As for the artifacts—the estate is so large I'm sure it holds many other historical treasures just waiting to be discovered."

"But I doubt there will ever be another find like King Arthur."

Laural looked across the hospital bed to meet her fiance's eyes. "No, there will never be another one like King Arthur."

"Thank you for coming," murmured Linda just before she drifted into sleep.

SEED OF HOPE

Nine Months Later

Andrew Gabriel, Sixth Marquis of Penbrook, paced agitatedly across the floor of his cousin's Georgetown brownstone. He cringed as another shriek of agony tore through the house. For what seemed like a diurnal lifetime, he had been impotently waiting and listening while his beloved daughter fought for her life.

For a moment his mind dropped back almost five decades to land on the day when he had been expecting the birth of his own child. Shuddering slightly, he relived the fear and anxiety which had gripped him while waiting for his wife's agony to end. Eventually he had been rewarded for his endurance. Overwhelming joy had replaced deep apprehension when his wife had come through the ordeal safely and he had held his baby in his arms. Now that same daughter was providing a repeat performance, and as the captive audience all he could do was wait for the drama to unfold.

Another scream echoed through the house. He raked his hand through his platinum hair and headed to the bar to pour a stiff drink. After downing the first scotch, he poured another. Sipping the second more slowly, he succumbed to temptation and projected his concern to Jordan.

Jordan Rush, Earl of Rockford, silently winced as he clenched his wife's hand. Bending forward he used a damp cloth to wipe the sweat from her face. Laural's eyes met his briefly then squeezed shut as another contraction tore through her.

"Your father wants to know how you're doing."

"Tell him," she gasped, "that I'm dying a prolonged tortuous death. Tell him I can now understand why Dana didn't want to have her baby. Tell him—aaaah!"

He grimaced. "She's doing as well as can be expected," he responded silently while attempting to keep his dread from projecting itself to Laural's father.

"One more ought to do it," coached the midwife. "Come on now—push!"

Laural glared at the woman. The midwife took a step back. Her eyes became unfocused and her jaw slack.

Jordan glanced between the two women. "Laural," he whispered sharply. "Laural!" He grabbed her chin, jerking her head around to face him. The midwife shook herself and sprang back into action.

Jordan felt the searing pain jolt through him as his wife's tortured gaze penetrated his mind. All her agony from the relentless ripping apart of her insides became his own. He staggered slightly but stood firm and tried to breathe evenly as he held her gaze.

Laural wasn't sure if she could go through with this. At first she had wanted to be a mother more than anything else. But now, with that possibility a reality, she was steadily becoming less certain. The only thing she knew for sure was, one way or the other, she wanted this ordeal over. At this point she didn't care if whatever was ripping her body in half survived or not. She didn't even care if she survived as long as the horrific pain came to an end.

She stared blankly at her husband's face for several seconds. Eventually, his strength, love, and compassion penetrated her pain-induced haze. Drawing resolve and endurance from his steady green gaze, she refocused. She squeezed his hand tight enough to break bones, and gave one last flesh-splitting push. A final scream tore from her lips as her eyes rolled up into her head and she fainted.

Several minutes later her eyelids fluttered open. Her father was standing on one side of her bed, her husband on the other. The midwife approached to place a pink bundle of blankets in the earl's arms. He smiled into the blankets and gently handed the bundle to Laural.

Laural blinked several times as tears swam in her eyes then spilled down her cheeks.

"She's beautiful," commented Andrew as he gazed down at his granddaughter. He stroked the barely discernable strands of chestnut brown hair, and allowed the newborn to grab his finger.

"And here," said the midwife, extending another pink bundle toward the earl, "is your second daughter."

Jordan held the baby so Laural could see her other daughter.

"She's just as beautiful as her sister," proclaimed the marquis, leaning across his daughter's bed to touch the baby's cheek. Sapphire blue eyes stared solemnly back at him.

"Have you picked out names?" enquired the midwife.

Both men looked to Laural. "Jordana," she announced, gazing lovingly at the baby in her arms, "named after her dad and in memory of a lost friend." Her gaze shifted to her second daughter.

Twins.

Her mind returned to considering the implications of her girls' birth. She shook her head.

No. This was a day of jubilation.

She looked up at her dad. "I'd like to name her Andrea."

Andrew leaned forward to kiss her on the cheek. "I'd be honored."

A few minutes later the earl and marquis sat in a pair of wingback chairs in the earl's living room. The silence stretched as they both slowly sipped their glasses of PS4 while contemplating the empty fireplace.

Jordan placed his drink aside. Exhaustion was clearly etched on his handsome face as he pushed his hand through his chestnut hair, and let it drop into his lap."There's a distinct possibility that Ravensblood is the father."

Turquoise eyes studied him for a long moment before Andrew placed the remainder of his supplement on the end table. "As I understand it, either you or he could be the father."

"True," admitted Jordan, turning tortured eyes back to the empty hearth. "But Nick had been drinking that supplement to enhance his fertility."

"So were you."

He nodded without looking up. Jordan had already told his father-in-law about his experience in the tower including that, during his captivity, Cynthia had forced him to drink the fluid.

But that had only been for three days.

"That may have been enough," offered Andrew, picking up on

his friend's worried thought. He laid his hand on his friend's arm. "Even if Nick is the father, it doesn't necessarily mean the children are predestined for evil. And remember, either way, your blood as well as Laural's runs through Jordana's and Andrea's veins."

"I hope you're right," stated Jordan, rising to check on his wife and daughters.

"So do I," said Andrew softly, watching as his friend left the room. "So do I."

BURYING THE PAST

The waves crashed and spewed foamy spray across the Cornish cliffs. The midnight moon cast an eerie glow over the English countryside. High above the coastline the ravaged remains of Penbrook Castle glimmered in the moonlight. The fortress stood as the last barrier between the rest of the world and the Penbrook family secrets. Secrets passed down from generation to generation. Secrets which, if allowed to fall into the wrong hands, would bring about the genocide of an entire species and irrevocably change human evolution.

A lone figure stood bathed in the moonlight. Cloaked and dressed totally in black, he blended in completely with the surrounding shadows. He listened intently as an owl cried out in the night. Twigs snapped and leaves rustled as the prey sought desperately to evade the predator. The figure stood motionless, a silent observer as the owl swooped down, caught the field mouse in its talons and carried it away. The smaller animal struggled fiercely at first, frantically trying to dislodge the claws buried deep in its flesh. Within moments the struggles became weaker, and finally ceased. The owl spread his wings to their full span, gliding with its now limp prize beyond the trees and out of sight.

His cloak swirled about him as the lone observer turned away. Striding further into the forest, he halted at the edge of a deep rectangular pit. His perfect night vision enabled him to see what had been laid to rest at the bottom of the deep chasm. Leaping with the agility of a cat, he landed easily on the ground next to the sarcophagus. As he straightened, the hood of his cloak fell back to reveal strands of platinum hair and skin that glistened, pale as alabaster in the moonlight.

He laid his hand reverently on the lid.

Someday humanity might fall prey to the predators, but not today.

Taking a firm grip on either side of the heavy slab, he heaved the lid down the length of the coffin. Stone grated against stone as the top slid back to expose the skeleton, bleached white by time. He studied what was left of his progenitor for a long moment. At last his eyes came to rest on the ring. The Penbrook emblem of the lion lying down with the lamb glittered as it was captured in a stray moonbeam. He compared the skeletal hand with his own. For a long moment he examined the twin image encircling the third finger of his right hand.

Removing his hand from the lid he placed it in his inner pocket. Slowly he withdrew three leatherbound journals. All the documents and personal observations of Arthur Gabriel, Fifth Marquis of Penbrook were bound together in a satchel worn smooth with age. Deliberately, he tied the leather cord around the skeleton's neck and stepped back. The turquoise eyes glittered with long-lost memories as he slid the lid back into place.

Leaping out of the pit as easily as he had entered, he turned his back on all that had gone before and strode purposefully toward the future. The swish of fabric and rustle of branches were the only proof of his passage.

After the figure vanished among the trees, a group of dark-clad followers entered the sacred spot. Silently they lowered their heads for a moment in respect as their hands rested on their shovels. In unison they straightened and, as one, began to bury the past.

About the Author

Valerie Hoffman is a psychotherapist who resides in Ormond Beach Florida. She was born in Brooklyn, New York and grew up in Syracuse. Dr. Hoffman moved to Florida in 1983. Despite going blind at the age of nineteen due to retinal detachments, Dr. Hoffman pursued her education and attained her doctorate in 1997.

She currently has a thriving private practice with two offices in Ormond and Daytona Beach. In addition to her private practice, Dr. Hoffman also is the Vice President of the National Board of Forensic Evaluators and serves on the interviewing committee to credential eligible candidates for certification as a Certified Forensic Mental Health Evaluator. This author has written several programs for professionals in her field to receive continuing education credits. She has recently published a journal article based on forensic psychology.

She is currently the president of the board of directors at the Center for the Visually Impaired. She also serves on the board of the Friends of the Library Access for the talking book library.

She enjoys writing, cooking, singing in her chorus and traveling in her spare time. She is currently at work on the fourth sequel in the "Vampire Royalty" series.

The Author's Notes

I was inspired to write this sequel thirty years after the previous novel ended because vampires are supposed to live forever. And in that case this series would be very long if I were relegated to follow each storyline year after bloody year.

I hope fans will forgive me for "killing off" Andrew Gabriel in the last book and be gratified to see that he found his way back in this one. I know many authors hold sacred the idea of not terminating any of their main characters in their books. However, I have always strived to make my "Vampire Royalty" series unique. People die in real life—even good people—even those we are especially attached to and I have chosen to maintain that element of reality in my books.

The idea to present the possibility that the Gabriels could be related to historical/legendary figures is based on one simple concept: if the Gabriels have been around for an eternity they are bound to have been caught up in many of the most interesting events in history. Besides, King Arthur was known for his lack of blood loss and not being able to be killed in battle—doesn't that sound just a little bit vampiric?

I hope readers have enjoyed traveling through the multi-layered plot of historical intrigue intertwined with modern day plot. If so, then stay tuned because we're just getting started.

For single copies or bulk purchases of
this and other books by
Valerie Hoffman:

Send your payment to:
VG Press
595 W. Granada Blvd., Suite H
Ormond Beach FL 32174

or call:
386-677-3995

or order via email:
drval@bellsouth.net

One book: $9.95
plus shipping and handling: $3.95
The total is $13.90

If you are ordering by mail within the United States, please add $11.20 for each additional book ordered at the same time. (This price already includes $1.25 for postage and handling.) For the mailing costs for non-USA deliveries, please call 386-677-3995 or send an email that includes the name of your country to: drval@bellsouth.net.

Please allow two to four weeks for delivery within the United States.

For payment by check or money order, please mail to the address above.

Please call or email to learn if the price or postage has changed.

You may order from most bookstores.